BED OF ROSE AND THORNS

LEE HUNT

BOOKS BY LEE HUNT

The Dynamicist Trilogy
Dynamicist
Herald
Knight in Retrograde

In the world of Dynamicist
Last Worst Hopes

In the world of The Dead Gods
Bed of Rose and Thorns

TESTIMONIALS FOR LEE HUNT'S WORKS

For Bed of Rose and Thorns

⚡ "This spectacular standalone fantasy from the prolific Hunt bursts with epic battles and avid romance." *Booklife Reviews Editor's Pick*

"A beautifully crafted setting with complex character dynamics and layers of political intrigue... A showstopper. Hunt's ambitious stand-alone latest has everything—a well-imagined fantasy world, great characters, incredible tension, and fierce love. The real genius here is the mixture of extraordinarily deep worldbuilding with relevant and complex themes, which include identity, intolerance, love, passion, friendship, integrity, honor and more." *- Prairies Book Review*

"An intriguing storyline, scenarios grounded in the real world, and a breathless pace make Hunt's latest standalone fantasy a must-read." *- BookView Reviews Recommended Read*

"4 out of 4 stars." *Online Book Club.org*

For Last Worst Hopes

"A great read with strong characterization. It's likely to appeal to fans of epic fantasy novels such as those of Brandon Sanderson and Robert Jordan." *- Reedsy Discovery*

⚡ "A superior epic fantasy, driven by strong characterization and a sense of utter desperation." *-Booklife Reviews Editor's Pick*

"A Cracking page-turner with an unlikely group of misfits."

"Hunt exemplifies how to make heroes shine within the large cast of a sprawling saga." *- Kirkus Reviews*

"A skyrocketing plot interspersed with deliciously entertaining and well-constructed scenes of fierce battles and magic." *- BookView Reviews Recommended Read*

For Knight in Retrograde

"Strong characters face a maelstrom in this intense, intellectually rigorous fantasy series finale. This final volume of Hunt's fantasy trilogy bursts at the seams with notions of science, spirituality, and politics pertaining to the 21st-century political climate. The unique pulse of this series remains the author's dedication to thematic sprawl and a hard-science magic system." *- Kirkus Reviews*

"This is a sterling end to a rich, concept-driven series. This trilogy finale will thrill readers who want thoughtful, inventive fantasy powered by ideas." *- Booklife Reviews Editor's Pick*

"I highly recommend the Dynamicist trilogy, and Knight in Retrograde in particular – Hunt has crafted something truly special here." *- J. Scott Coatsworth, Liminal Fiction*

For Herald

"Surrender yourself to Lee's fantastic world of magical physics to rediscover what you thought you knew about reason, morality and the unbreakable bonds of friendship and love. As an innovator and physicist, I found myself reflected in the characters of *The Dynamicist Trilogy*. I felt chilling empathy for their challenges when fear shot up my spine and a strong sense of tribalism with their desire to invent and change the world. Wisdom grabs at the reader from every page." *- Amanda Hall, CEO of Summit Nanotech*

"A bold fantasy sequel that delivers on the first volume's call to action. This has deep relevance to life in the early 21st century." *- Kirkus Reviews*

"This is an exciting, expansive, and ultimately satisfying exploration of the meaning of heroism, the economics of magic, and the role of innovation in society. Readers looking for a thoughtful take on the wizard-school story will enjoy this mix of philosophy, mathematics, and action." *- Booklife Reviews*

"*Herald's* quite a ride, one I'd recommend taking if you love fantasy and want something that's not like everything else already on your SFF shelf. And that's one of the highest compliments I can give to a well-written, page-turning book like this one." *- J. Scott Coatsworth, Liminal Fiction*

For Dynamicist

"I highly recommend Dynamicist – it's a well-thought-out, high-minded fantasy with a very satisfying set of twists and turns that's not quite like anything else I have read in high fantasy. And to me, that's a great accomplishment indeed." *- J. Scott Coatsworth, Liminal Fiction*

"This is a compelling story for readers who crave complex worldbuilding. This intricate, philosophical update to the wizard school story will appeal to fans of cerebral fantasy." *- Booklife Reviews*

"A philosophically minded series opener that deftly merges science, fantasy, and college life." *- Kirkus Reviews*

FIRST EDITION

Bed of Rose and Thorns © 2022 Lee Hunt

Cover art by Jeff Brown

Interior design & typesetting by Other Worlds Ink.

Distributed by Ingram Spark

Printed in Canada by Blitz Print

Library and Archives Canada Cataloguing in Publication

Title: Bed of Rose and Thorns / Lee Hunt.

Names: Hunt, Lee, 1968- author.

Description: First Edition. 2022 ISBN 978-1-7779734-3-8 (soft cover); 978-1-7779734-4-5 (Ebook/PDF); 978-1-7779734-5-2 (Audiobook)

Edited by: John McAllister (mcallister@gmx.ca)

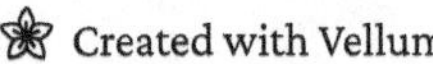 Created with Vellum

For the leaders.

CONTENTS

Characters   xiii

1. Eleven Years Ago   1
2. Eleven Years Ago, Later That Night   3
3. Redirection   6
4. Fit to Ring   17
5. Shadows of the Past   32
6. Doorway to Time   42
7. Lessons   54
8. Taking Advantage   63
9. Liar's Lesson   74
10. Negotiations   82
11. Discouragement   93
12. Audience   104
13. Discovery   115
14. Agent   124
15. Iceberg's Tip   137
16. Frustration   146
17. The Second Note   160
18. Garden   172
19. Moment in a Bottle   180
20. The Tallest Tower   190
21. Vampire   199
22. By Any Other Name   210
23. Eleven Years Ago   228
24. Untombed   232
25. Force of Nature   251
26. Eleven Years Ago   254
27. Love of Another Kind   262
28. The Dread Queen   266

Acknowledgments 279
About the Author 281

CHARACTERS

11 years ago

The Queen
Sir Ezra, a banished Knight of the Queen
Lady Kay, the Queen's Advisor
Sir Marigold, a Knight of the Queen
The Prince of Erle, husband to the Queen

At Province

Lady Kristen Province, noble woman Ezra was sent to guard
Lady Rachel Province, the youngest daughter of Lady Kristen
Pontes, Lady Kristen's secretary
Danielle Stonehouse, owner of the Stonehouse
Brendan, an assistant to Danielle
Gilbert, a squire at Lady Kristen's estate
Sergeant Estes, a sergeant at Lady Kristen's estate

At the capital

CHARACTERS

Constable Bobby Archibald, a senior member of the constabulary
Sir Jennyfer Shryke, a Knight of the Queen
Sir Roger Corning, Knight Captain
Sir Valerie Simons, a Knight of the Queen
Sir Kenneth Kantor, a Knight of the Queen
Lady Jayne Orton, senior treasurer to the Queen
Lord Seltser, secretary to the Queen
Lady Jacqueline Paron, a noblewoman
Lord Ronald Paron, Lady Jacqueline's cousin
Sir Castel, huge champion of the Parons
Sir Eaton, a knight of the Parons
Professor Olivia, a professor at the Pyracantha Institute
Adjunct Professor Parsons, a professor at the Pyracantha Institute
Lady Beatrice Whall, a member of the Queen's Council
Sir Gregory Whall, Beatrice's cousin and champion
Lady Alanna Gill, a noblewoman performing the role of "Thorn" at the Queen's Council
Lord Jonathon Sutton, a member of the Queen's Council
Keavan Fawcett, the Queen's armorer
Brayden Fellows, a dead actor
Saraith, the name of a figure of legend, and ... an actress

CHAPTER 1
ELEVEN YEARS AGO

A loud, unwelcome sound, something hard crashing, jolted Sir Ezra. It told of some new act of violence, some new brutality to initiate a fresh breaking of his heart. It was deafeningly loud, even though it came muffled through the door. His eyes moved from the door to the four Knights of Erle who stood opposite to him with their hard eyes, curved swords, and straight allegiance to the man on the other side of the thick wood of the portal. He willed a tremor out of his hands, hands that wanted to reach of their own volition to the door and open it. The trembling warned of a potential that he could not allow to become real. Those hands that always wanted to reach against will and propriety to the woman, the Queen, on the other side of the door, and touch her.

I never have. I never will.

It was a burning pain, a heart-fluttering disturbance, but loving someone so great, so lovely, driven, strong, intelligent ... so perfect ... was a reward of its own. Honor was said to be a gift that you gave yourself. If so, it was one that Ezra gave himself every time he stopped his hands from reaching out, every time he stopped his lips from speaking forbidden truth, but it was a painful gift. Almost as painful as love.

Honor was the gift he needed to give *her*, more useful than giving her his useless love, because if he kept his honor he could stay here. He could guard her.

I'm the only one. The only one left.

The other Knights of the Queen had been sent away at the Prince of Erle's insistence. His supposed fear of betrayal.

Ezra had refused to go, was now her only guardian, and his ears strained to hear through his helmet of heavy-gauge steel for any sound she might make. The armor had always been a barrier between Ezra and the world, between him and *her*, but it was far from the only one. The door to her royal bedchamber was thick oak, an eternity of thickness, but not half as deep as the distance his choice had made between her and him.

There was another crash and now a scream.

Her scream, but different from the others he had heard, those screams of passion and release that had dashed and broken his heart so many times. *This* scream was of fear, and it was accompanied by a dark undertone he had only heard once before.

"Don't touch it," came the flat tones of one of the Knights of Erle.

Ezra had not realized that his hands had moved to the door on their own, that he was beginning to vibrate again, almost imperceptibly for now, that the potential was once more building.

The knights opposite to him all had their hands on their sword hilts, their knuckles white with tension.

They knew. They expected the scream.

Faster than thought, in unity of mind and body, Ezra drew sword, let slip his power, filled the room with a deep, violent bell sound—a sound like ringing thunder—and swung with all the resonant love and strength and ferocity he carried within himself.

CHAPTER 2

ELEVEN YEARS AGO, LATER THAT NIGHT

"It will be war, plain and simple, bloody and violent, the ending of which we cannot know the where or when of," said Kay, calm and even despite her dark words and rhetorical eloquence.

"What will it take to win?" asked the Queen, her long blonde hair hanging down like drooping flowers around a tired garden. That delicate, limp, arresting fan of hair hid a darkening bruise over one blue eye and puffed lips.

Seeing the injury nearly set Ezra to trembling and chiming once more. But exhaustion aided will this time, and he kept his love and concern for her caged inside. Enough passion had been loosed, enough death delivered, for one night. He was utterly spent. It had taken hours to scour the palace with his one precious ally and hunt down and execute the remaining Knights of Erle. And kill their prince.

His Queen's husband.

Morning had nearly come before Ezra was able to force open the gates that had been stealthily locked by Erle—locked by armed men in the hours that Ezra had stood guard, ignorant of the unfolding plot— to allow Sir Marigold and everyone else who had been sent away by

Erle back into the palace. Some, like Marigold, had never lost sight of the palace walls, while others had been spellbound by the deep-pitched, ominous sounds of thunder coming from the Queen's home.

The sounds of Ezra's soul, unleashed.

Kay smiled unhappily. She had been among the first to reenter a secretly emptied castle, though she was no knight. "In war," she said, "there can only be losers. Though perhaps we can ensure that we lose less than Erle."

"What can we do?" asked Ezra. He was sitting in a chair in his now ruined plate armor. He should have been standing. In either woman's presence, he should only ever stand, but he had lost too much blood.

Why am I here?

Ezra knew why. He was the only one who knew what had happened. He was the only one who had, bleeding and half-dead, burst through the Queen's door to confront her and the Prince of Erle.

No, that wasn't true. *Kay knows.* The Queen would have told her some of what had happened while his lacerated hairline, shoulder, hand and thigh, and knee were being sewn up by Sir Marigold, and the broken metal loops dug out of his skin where they had been hammered through plate and chain and soft underlayers from some subset of the numberless blows he had taken.

"You should be dead, idiot," Marigold had said. "This artery," she spat while sewing the inside of his upper left thigh, "I don't know how you didn't bleed out. It was too close."

Kay and the Queen would have had plenty of time to talk while his only friend had cursed him, finished sewing the ripped skin closed, helped him hastily to don once more his scrubbed, dented, grievously fatigued armor and return to his apprehensive position beside the Queen.

"There is a way out of war," said Kay, looking sadly at Ezra. "Perhaps."

Ezra knew that whatever that way out was, it had already been decided by these two great women. Both ladies were gazing directly at him. He asked, "What must I do?"

As the Queen abruptly looked away, thoughts hidden by bruises and hair he would have died to touch, Kay told him.

IT FELT LIKE DEATH. But death would have been less painful. Death would have been without the broken heart that preceded the end of thought and self.

Honor is a gift I gave myself.
Gone now. I have one gift only left to give.
Love is the gift you give to someone else.

CHAPTER 3

REDIRECTION

"Don't fight the steel, Gilbert," said Ezra, his words echoing from within his own steel helm. "It has a way that it wants to move. Denying that won't help you in a fight."

Gilbert paused, sword over his head in position to strike downward on the thick wooden dummy. "My sword has a will?"

He was only thirteen years old, so Ezra tolerated the silly question. *It's my own fault, anyway.* "Not exactly. Come to rest, and I'll lay this out more objectively for you."

Ezra knew that he could not be perfect, no one could—not even the Queen whom he tried so hard not to think about—but it was important to *try* to be perfect. And although he held a lie deep inside himself, although he hid his feelings every moment of every day, he knew that the truth should be spoken whenever possible. Even against such romantic half-truths as personifying a weapon. Fairy tales would help no one.

"Your sword has no *will*. There is no magic in the world."

None without a cost.

"Magical swords are not real—but momentum, mass, weight, speed, direction are all real things that you *must* understand and know how to make use of. How you change the direction of your blade is affected by its balance, and your balance by your feet, your shoulders, and your wrists. To move from one direction to another, quickly and with killing force, must be done correctly."

"Or *you* will be very unhappy, like our knight and your master, Sir Ezra!" came the bright girlish tones of Rachel, Lady Kristen Province's youngest daughter, from the edge of the practice ring.

"I'm perfectly happy," Ezra lied, then regretted letting himself be baited by her. She had been—bit by bit, through her increasingly aggressive attention—forcing his lies to the surface. Rachel was older than Gilbert by more than four years, but about the same height, though she appeared much more the finished of the two. She was a woman, and Gilbert was a boy. She had very long dark hair. Beautiful hair, Ezra had to admit, and was fit and strong in the way of active youth. It was her bright eyes that were the problem now. Eyes that followed him.

Ezra checked that his many layers of armor were strapped tight about himself.

"I see you are dressed for training," Ezra said to her. These words, at least, he could speak truthfully. She wore long dark hose and one of her old tunics with an additional over-the-shoulder padded piece. "Throw on a vest and a leather skirt and join us." Though paying attention to her training when he first arrived at the Province estate eleven years past had likely been the mistake that initiated her infatuation with him, he could hardly deny her interest in sword combat now.

It would have been wrong to do so.

He turned back to Gilbert, who was waiting, eyes flickering between Ezra and Rachel. Gilbert had a huge bent nose that would have put some trainers off; it was proof that accidents happened to the boy. And they might happen again. But Ezra had often thought that others jumped too quickly to conclusions. No one knew what might come of the boy, just as being kind to an ignored youngest daughter should never be viewed as a mistake.

Kindness and love are never a mistake.

Ezra still believed that, even if it had resulted in misdirected affection from Rachel and a deeper love in him that he was forced to hide.

"Where were we, Gilbert?" he asked, seeing that Rachel had donned the vest and skirt. "Helm," he said to her and gestured to the leather-lined helmets on the rack to her right.

"Uh," Gilbert said, "don't fight the movement of the metal?"

"Yes."

"There's something I don't understand about that," the boy said.

"Okay."

"Well, if there are right and wrong ways of redirecting—"

"Let's say better and worse, faster or slower," Ezra said.

"Right. Well, if these ways are known, won't it make us predictable?"

Ezra did not rush to answer such a good question. *The boy might have more potential than I thought.* It was a naive question, but also one for a wise master to heed. "It could, Gilbert," Ezra admitted. "You might say that we can be anticipated and manipulated by our tendencies. The tendencies of physics, scholars would say. But there are enough movements and transitions between movements to confound prediction. Especially once you master the basics and can move on to style and expression."

"Can we spar?" asked Rachel.

She wants to beat Gilbert in front of me.

"Let's try a new form first." An old form came to mind, one he had used once in real combat. "This is called Carried by the Cyclone."

"Ohhh, I like the sound of it," said Rachel with a sly edge. Gilbert looked away from her.

"I will demonstrate," said Ezra. The cyclone form was arguably not well suited to either of his students. It required tremendous amounts of energy and balance, but it was good for building both, and also ... it might help him. He had been called out quite accurately by Rachel.

He was unhappy.

He took a long slow breath and deliberately stilled his mind. *She* had told him he must, all those years ago, and she had been correct.

The only escape from the bottomless well he found himself in, the hole in his soul caused by his banishment from *her*, was to still his mind.

Without judgment, he took in his surroundings. A man who wanted to ride a cyclone should know what was within reach. He was positioned inside a set of stone buildings, in a ring of sand, bounded by a cobbled square with equipment and weapons stacked in wooden shelves and racks. A tall, open building stood adjacent. A few men and women trained inside, Ezra's older students and members of the household guard, all pupils in one way or another. The shadow of the Province castle fell across the building opposite the square. This was where Lady Kristen and her daughters lived, where the business of the earldom was conducted.

Of all the stone buildings in the compound, Ezra's private residence was farthest from the castle. It was set apart from the others, nearest to the gate, farthest from people, as Ezra had requested when Lady Kristen had taken him in. This was where he had lived for eleven years, though his idea of home was elsewhere, along with his heart.

Ezra drew his sword and set himself in motion, stepping and thrusting as the form dictated, in a set of movements not unlike a dance, but with a very different meaning. The cyclone form involved many spinning moves, spinning blocks with a special hardened and flattened vambrace, and spinning attacks in which incredible retracted speed and torque were translated into terrific rotational velocity at a suddenly extended sword point.

A stilled mind was one of two things that protected Ezra from the pain and unhappiness of his banishment by the Queen. The other was its diametric opposite and incongruous equivalent: a mind perfectly and fully occupied. Such perfect attention also left no room for pain or obsession.

Only when perfectly still or completely focused, did Ezra escape the fact and consequence that his heart beat only for the woman who had sacrificed him.

He spun his sword in a tight whirl about his wrists, within a spin about his shoulders, within a rotation about his hips. There was a joy in it, an unwinding of tension and a release of kinetic energy. A high-pitched whirring followed the sword's blurring motion, splitting the quiet morning air. It sounded like a sharp birdcall or the wind of a storm through a pipe.

It was the closest to a chime that Ezra could allow himself, emanating partly from his being and partly from the incredible angular momentum of the sharpened metal. It was an expression of joy in the world, a release of power and freedom, which the man, encased so tightly in layers of metal, so badly needed.

The form built to this release nine times, one for each of the silent, dead gods. Nine times, Ezra split the air, parted its heavy stillness, and brought it to singing life.

Rachel and Gilbert both clapped when he finished, as did the guardsmen who had come out to see what could possibly be producing such a piercing, lonely, haunting sound.

"Now I will show you how to do it," said Ezra, panting.

"Sir Ezra, you are summoned," came the voice of Pontes, Lady Kristen's secretary, through his door.

Ezra was deep in the rows and columns of the treasury book that Pontes had entrusted to his care, and he had been working by lantern light. "I'm almost through, Pontes. Does she need me right now?"

Since being banished, Ezra had learned accounting and devoted many long evenings to performing audits for Pontes. It occupied his mind in the darker moments, which he desperately needed. But this was not the only reason Ezra did it. Someone he loved had also spent long hours poring over ledgers. When he was occupied in the late hours of the night by the procedures of finance, he could almost imagine that, instead of sending him away, *she* had kept him by her side to help her with her endless tasks.

"I am afraid so, sir," came the muffled tones.

"Are you alone?"

"Yes, sir."

Ezra walked to his barred door. His outbuilding had few windows —and those with tight shutters and heavy curtains—and an even heavier woolen carpet. "Then come in, Pontes," he said, opening the door.

Pontes was perhaps thirty, with a dramatic widow's peak of thread-thin brown hair and a spare build. Ezra had thought many times that the secretary's careful personality suited his looks. Both had a kind of parsimony about them.

"Take a look at the ledger while I change, would you," Ezra said as he went to find something more appropriate to wear than old pants and a sweater with holes in the elbows.

"This is excellent work, sir," Pontes said wonderingly after a moment, though Ezra had helped him many times in the past.

Shrugging into his padded shirt, Ezra said. "Well, it's important that we account for every horseshoe, every pickaxe, every plank of wood, isn't it?"

"You may be the only other person here who would say that," Pontes said under his breath, still looking at the book. He ran a long, bony finger along a row of numbers. "Every number does tell a story."

"It does," said Ezra. "A story with no words." The phrase reminded him of something the Queen had said to him eleven years in the past.

Pontes closed and locked the ledger, turned around smiling, and froze.

Ezra was halfway into his plate armor. "I need you to help me with this," he said.

"Sir," Pontes said in his always proper, always deferential tone, "I believe that Lady Kristen would like you to attend her without your armor."

Which meant that she had given the secretary explicit instructions.

"I can only give her my best effort," Ezra said, organizing his helmet and gauntlets.

It's safer this way. For everyone.

"But sir ..."

"Formality is important, wouldn't you agree?"

This Pontes could not argue with. He was the soul of propriety. Without another word, he lifted—with some difficulty—Ezra's double-strength breastplate.

A quarter of an hour later, Sir Ezra and Secretary Pontes stood on the verge of the great stone hall of Lady Kristen, looking through its open door and down a long, straight passage.

"We cannot go until we have conducted our interview," sounded a querulous male voice from within. "We simply *will* not. This is too rare an opportunity, and we have been put off for far too long. Give us just two days. *One* day to interview him, and it will be done. As a service to natural science."

Ezra did not recognize the pedantic voice, but he knew that speaking in that way to Lady Kristen was a hazardous breach of etiquette. He did not hear what she said in response, but—looking down the long aisle—he saw what happened next.

Sergeant Estes and another guard had taken the man by either arm, hard enough that he yelped and dropped a strangely shaped something. It was, unaccountably, a birdcage to judge from the squawk that echoed down the hall. There was a scuffle, and the man's companion, a woman, crouched over the cage, made some comforting noises, picked it up, and followed the man as he was bundled ungracefully down the hall toward Ezra and Pontes.

They retreated a pace to hold the doors open as this strange quartet approached. The bird began to sing, warbling beautifully from within its shrouded two-foot-tall cage. Sergeant Estes grimaced as he neared Ezra, his face-wide mustache turning up with it.

No helm. Ezra pointed at his own heavy helmet and Estes bobbed his head, knowing he would hear of the breach in protocol later.

The two guests looked out of place. Both wore long robes, like some sort of priest or academic. An embroidered patch above their right breasts showed a tall rose bush sheltering a large, stalking cat —a puma perhaps. Neither of the two was young, though the woman's face told Ezra she was older despite her full red hair and slim build. "You played that ill, Parsons," she muttered as they passed by.

In seconds they were gone, though Ezra could hear the bird singing long after the night swallowed them all.

"Academics, I would hazard," said Pontes.

Setting aside the strangeness of academics and birds in cages, Ezra stepped fully inside. Except for a few servants and the lady herself, the hall was now empty. As they crossed the long open space between door and dais, Rachel rushed in from a side door and went to her mother's high, padded throne. Both women wore sleek blue dresses, and their faces were animated in discussion.

"I must leave you now," whispered Pontes, "but thank you for your help." He gestured with the ledger in a kind of salute.

"You're welcome," Ezra responded, sensing a strange gravitas from the other man.

Pontes smiled fractionally. "Good fortune to you, Knight." He carried the accounts that Ezra had been reconciling with him but, instead of leaving, as Ezra had expected, he seated himself at a side table. Close enough to be called upon by Lady Kristen but far enough away to feign ignorance of what was said by her.

"Why?" Ezra heard Rachel cry. "No!" she hissed to her mother.

He looked closer and saw that there were tears in the girl's eyes.

Ezra slowed as he neared the lady and her daughter, giving them time to end or escalate their argument, halting at the edge of the dais. They abruptly ended their discussion, and as one, gazed directly at him. Rachel's eyes were wet. Kristen's were ... difficult to read. Lady Kristen was a striking woman. Raven-haired like her daughter, but wise in the ways of the world and infinitely more sophisticated.

"Come closer, Ezra. Kneel at my feet."

It was a command both intimate and domineering. Ezra had always wondered if Lady Kristen might have meant it to be taken both ways, for when her halls were empty, she always asked him to take a knee before her. At first, she had done it a few times in front of others too, but this had stopped when, during one of her periodic visits, Sir

Marigold had witnessed the request. She had called out, "What is it precisely that you would like kissed, Lady?"

That was the only time that Ezra had ever seen Lady Kristen blush.

Kneeling in plate armor was difficult, but Ezra wore his armor every day. When the Knights of Erle had taken him down and tried to murder him on the ground, he had regained his feet despite their numbers. He suppressed feelings and memories of that night every day, every hour. But some part of him remembered and would not allow weakness to creep in. Some part of him dreamt that the Queen would one day call him back, and if she did, that part demanded that he stay strong for her. He sank quietly and gracefully to his knee before the lady.

"You wore your armor," Rachel complained, which caused her mother to scowl at her.

Ezra did not answer. He was here for Kristen. When she returned her gaze to him, he said, "To better serve you, Lady."

Kristen extended her left hand, and Ezra removed his helm, placed it on the floor to the side, and kissed her gently on the knuckle. He maintained eye contact with her as he did this. Her fingers very lightly covered his and held him there.

"Knight, do you enjoy your service here?" she asked, her hand still in his, her eyes not leaving his.

"Yes, my lady," he said, though the truth was more complex. He did not wish to hurt her or Rachel with his past, or with truths they could not hear. He wanted to release her hand. The contact was uncomfortable. It implied a relationship he did not want, but she was the lady of the house, and he did not wish to embarrass her. Ezra was certain that Pontes was surreptitiously watching, but the secretary was no brash spitfire in the mold of Sir Marigold, who would have spoken up no matter what.

What is the etiquette?

"Good. Pontes tells me that you have a keen eye for finances."

"That is generous of him," replied Ezra, meaning it. Few were kind to the bookkeepers. "It is my pleasure, my lady."

Lady Kristen smiled. There was something of the predator in her upturned lips. "He also says that you work long into the night, every night, on my behalf."

What is happening here? Ezra knew that his work habits were well understood by the lady. He did not break his shared gaze with her to check Pontes's expression, but he thought of the lesson earlier with Gilbert and Rachel. He suspected some manipulation was coming, and he worried that he had never mastered the basics of the game being played to even hope to turn it aside.

"I have decided to make you my seneschal, Sir Ezra. What do you think of that?"

Dread seized Ezra, but he suppressed any show of it, as he knew he must. "I am . . . surprised. There must be better men for that than I."

Lady Kristen released his hand, finally, and said, "I think not. You will have to move into the castle proper."

No, no, no. That would not do. *What if I dream of her? What if they hear? What if they feel it?*

"May I think on this, my lady?" he asked, wondering how to get out of it. Trying to think what act of physics or momentum might redirect events.

She smiled again. "By all means, Knight. Consider it on your trip to the capital where you will assist Pontes in negotiating our new wheat taxes and iron rates."

"No!" said Rachel.

Ezra was too shocked to say anything. He closed his eyes and clenched his fists to still the vibrations welling into life in the core of his being.

Lady Kristen maintained her smile, only widening it, sensing and seeming to enjoy his discomfiture. "You will need new clothes. You know Danielle Stonehouse, of course. She is the finest seamstress in the earldom. Go into town and have her fit you with formal dress." She caressed his metal clad shoulder with the hand he had kissed. "You won't need this armor anymore."

"But I have been banished," whispered Ezra, struggling to hold old wounds closed. He felt like the air his sword had split so often. Sundered. Exposed.

"No," said Kristen. "That has been rescinded."

Ezra felt like he was in a dream. *Rescinded?* He wondered what had changed politically to allow his return. His banishment had been the sacrifice necessary to avoid war with the Kingdom of Erle. Had enough time now passed to allow his return? Had Erle forgotten about his murder of their prince? Or was the Queendom now powerful enough that his banishment was no longer required?

These were surface thoughts. Deeper down, Ezra was reeling, fighting the wound that had suddenly burst. He struggled to hold his feelings inside and listen to what Lady Kristen was saying.

"Go to the city of the Queen one final time." She leaned forward and presented her hand to him for another kiss. "And put it properly behind you."

Ezra did not remember if he kissed her hand or not before he took to his feet. He could not say whether he had nodded to Rachel or Pontes. His mind felt like it was whirled in a cyclone, turning on Kristen's ill-conceived notion that going to the city would allow him to achieve some sort of closure, turning on the question of why his banishment had been rescinded, turning on his suppressed memories of the Queen, and on the decade and more of feelings he had denied.

He turned and turned inside, fearing that his carefully nurtured balance had been lost, that a massive, dread potential was building in him again to some new, unknown, uncontrollable purpose.

CHAPTER 4

FIT TO RING

It had been some time since Ezra had been stabbed by a sword, but this other weapon now poking into his shoulder felt no less deadly than cold steel. And the timing of *this* assault could not have been worse. His body could not have been less protected.

"This is, let me see, the fourth time, I believe, in eleven years, that I've seen you without armor, Sir Knight, and here I find you quite disarmed," the voice of his attacker said. "Whatever are you going to do now?"

The hard nipple of Rachel's right breast was poking his left shoulder quite firmly through the thin fabric of her dress.

Ezra struggled to still himself. He did not know what to do about the young woman, or her breast, given his state of undress in the Stonehouse fitting room. Worse, Rachel had sprung another surprise. She had not just caught him unawares—out of his armor and distracted out of his mind by the recent turn of events—and was not merely pressing herself close against him while he was trying to hold still and be measured. She had also dyed her raven-colored hair blonde. Just like the Queen's.

Why?

He had a powerful autonomic reaction to this, the same reaction he had experienced on the few other occasions over the last decade when he had accidently crossed paths with a woman who bore a resemblance to the Queen.

It had been eleven years, but some reactions never faded. Some injuries never healed.

We are slaves to our pasts. Even those we have banished.

This time, the reaction was so much the worse. He was being sent back to the capital, the city of the Queen. His banishment was apparently over, and he had already begun to fantasize about catching some fleeting glimpse of his Queen, just a momentary glance at her long hair, of the sun's rays reflecting off its golden, heavenly sheen. And then Rachel had arrived, pressing herself against him, looking too much like the woman he could never forget.

The lady of the house, master seamstress Danielle Stonehouse, was just at that moment measuring his inseam, precisely the wrong place for her gentle fingers to be while he was being poked by a young woman's high, erect nipple and remembering the Queen. Ezra looked down at Danielle and saw her eyes narrow at the gravity of the situation.

"Rachel Province," she said with something of exasperation and something of wickedness, "a little close and personal, are we not? Have you come to pick something up for your mother?"

"For *me*," Rachel said, still pressing shamelessly into Ezra. "I would like a new scarf. It's positively *dusty* out there."

"Well, I'm done with Sir Ezra's . . . measurements," said Danielle standing up. She was in her late thirties, just a little older than Ezra but, unlike him, fully dressed in a smooth, dark, semi-formal outfit. Ezra was wearing only a thin pair of shorts. Whatever Danielle's thoughts, they were hidden, unlike Sir Ezra's. His were on full display.

She looked from Ezra's straining, uncomfortable shorts to his more uncomfortable eyes but spoke without expression. "I will have your formal clothes ready later this afternoon, Ezra. Why don't you get dressed, go get those supplies you need for your journey, and then come back?" She walked across the dressing room, and at the door, gestured to Rachel. "Come along dear, I'll help you find something safer to drape around your pretty young neck."

"I'll be there in a moment, Danielle," Rachel said, pressing harder, as if it was her strength and aggressiveness that counted. Once a man felt a woman against him, her power was known. But she seemed to think, incorrectly, that Ezra's discomfiture was only the result of his arousal and—also incorrectly—that his arousal was entirely the result of the life-affirming power of her breast.

No one but the Queen, and possibly Kay, could know the depth of his feeling for the woman who had banished him. The woman who created the necessary lie that had separated them forever. No one but the Queen knew her power over him, the bite she had left on his neck and his soul, the power that even now raised his shorts because a young woman had dyed her long locks into a passable resemblance of a distant Queen's wild, blonde hair.

Rachel had no way of knowing how she was at once raising his arousal and grinding her soft leather boots into his broken heart.

Ezra was not about to tell her, either.

"I think you should come now, young la—" Stonehouse began, then stopped when she saw Ezra's nod.

I'll deescalate this.

He knew that he should, that he *must*. Rachel had been a little girl when he was sent to be her mother's knight and guardian. He had made the mistake of being kind to the youngest daughter, instructing her in the sword when her tutors had ignored her. Sometimes, attention, reputation, and bad timing have a life-changing effect. He needed to find a gentle way of dealing with her infatuation.

Danielle Stonehouse sighed. "Don't be long, or your mother will hear of it." She swept out through the door without another word or a backward glance.

Ezra put his hands on Rachel's lean shoulders then and held her away from him. "Rachel," he started, but she burst into tears, wriggled out of his gentle grasp, and wrapped her arms around him, pressing all of herself against him.

"Don't go!" she wailed. "Do not go back to the evil Queen in her evil castle."

"Come now, Rachel, the Queen is not evil." Ezra said, still hoping not to have to use real force to push her away. "And there is little chance I will see her in any case."

She looked up at him, her eyes a mess of red from tears and black from smudgy paint. "Yes, yes she is. She *is* evil. Everyone knows she eats men alive. How many dead husbands is it now?" Ezra flinched.

"Don't go," Rachel cried again. "She threw you out like slops, but you were lucky to get out. Stay out. Stay *here*." She breathed seductively, "*With me.*"

She ground herself against his erection then, an escalation far beyond anything she had ever managed back at the estate. It was intensely pleasurable. And very, very wrong.

I must be extremely careful.

As good as Rachel felt, he did not *want* her. He had only ever wanted one woman since Lilly, his wife, had died. Lilly had been about Rachel's age too, and feeling her young love now only made him sad. The erection was the result of long blonde hair and memories of the Queen, the return of dark memories prompted by this prospect of returning to the capital. But Rachel's youth and earnestness, her fragility, was not something Ezra wanted to test. He did not want to hurt her. He hoped he could talk sense into her, though she was not making it easy.

How can I do this?

A tricky question, with Rachel pressing so hard against him in the dressing room, dressed up like the woman who owned his soul. It was not as if Ezra had much experience with women. His wife, yes, but that had been nearly twenty years ago. The Queen, but that relationship was complex, and he had been on the other side of a grossly asymmetric set of feelings. Rachel's mother, Lady Kristen, may have wanted him, always asking him to kneel close to her and kiss her hand, but her attentions had been easy to avoid while in his steel plate. He always made sure that touching him would be unpleasant for her, had always kept his hardest armor strapped tight, so tight that only a squire could unbuckle it. No other woman had ever shown any interest, not Rachel's five sisters ... not anyone. There was Sir Marigold, of course, who came to visit every few months, but she was a friend. Perhaps his only friend aside from Danielle.

Rachel started pulling at the long fabric at the front of her dress, raising it out of the way. An old vibration, still mild, stirred in Ezra then, a shadow of bell notes brought by long blonde hair, the coming trip, and persistent memory. The spell of the Queen was long and deep.

No, this is not happening. Dear gods, no.

He grasped Rachel again by the shoulders, but harder this time, knowing he needed to put a stop to matters. "We cannot do this, Rachel."

"Why not?" she asked, teeth barred. "I can feel that you want me. You're harder than one of those ironwood canes that Lady Stonehouse keeps out there."

The sharp, barred teeth also reminded him of the Queen, of her shocking aggression, her painful bite. The vibration sounded again, still soft but growing. It came from within him, he knew, from his passion, but it was an exceedingly rare and very poorly understood phenomenon, the tolling of a vast potential energy inside himself.

NO!

"Rachel, you . . ." he wanted to say that she was too young, except that age was not the true issue. She was just wrong, for him.

I already have an owner.

He looked down at her, at her long blonde hair, trying to think of what else to say. He had been sure he could manage her, always had before, easily, but thoughts of the Queen and her hair, her hypnotic smile and bared teeth, had undone him. And the more he thought about those things, the more he struggled to put them from his mind, the more fully he fell under that old power.

Eleven years away from her, deprived and abandoned, had hollowed out a great, unfillable hole in his soul, a soul that yearned, despite this, to speak love to the heavens.

The first chime rolled out.

It came from within him, from his feelings, from his body, which had just, almost imperceptibly, begun to vibrate. But the sound came also from the air above, from some continuum that resonated with his passions.

Another chime thrilled the air.

"What was that?" Rachel's head cocked and her eyes narrowed. "You've started chiming!" Her eyes widened. "There have always been rumors that you might be a Bell, but I never believed them. ... That you ring before battle, before terrific violence, and . . . from deep, true love." Her eyes flashed, open and wider still, her pupils suddenly filled them, black and large. "You *love* me!"

No, no, no, no, no.

This was bad. Even without the harmonic, having a confused and unwanted would-be lover was not a problem Ezra had experienced often, though he knew that sexual misadventures and misunderstandings were common between people. It was rare for him to be molested by an amorous, delusional partner, but he was well aware that such things were not rare for others. Sexual misattention happened all the time, often to even worse ends than this might lead. It was worse when it was a man who was obsessed. Men resorted to violence. Some of them, anyway. Too many of them.

His Bell nature he really, really did not need right now, though. It was the incarnation of a romantic legend that he had always tried to hide—a poorly kept secret that probably had not been believed—but if now confirmed and on full display would do nothing to deescalate the situation. Depending on what stories Rachel had read, it could make things worse. A *lot* worse.

"Oh, you are *mine*! My Bell lover, the only one in the Queendom!" Somehow Rachel had slipped from his grip once more and was pressing into him again. He looked down at her long, dyed blonde hair so like the Queens's, and chimed louder.

I'm in trouble. I have lost my grip on reality.

It would have been funny, because it was getting damned ridiculous, except that this was also damned serious.

"Rachel," he said, pulling free and taking a knee before her, holding her hips away from him, trying to calm her down and show seriousness. He looked up, and her hair made a fan, so like the Queen's, and his mind spun, reverting to those days, eleven years ago. He remembered daggers of long, blonde hair trailing into his face as he kneeled before her in the blood of Erle.

The quiet air of the room erupted in a deep, rolling, bell-like tolling sound, shaking the building, shattering something in another room. His body spasmed. He lost time, then found his face in Rachel's stomach, his hands under her dress, his fingers roaming desperately up and over her thighs, over her ass, and down and around, his thumbs hooking over her hips as he pulled her toward himself, crying.

Oh, my Queen! What have you done to me?

"It's okay," Rachel crooned, her hands tangled in his hair, holding his face hard against her. "I love you, too, I've always loved you Ezra, since first we met."

"Rachel, this isn't wh—"

"Oh, I can feel it through your hands, through your face. It's love from *heaven*. Don't stop, Ezra, it feels wonderful. Mmmmmm, so wonderful. Dead gods, get this dress off me!"

She tore her bodice open, knelt down, and pushed her breast against the side of his face, against his lips, just as the dressing-room door opened.

"What in the names of the lost gods!" bellowed the normally cultured voice of Danielle Stonehouse. She ran across the room and pulled Ezra away, pausing only to stare in shock at her hands where they had touched the vibrating knight. "There will be no noonday chiming of Elysian Bells here in *my* store! Go wait in the private room, Rachel. Now!"

"Wʜᴀᴛ ᴛʜᴇ ʜᴇʟʟ, Eᴢʀᴀ!" Danielle Stonehouse exclaimed. "The Queen banished you here to look after her mother, not fall in love with her youngest daughter."

"I'm not in love with her," Ezra said miserably.

Stonehouse put her hands on her hips and bent toward him, brows raised, "My front window *cracked*, Knight. It's in the other room. I lost five antique vases, and I don't know what else out there. You love her like nothing I've ever heard of from a living person."

She paused, face harder, and added, "You love her like the god in one of those stories young women read, stories that are left behind because the woman grows up and finds out there is no such thing as storybook love like that." She scowled. "Except you just showed Rachel that such a love *does* exist, and for *her*."

"No!"

"Yes!" If anything, Danielle only looked more exasperated. "As far as that young lady thinks, you just pledged yourself to her. You knelled for her and touched her. You chimed Elysian Bells. You announced your love to heaven. There are a few backwater courts where that would mean you just *married* the girl." She straightened up and shook her head. "How am I going to explain this to Lady Kristen?"

"I. Don't. Love. Her."

"Horse. Shit. Everyone in the store just had their teeth cracked by your love. People as far as the third well probably heard it. Word will be spreading through town that a Bell went off. A crowd will be gathering outside my store by now."

"But I don't."

Danielle looked at him skeptically. "Are you embarrassed, Ezra? You shouldn't be. I don't know why it has to be her, a slip of a girl, and not someone more . . . mature." She glared meaningfully at him, then shook her head. "But it's a gift that your feelings manifest like this, an *amazing* gift. Explore it, yes, but *outside* my store, if you please. And *after* you marry her."

"She looked like the Queen," Ezra said.

"What?" Danielle froze.

"Her blonde hair, it made her look like the Queen, just as she looked eleven years ago."

"The Queen?" Danielle's face was aghast, her eyes wide, mouth caught between skepticism and horror.

"Yes."

Danielle caught her breath, smoothed her face, and reached unsteadily for a chair to catch her balance. "You chimed for the Queen?"

Ezra looked down. "No one can know." It was an enormous secret, though not his darkest. "I never touched the Queen," he lied. "No one can *think* that I did. I just loved her. A secret I kept from everyone. Especially from *her*."

"Really?" Stonehouse said, face skeptical again.

"Yes. She didn't know. It was never acted upon. My nature, too, I kept secret."

Daniella shook her head in disbelief. "Well, not from the Prince of Earl. You ripped his head off and kicked it down the royal halls. He might have had an inkling before his head came loose." She looked up at the ceiling, rolling her eyes. Ezra could almost see her putting it all together, his public history and his poorly kept secret.

"The whole story, your banishment, makes sense now! You killed the prince, then you stormed through the palace murdering whoever you could find in his livery, nearly touching off a war. So they all might have figured it out before they died. It's so *obvious* now." Danielle thrummed her hands on the chair back. "The only reason no one saw this is that no one alive has ever actually *seen* a Bell. No one really believes the legends about them anymore."

Stonehouse pulled up the chair and sat in it. She looked Ezra up and down, considering. "So when someone looks like the Queen, whom you love," she squinted skeptically, "*secretly*, even from her— you chime for them?"

"No ... uh ... not until now ... not really."

Danielle looked at him flatly. "It has always been possible, then, but you managed to contain yourself?"

Ezra nodded. "This is the first time it's ever gotten away from me. I stay in my armor, as you know—except for here, today—I don't touch people. And Rachel surprised me, as you also know."

Danielle sat back thoughtfully. "It almost makes me want to invest in a blonde wig." An eyebrow arched, "Though it's hard on my merchandise."

"I'm not marrying Rachel."

I have another owner. Even if she sent me away.

"No, no, you can't," said Stonehouse soberly. "Once that hair dye came out, she would be a very disappointed young lady." Danielle held an apologetic hand up toward Ezra and added, "I just measured you, Sir Knight. You, uh, have what it takes, but the young lady thinks she has a love made in heaven, perhaps the only one in this generation . . ." She thought some more and added, "And what if the Queen wants you back?"

"She doesn't."

"Yes, I suppose it's been eleven years . . . This is all very damned strange," said Stonehouse. "We need a really good lie."

Ezra had heard that line before. It made him sick.

"We have to tell her it's all a mistake," he said. "Then I'll leave on this trip. By the time I'm back, she'll have forgotten all about it."

Danielle started laughing. "Oh definitely. It's not like this isn't the prettiest love story on earth that you've given her." Abruptly, she stopped laughing and stared maces at Ezra. "A storybook knight who chimes like heaven with love only for her while dispensing hell-shattering violence against all enemies. And you *touched* her with your resonance! She's never going to forget that. *No one* would. Do you have any idea how that must *feel?*"

"Yes," Ezra said miserably. "I feel it first, so yes, I do know."

Danielle looked down at her hands, hands that had touched him while he had chimed. "You've really messed up, *Sir* Ezra."

"So . . . back to a lie?"

"A lie."

~

"You could die?" Rachel exclaimed.

Ezra was a terrible liar. Everyone who played cards with him knew it, and Stonehouse was one of them, so she jumped back in. "That's right, Sir Ezra needs permission from the Archbishop and the Queen, and he needs to ask his dead wife, Lilly, at her gravesite. Otherwise . . ." she shook her head sadly.

"Otherwise he'll die?" Rachel said through tears.

"You've read *The Last Tolling*, you know that he could," Danielle said. "You felt how he got louder and louder. It wouldn't have stopped. You could also have been hurt."

Rachel dried her eyes on the scarf that Stonehouse gave her. "So what are we going to say happened?"

"Well—" said Ezra, uncomfortable and ill at ease. He hated himself for lying.

"We are going to say that there was an accident," Danielle interrupted. "A robber came and Sir Ezra fought him. It was the chime of violence. The thief went out the back, scared to death, and ran away. And that's *all* we'll say."

Rachel wailed, "But I *love* you, Ezra."

Her sincerity took the knife of their lie and plunged it into Ezra's stomach. Danielle was undeterred. "There are no other Bells left, Rachel. This is why. Conflicted loyalty, such as between the fealty he owes your mother and you, or the Queen and you, could rip him apart."

"No," Rachel breathed.

"If you love him, you will keep silent and be patient."

Rachel nodded.

"Now go out there and wait. Sir Ezra will come out in a moment, and then you will each leave separately. And. Stay. Away. From. Each. Other."

Rachel lurched toward Ezra, stopped, seemed to quiver. Her dress had been repaired. She was in the right place for that at least. Her throat spasmed with some barely contained outburst before she turned abruptly from Ezra and marched out the door.

Ezra looked at Danielle and shook his head

She only shrugged. "It was in a book. A book I know she has read. What else could we have said? It might even be true for all you know."

The door swung open. It was Brendan, one of Danielle's assistants. "There are a couple of gentlemen outside," he said, "asking to see Sir Ezra." He nodded and left as quickly as he had arrived.

"Must be the constables," said Danielle.

It felt more than strange being out of his armor, dressed in thin pants and a shirt anywhere but in his private rooms, let alone heading out to see officers of the law. And preparing to tell them a lie.

No lie has ever made my life better. This one won't either.

But Ezra could not think what else to do.

My honor was destroyed eleven years ago anyway.

This lie was a consequence of that first one. He walked across the storefront with Danielle.

The Stonehouse was a beautiful shop, the finest of its kind in town. There were elegant hats and scarves, expensive canes, exquisite black calf-leather gloves, everything displayed with style on carefully posed mannequins among expensive cherrywood furniture and artfully arranged vases and pictures. Ezra flinched when he saw the broken mirror and shattered vases.

Rachel was standing near the door. Its small stained-glass window was indeed cracked, just as Stonehouse had claimed.

"I'll help tell them what happened," Rachel said, staring intensely at Ezra.

He could feel Danielle stiffen beside him. Rachel was already finding excuses to be with Ezra. For his part, Ezra did everything he could not to look at her face or her long blonde hair.

If I start vibrating again, it's all over.

Rachel insinuated herself just ahead of him as he swung the door open.

A festive-looking crowd had gathered outside, leaving only a little space directly in front of the shop. Two men in rich clothes and long cloaks stood a little apart from the crowd, perhaps twenty yards away. They had the look of Erle, though probably only Ezra recognized those long cloaks favored by that country's assassin-knights.

In unison, the two men threw back their bulky cloaks to reveal loaded crossbows and aimed them at Ezra and Rachel.

A deep gong-like sound erupted from Ezra as he pivoted in front of Rachel to shield her with his body and slammed the door shut again in front of them. At the same instant, two heavy bolts flew from the assassins. One hit the door dead center, just below the cracked window, and punched through the wood to pierce deep into Ezra's back. The other bolt hit the edge of the door as it closed and careened into the store, narrowly missing Danielle but hitting a male mannequin in the stomach, sending it flying with a clatter against the wall.

"*Cane!*" roared Ezra over his own ringing, pulling himself painfully off the bolt.

Stonehouse reacted quickly and threw one of her heaviest canes, a polished ironwood piece, to Ezra. He snatched it out of the air, pushed Rachel to the side of the door opposite to its opening, flung the door open again, and charged outside, making a straight, hard line for the two Knights of Erle.

The crowd was panicking and scrambling to clear the area, but their footfalls and their screams could not be heard over the thunderhead of deep peeling sounds exploding in the air around Ezra.

The assassins were frantically trying to reload. A fatal mistake, because Ezra was on them, a deep, terrifying sound emanating from him as much as from the air around him, like rolling thunder, well before their next bolts were ready.

He hit the first man across the top of the head and broke his skull in a spray of bone, hair, and blood, stoving it in. The second man had drawn an arming sword, something short and fast, and swung it with evident haste and panic at Ezra, hitting him in the side. Ezra had been moving away and vibrating, so the blow, though sharp and painful, did not appear to cut right through his ribs and did not immediately fell him. The man's eyes were wide as he drew back for a second swing, but Ezra caught and held the blade with his cane, which proved to be remarkably hard. His arm vibrated with a speed out of mind, and he spun the cane around the man's guard, then struck him savagely in the temple. The would-be assassin collapsed like his strings had been cut, dropping his sword into the cobbles.

"Stay down!" Ezra roared. The man lay still on his side for several long moments before twitching into motion, his hand scrambling for his sword.

Ezra hit him in the head again, busting the left side open in an explosion of blood and brain matter. The cane was almost invisible as it resonated with Ezra's vibrations. The assassin lay still.

I have been lucky. This time.

Ezra looked down at the wave of blood streaming down under his shirt, registered the pain in his back from that first bolt, and reconsidered his luck.

"Murderer!" cried a new, tense voice in the accents of Erle. "You won't escape retribution forever!"

The voice was enraged and loud, but Ezra almost failed to hear it over his own deep, angry ringing. Out of the corner of his eye, he saw the man. The plan made sense now. Two lesser assassins to distract him while the real threat lurked in the crowd with a lighter, quicker crossbow.

As plans went, it made sense, but the assassin's need for emotional vindication had been a mistake. "Drop it," Ezra heard Danielle Stonehouse call. She had appeared from nowhere with her own, smaller crossbow, and pointed it now at the third assassin's torso.

Ezra took a chance and cautiously turned to get a better look at the man who was about to kill him. He was only a few steps away to Ezra's left, in close. Too close, maybe. An opportunity? The skin on the assassin's face rippled from the heavy, low keening sound that emanated from some halo around Ezra, and his eyes squinted against the pressure, but they were hard. His finger was on the trigger of the weapon, and Ezra knew he was about to pull regardless of the threat from Stonehouse.

Ezra's blurring hand shot out just as the assassin pulled his trigger and Danielle simultaneously shot the man of Erle in the chest. Ezra's hand was vibrating so quickly it was nearly invisible. In a flash, he tilted the end of the crossbow up even as the bolt was launched, affecting its trajectory. Even so, the missile hit him, shattering into two pieces. One ripped a trail of broken skin along his left arm and the other penetrated the top of his shoulder. Two spinning paths of red blood followed the pieces as they flew off down the street to the sound of rising bells.

"Oh my love, you're hurt!" exclaimed Rachel, rushing to him.

He saw her long blonde hair and remembered another day in the past with the Queen, also filled with blood and secrets. He chimed from deep roaring anger to high soaring love and lost consciousness.

CHAPTER 5

SHADOWS OF THE PAST

He bobbed in an endless ocean, moving gently in the long, slow swell of idea and mind. Ignorant of how he had gotten there or what his purpose might be.

Bereft of any internal recognition of the world or himself at all.

The great risings and fallings of dark, fathomless water ought to have been frightening, for those who bobbed near its surface were entirely at the mercy of the waves, and the ocean was infinitely powerful. Nor could they know what leviathans might swim in the deeps below.

The man, however, felt no fear, only a sharp, heavy loneliness. The endless sea seemed too vast a body not to host other travelers. Or signposts. He splashed, turning to look in every direction. There was no road, no marker, no other person. No discussion, no idea. Only more water. It was so featureless that he could not even be sure if he had turned one, two, or even three circles in the water. It felt wrong, as if something even more important was missing. But what? He considered this in the long unending time that lay before him and concluded that something so puissant as this vast ocean should have a purpose, an effect. Or failing those, at least some other witness to its infinite majesty.

But there was only him.

Moving slowly and purposelessly in the inexorable grip of an unknown tide within a trackless and endless sea. Not knowing what he loved, what he thought, or even the product of both: his identity.

"How long can I live here?" he asked the body of water. "Who *am* I?"

There was no answer, not even the possibility of one. The sound was simply lost without echo to the boundless, open sky and bottomless sea.

Eventually, there was pain. In his back, in his side, along one arm and shoulder. He whirled in the water, looking for the tiny fish he imagined might be devouring him. There was nothing, no little predators with long, sharp teeth and quick movements.

"Damn."

He had hoped to speak with the fish, even if they were slowly consuming him.

Time passed, increasingly in pain and loneliness. The sense of absolute isolation was by far the worst of the two torments. "Destroy me, only end this abandonment!" he shouted to the infinite water.

Destruction did not come—at least not in the swift form he looked for—only the continual rising and falling of the swell.

There was no sun that he could see, just a brightness in the sky. There was no way to tell time, except through the persecution of unending solitude in a wet, endless desert of self.

An eternity later, a tall, pointed shadow slowly crept up and came over the man. It looked at first like a thorn moving across the water, sliding silently toward his impalement. As the dark silhouette moved over his mind, he turned to see a massive iceberg behind him. He never considered that it may have approached stealthily on currents of its own, for purposes of its own. The shadow was merely its tip, and not a thorn at all.

Though the tip pointed toward heaven, the man understood that the vast bulk of this creature was hidden beneath the surface of the dark waters. He rejoiced that he had found company. He spoke questions and made observations to the silent, inscrutable mass. He swam all around its enormous bulk, admiring its smooth lines and how beautifully blue the upper sections looked before the water turned cold and dark. He dived down a few body lengths to see how deep the clean, crystalline structure went and was amazed at the endless, vertiginous expanse of ice below him.

There is no bottom to this creature.

I could spend a lifetime exploring this iceberg and never know or understand her completely.

Emerging from the water, he realized that he had found more than just a vast and complex companion, he had found out something about himself. Some knowledge had returned to him, the most important kind. *Love.*

He said to the iceberg, "You are beautiful."

Ezra sat up, trying to remember the dream.

He had been lying on his right side.

"Lie back down, Knight," said Danielle, "I don't want you bleeding your last on *my* bed."

Ezra lay back on his side but turned his head. There was no indentation beside him, which was a relief. He turned his head farther to look at Danielle Stonehouse, dressed in a simple green dress and lounging in a very peculiar but comfortable-looking chair beside the bed. The chair was long, almost the length of a bed, but had a soft back and a folded-up blanket near one of its arms.

She slept there.

"Yes, I stayed with you after the surgeon finished," she said, noting his gaze. "Someone had to protect you from all the blonde women of the world who might scale the wall, climb through the window, and find you without your armor."

Ezra knew there was little point in protesting or defending himself. *Events have truly taken a ridiculous turn.*

"Thank you," he said, vowing silently to control his feelings and still his mind in the future. But making a vow would not erase the damage he had already done to Rachel.

"There are also two academics who seem almost as aroused at the idea of seeing you. They *heard* you yesterday, Ezra, and now insist on speaking with you." She smiled sharply. "*Exigently*, they said."

"I don't know any academics," Ezra said, then stopped himself. "Did they have a bird?"

"With them," sneered Stonehouse.

"I don't know any birds, either," he muttered.

"Well, I've traded messages with Lady Kristen, *your* lady, and she says that she will see them off and send your armor as soon as you are again capable of wearing it."

"Thank you," Ezra said. He tried to sit up again, but Danielle was out of her chair quickly and had one hand on his chest and another on his left shoulder before he got far.

"You are here rather than at the Province estate where many feel you rightfully belong, because of grievous injuries." She sat on the bed, her hands still resting upon him. "Your trip to the capital will have to be postponed a few weeks." She removed her hands and stared at them for a moment. "Perhaps by then I will have sorted out who is going to pay for my shattered merchandise."

"A few weeks?" Ezra said. "No, I can go tomorrow."

"Is that so?" said Danielle. She lifted her hands from his chest and, without another word, climbed onto the bed, pulled up the hem of her dress, and straddled his hips, careful not to put too much weight on him.

What are you doing?

She smiled as if she could hear his thoughts. Placing her hands back on his chest again, she said, "Can you . . . get up *now*?"

Despite the pain in his back, side, arm, and shoulder—despite knowing he had nearly died a few hours before—Ezra could not ignore the delicious sensation of her thighs hugging him. Halfheartedly, he attempted to push her off but found himself utterly powerless to do so. "Well, this is a situation I never imagined," he said at last, surrendering.

Danielle's eyebrows arched. "Me neither, though you *are* stronger than I imagined you could be." She put one hand on the bed on either side of his face and said, "You started chiming again, very softly, just before you awoke."

"I'm sorry."

"Don't be," she said with a predatory smile.

"Danielle," Ezra said, intensely aware of how close she was and how little he could do about it. "You saw what happened to Rachel. I'm dangerous. You should not touch me."

With a sigh, she dismounted him and walked to the door. "If you promise to stay there, I will send Brendan to find the surgeon so she can have another look at you. Perhaps there can be a new prognosis somewhere between three weeks and tomorrow."

After this, it seemed to Ezra that he was alone there for a very long time. Solitude was nothing new for him, of course, but normally he spent his time productively, patrolling the estate of Lady Kristen Province, guarding her person, or training her guardsmen. These had been his tasks with the Queen too, for years. Being alone, living silently in his thoughts, had been quite pleasurable until he had fallen in love with her, until he had become *hers*. After that, it never occurred to him that he was alone or that he rarely spoke in her presence. He was with her, which he loved and needed, and everything she did fascinated him.

Or hurt him.

In the back of his mind there was a resonance of thought, some idea that this state of mind paralleled some other recent mindset or memory, but he could not connect it.

The surgeon arrived at some point, with Danielle Stonehouse, and opened the curtains and shutters wide—the glass windows had been removed—to let daylight in. She lifted the blankets and examined his wounds, starting with his back.

"Strange," she said. "Fast. Not exactly pretty, but very . . . unusual." She continued poking at his back while she spoke. "This is a consequence of your . . . condition, yes?"

"Of being a Bell?" asked Danielle, for him.

"Quite," said the surgeon.

"It is healed enough that I can travel tomorrow?" Ezra said.

"By no means," the surgeon said. She moved to his ribs. "Are your bones stronger than normal, I wonder? Like a cat that purrs?"

"I don't purr," Ezra choked. *And I'm not a cat.*

"More like a thousand cats," interjected Danielle.

The surgeon snorted, showing the first sign of a sense of humor. "Cats have strong bones because of the vibration of their purring. Perhaps that's why the cut didn't reach your lung and kill you on the spot."

She moved to his arm, unbandaging it from wrist to shoulder. She inspected the cuts, then bandaged them up again. "Your arm has scabbed over too fast. It's going to look like hell."

"At least it's my left."

"You are fortunate no tendons were severed."

"What does this mean, doctor?" asked Danielle.

The surgeon packed up her instruments before answering Stonehouse. "This is new territory for me. I don't know if this rate of recovery will continue." She pursed her lips. "This knight is still in a serious condition, but he is better than anyone could have expected. He's *alive.*" She looked at Ezra, considering. "He will not be able to sit on a horse for more than a week, even if he continues healing at this rate. The bolt punctured the key stabilizing muscle between his hips, ribs, and spine."

"But I could sit in a carriage?" asked Ezra to an annoyed look from both women.

The answer came hesitantly from the surgeon. "Perhaps in four or five days, under best-case assumptions," she said slowly.

"Two," said Ezra quickly.

The surgeon's expression grew almost as malevolent as the assassins' had been. "Then it would be best to die now and save us further trouble."

Ezra was about to protest again, but Danielle once more put her hand on his chest and said, "Why don't we alert Lady Kristen's secretary? Pontes, right? Let's instruct him to ready the carriage and this knight's warhorse—in tow—for some time in the next five days, subject to notification. Then we can see how he fares."

"That is reasonable," the surgeon said to Danielle, once more ignoring Ezra. "I will visit every morning and evening to assess his progress."

"Thanks for not straddling me," Ezra said to the surgeon, but looking at Danielle.

"What?" the surgeon asked.

Danielle smiled but looked, for the first time in Ezra's experience, uncomfortable. "He's confused by the poppy you gave him earlier," she said hastily.

"Hmm," said the surgeon. "Well, straddling of any kind would do him no good right now. Your proposed timeline is extremely optimistic. He could still die of infection."

Stonehouse pulled the shutters and curtains tight, plunging the room into darkness, then took the surgeon by the elbow and guided her to the door. "There is a young woman lurking on the street outside my establishment."

"You can only mean Lady Rachel," the surgeon said flatly.

"Correct," said Danielle opening the door. "If she were to visit our knight, infection is the least of what might happen." The door closed and their voices faded. "And that is why it is important that you tell her that . . ." were the last words Ezra could make out.

He was alone in the dark. He was used to that from his past life. The Queen had been, and still was, the center of his universe. She did not act in consideration of *his* benefit, he acted in *hers*. Being cared for by Danielle Stonehouse and the surgeon was an unusual pleasure for him. Such solicitude had not happened before in his life, except perhaps sometimes from his friend Sir Marigold. But from her, it was always accompanied by cursing.

The world does not revolve around me.

He wondered what he would find when he returned to the true center of things, however briefly. A rising feeling, deep in his stomach, told him that he should not delay.

He lay there in the dark, through long silent minutes and hours, willing strength into his body.

"You are sleeping in my bed," Stonehouse said that night from the doorway. A sliver of lamplight coming through the shutters cast an amber glow over her. Ezra saw that she wore a white sleeping gown of some expensive cloth. He worried that she would put her hands on him once more, but she walked softly, her nightgown swishing, to her lounging chair and lay back upon it.

"Be guarded while you sleep, Knight," she said, pulling the blanket she kept there up to her neck.

"Thank you."

"Someone needs to protect you from the world. And the world from you."

Ezra closed his eyes.

She was gone before he awoke the next morning.

Feeling stronger and less worried about what might happen with Danielle, Ezra eased himself carefully out of bed. He felt steady on his feet. A basin of warm water, a pearl-handled razor, clean clothes, and a towel waited on an elegant wooden table. He felt still stronger after making use of these items. Cleaner, better defined.

The wound on his back hurt worse than the others, though Ezra understood that the sword stroke to his ribs had come closest to ending his life. Blood no longer spotted through his bandages, though he had not truly tested the stitches or the dressing. He had not stirred from Danielle's bed until now.

The door opened on silent hinges as Ezra emerged from the dark room for the first time. He stood at the end of a long hall. Along one side, windows allowed sunlight in, and Ezra could see that he was on the third and top floor of her shop.

Why don't I test my legs?

Walking was not easy. Ezra found his balance a little off. *The poppy?* And he was stiff. But as he marched back and forth down the hallway, a feather's weight of strength and coordination returned. And more than that, a feeling of control. A feeling that he might soon fly again by his own wings and return to the capital. For business yes, but perhaps also to catch the smallest glimpse or sign of *her*. The Queen.

He caught his reflection in a hallway window. He looked gaunt. Chiming for the Queen—even if it was *to* Rachel—and then against the assassins had stolen energy from him. Being injured had taken more of his reserves.

It reminded him of how dangerous it was to chime. A child's story to some, a fantasy of sex or violence to others, the curse he had been born with was perilous to everyone who felt its touch. *Poor Rachel.* There were so many reasons to avoid losing control, so much unnecessary pain to avoid inflicting.

I must control myself if I am to do any good in the world.

With a fantasy of control in his mind, Ezra continued exercising.

When he heard footsteps on the stairs, he returned to his room and lay on the bed. It was Danielle with a tray of meat and cheese.

"You have been up and about," she said, her expression melancholy.

Why does she look sad?

"Yes. Please tell Pontes th—"

"Please walk softly, Knight. I have spoken to Lady Kristen again about Rachel's intentions. She has agreed that Pontes will wait on the next street every morning for the next few days. I haven't lied to you."

"I know," Ezra said. "Where is my armor?"

"With Pontes," Stonehouse said. "If you leave this week, you won't be in condition for that much steel."

Probably true.

She took the tray with her when she left.

As soon as Ezra was sure she was gone, he returned to walking the hall and exercising quietly there. He could not perform a sit-up, would not have dared to try, but he could manage a push-up now, though it came with sharp and immediate pain, and he could squat. Stretching his heavily scabbed and still bandaged left arm was out of the question.

"*Back to my room,*" Danielle hissed sometime later, surprising him. Ezra had been too intent on a stretch to hear her. She looked distressed now. The knight obeyed without question, trusting her concern.

"Get undressed," she whispered urgently.

"Bu—" Ezra reminded himself that she had to have seen him naked already, that she had, in fact, slept only a scant few feet away from him. His sense of normalcy was askew, he knew, but he did what she asked. The intensity of her expression demanded his obedience. "I will be able to leave soon," he said once she had tucked him under the covers.

"Yes, you have progressed amazingly quickly, Ezra, but you must rest now."

"Okay."

"Just lie back, Knight, and relax," Danielle said. "When you are ready, Pontes will be there, out back, waiting." She produced a spoon of poppy milk. "This is at the orders of the surgeon."

"Thank you for looking after me," Ezra said.

Stonehouse's eyes were wet, which was odd. *She is not a very emotional woman.*

He had never thought to see her cry.

A strange lassitude rolled over him. The physical pain receded, and his mind left the present, returning to memories, burnt into dreams, of a night twelve or more years in the past.

CHAPTER 6

DOORWAY TO TIME

Sir Ezra had stood watch at the Queen's door for years. Ever since Lilly died. From before she had even been Queen, back when she was still a princess. He had seen young men come to her chambers at night—a few women too—though he rarely saw them leave, which was strange. As painful as seeing these lovers had been, their visits were few compared to the many long nights of labor on behalf of her Queendom. She rarely stopped working at all, always in meetings with Lady Kay and other advisors, in argument with a hundred lords, studying the finances, drawing up plans. Sometimes just sitting by herself, thinking. Once he saw her brush her long, blonde hair and dreamt of being the brush.

He could not pinpoint the exact moment that he fell in love.

Perhaps *falling* in love is an apt term, he thought, for the intensity started slow and became stronger the longer the fall persisted. He knew that he had already fallen an infinite distance into love with her on the night he heard her quietly crying, the night she left the heavy chamber door open.

He strained to hear her. These moans were not the loud, breathless ones the Queen produced during sex. Or the angry shouts of frustration when her lovers disappointed her and she ordered them to leave. Those screams and shouts had hurt Ezra viscerally. It was not simple jealousy. He knew the Queen did not love her lovers, but it hurt that she was not loved during such moments of excess feeling. When she was vulnerable.

She should be in loving *arms. My* arms.

The sound coming from her chambers on this evening had not, at first, hurt the knight. He had not immediately made sense of them. His helm was on, muffling the sound. But there was something, something not right. The feeling worked on him until he did what he had never done. He removed his helm and put his ear to the space left by the open door.

She was crying. Quietly. In the dark, alone.

This was the worst pain that his love for the Queen had yet produced. It was like being stabbed in the guts. It reminded him of his helplessness at the death of Lilly in childbirth but was perhaps even worse. Lilly had died, but in her last moments, after Ezra had sent everyone else away, he had chimed for her. She had died feeling his love, had left the world to ringing glory. The Queen was alive, but suffering and alone in the dark.

Her pain and aloneness called to his own and worked upon his discipline, his sense of duty, even his sense of self. There was nothing more frustrating and soul-crushing than hearing someone he loved in pain that he could not assuage. Her tears were the small sounds that shattered his armor and ruined his restraint.

Steel-encased men can only move silently with great care, but great care was what Ezra had for her. The heavy metal was good. It made him cautious, kept him safe, helped him keep *her* safe. He thought of his armor as his discipline, his overmind, the conscious effort that kept his internal passions from inflicting themselves on the world. His armor was the tool and symbol that he used to lever his emotions into stillness, into quiet.

It held his feelings in and bounded their immense potential energy. And yet, when he walked so carefully across the thick rugs of her darkened bedchamber, the only faint sounds came from inside him, a barely perceptible humming. The sound of a vast choir of angels singing love on the edge of hearing.

She sat in a chair. Papers were strewn across a desk behind her, but she had turned her chair and herself away from them. She was hugging one knee to her chest, exhaling deeply, chin lifted proudly despite the tears flowing down her cheeks. Struggling to regain control of her emotions.

An answering resonance sprang from Ezra and a clear chime echoed off the vaulted stone ceiling.

"What sound is this?" the Queen said, dropping her knee and turning her face toward him.

Ezra desperately clamped down on his feelings, ruthlessly suppressed them, forced them inside. He fell heavily to his knees beside her, making his armor clang, attempting to disguise the sound of his love echoing across her world. "I am sorry, my Queen," he said. "I heard you and thought I should see what I could do."

"You can do nothing, Knight," she said in a small voice. "I must solve these challenges alone."

"What challenges?"

In the dark, it was impossible to see how wet her eyes were, but Ezra knew tears still flowed. There was a thickness to her voice when she replied. "Easing the pain and suffering of my people, preparing for threats, recognizing opportunities before they slip away, sensing counterforces, determining who is an enemy and who is a friend."

"Tell me whom to destroy," Ezra said. A new, deep sound rolled out of him now, so deep it was almost beyond human hearing.

The Queen looked up suddenly, and Ezra crushed the sound of his soul into silence once more. She frowned, then seemed to set aside her confusion. "If only it were so easy. It falls to me, and me alone, to find a way through this, Knight. I am the purpose that aims to save the Queendom."

She stood up, towering over him though she was not tall. "I am the Queen," she said in a voice grown strong. "I will do what needs doing, sacrifice what needs sacrificing, give what needs to be given. It is my duty, my honor, and my pleasure to do so! For a better world, Knight."

"But not alone, surely?" Ezra said in a small voice, trembling to hold his raging feelings bound.

"Yes, alone," she said.

"But why?"

"Fewer people get hurt that way."

"No, no." Ezra could not accept this woman crying alone in the dark. "Tell me how I can help," said Ezra, his teeth clenched with his effort to hold his feelings inside. "I would sacrifice too."

"You would sacrifice?" she asked in a new voice, still towering over him, now very close.

"Yes."

There was a pause before the Queen, in a new voice, deep and frightening now, said, "You do not know what you are saying."

"I will do anything for you."

"Take off your armor."

"W-who will guard you?"

She laughed now, a brittle sound, "I need no guards for this."

Ezra put steel arms around her narrow waist and said, "I love you, my Queen."

"**Rose**," she said in her new voice.

"I love you, Rose." A deep, penetrating bell-like sound manifested in the air, shaking the room, shattering a tall narrow mirror on the wall. "I love you, I love you, I love you."

A painting on the wall fell with a crash, a crystal figurine on a pedestal disintegrated, but the great ringing sound only grew. With strength unimaginable, the Queen broke his metal grip and ran to the door of the bedchamber, slammed it shut, and just as quickly rushed back to him.

"Stop, stop, stop, Knight, stop, *Bell*. Keep your armor on, hold it in," she said, voice desperate now, her arms around his neck, hugging him.

"I love your pain," he answered, and a clear sound of heaven keened, not painful to the ears but damaging to stone.

I love your complexity,
I love your tears
Your hard relentless work,
Unyielding will
And your exhaustion.
I love your passion
And the look
Of determination
On your face.
I love your hair,
It falls from heaven.

With every word, the room shook with a reverberating, heavenly sound. And with every word, it seemed, the Queen shouted "Stop!"

He paused, and she seemed to come to a decision. Taking a deep breath, a step backwards, and summoning some profound power from deep within, she responded to him. Her voice was low and dark. It issued from between teeth suddenly long and sharp like thorns of bone, her quieter tones not ringing like his, but with a power of their own.

I am the Queen
And float alone
Unseen on endless seas,
On missions of my own
With sins aplenty to atone
Yet full and strong, complete.
These are my tasks
Your sympathy, I do not ask;
Your assistance would be wrong.

Ezra was entranced by the dark sounds and the unyielding words. His heart leapt. *She is like me, only darker, more alone.* He sang back.

I know that you are vast,
An iceberg floating past.
But let me swim within your wake
And follow in your journey,

I will take no space

I will help you with good grace.

The Queen shot back, not nearly as loud, but darker even than before.

You cannot survive on my ice

My life is only awful sacrifice!

Ezra responded in ever-rising chimes and ever-growing volume.

I love your selfless sacrifice.

Let me only stand beside

And lift your obstacles,

Not because you need me

But so that you can do still more.

I love you, Rose.

The entire palace shook now, and the dust of breaking rock fell from the ceiling.

She ceased replying then and stepped back into him. She reached her hand out to touch his face and ran her fingers behind his head. She clutched a handful of his hair and bent his head away from her, exposing his neck. Her lips pressed gently against his flesh. He could feel her tongue against his skin. She breathed in and bit his neck. Hard, drawing blood. Then, in a voice once more human, she said, "Stop, Ezra, stop Knight, stop or we both shall be destroyed!"

"Aaahhhhhhh!" Ezra screamed, fighting to draw in the rolling sound of bells and vibrations that shook the walls of the room.

"Shhhh," she whispered, holding him tight, her bloody lips still at his neck. "Quiet your feelings, still your mind."

"Why?" he said, struggling. Now that the power was released, it seemed impossible to contain, harder yet to step back across the line he had rung into oblivion.

"No one can know what you are and that you love me. No one, ever."

Hot tears accompanied the effort to deny love, to create a thin, transparent wall between it and the world, to still the heavenly announcement of a sacred passion.

"Shhhhh, now. Shhhhh. Quiet." The Queen's dagger-like hair fanned around his head, and she whispered to him, "You can do it, and you will do it. You are strong, the strongest I've ever seen. *Be* strong then, take it back inside, hold it in, hold it, hold it fast."

By degrees, the sounds lessened. Slowly, slowly, until there was only a man on his knees in heavy armor being held by a woman with long, golden hair, in the dark.

~

"Rose!"

Ezra tried to sit up, but he felt a great, heavy lassitude bearing down upon his mind and body.

Rose?

I've just uttered the name I must not utter. Ezra lay still and attempted to collect himself.

"You were chiming again. Loudly," Danielle said languidly from the sleeping chair. Despite her dream-like tone, she was breathing rapidly.

"Why don't I remember falling asleep?"

Why am I so confused?

"Mmmm," breathed Danielle, "because Rachel wanted to see you, and I couldn't prevent her any longer." He heard her get up out of her chair and slide into the bed beside him.

That explains little.

"So I multiplied your poppy to ensure an appearance of near death when she came in." He felt Danielle slide underneath him and place his head on her stomach.

She sent me backward. And didn't tell me.

Ezra tried to sit up again, but he still felt disoriented from the poppy, and Danielle's hands easily held his spinning head where she wanted it. "I've had quite a nice set of dreams myself . . . in response to your chiming," she said wistfully. "It has been years since I felt even a tiny fraction of such release."

Why are you doing this?

"Why are you speaking to me this way?" Ezra asked.

Danielle's hand gently caressed his jawline. "I am keeping a great and dark secret *for* you, Sir Ezra, I won't keep one *from* you." Her hand stopped. "Have you read *The Glass Empress*?'" she asked. "It is about Empress Jessamine and her quest for a Bell lover. She dismissed her entire harem when she heard stories about a young man who rang death in battle. She devoted her life to winning his love, which she later said was the sound and feeling of heaven."

"No, I haven't," Ezra choked. He avoided such stories.

"When they married," Danielle continued, caressing his face once more, "there were no musicians, save for him, knelling his love. They called the sound *Elysian Bells*. They were so powerful, so impassioning, that every woman in the city, it is said, became pregnant on their wedding night. You've heard the legend."

Yes, a children's fantasy. Ezra cleared his throat. "In all the years I've known you, Danielle, I have never heard a word of sentiment from your mouth."

"Hmmm," she said. "Perhaps I have changed. Or have *been* changed."

"I am sorry," Ezra said.

"Too late," she whispered. "You say that you know how your chiming feels, but I don't think you do know. I can *feel* your love for her." She kissed his head through his hair. "Only it is not at all apparent to me that it is for the Queen. It feels like *mine*."

Ezra felt a great wariness, a concern that burned much of the poppy away. A concern that forced him to think carefully before responding to her. "I don't want to hurt you like I hurt Rachel."

And then run away. Dead gods, what am I doing?

"I'm not Rachel."

"I think I should speak with her before I go."

Danielle sighed. "That is a *very* bad idea. She needs to forget you."

"Will you arrange it?"

"Yes." She kissed his neck, reminding him momentarily of the

Queen. "I'll tell her to wear a hood to hide that blonde hair of hers so you don't make things worse."

"Speaking of that, I—"

"And I'm not you, Ezra, sweet man that you are, to waste a decade of my life dreaming about a woman who rejected me." Her hands swept along his sides. "In fact, I don't think I'll see you again after tonight. I don't think you're coming back at all. We won't be friends, we won't be lovers, but we could still be . . ."

Ezra found himself responding, but after Rachel he feared harming her. "I *like* you Danielle," he said, bringing a hand around and sliding it over her hip.

She trembled under his touch.

"But I am a possession of the Queen."

And I don't want you to feel as hopeless as I feel.

But you said you would not.

"And I don't want you to feel the same pain I feel."

I don't want to hurt you.

Danielle kissed him on his chest, then his mouth, each touch erasing a little more of his guilt and worry, almost as if she could read his thoughts.

There were few women cannier than Danielle Stonehouse, and few of those could also have produced a crossbow and summarily executed an assassin or saved Ezra from further harm with Rachel. Only the Queen and Marigold were tougher, as far as Ezra's experience went, and he *loved* the Queen and was close friends with Marigold. But now this woman had secretly taken her own possession of him. She had gone from staring at hands that had touched him when he chimed, to guarding him, to submerging him in sleep with poppy, to sliding into bed with him and holding his head in her lap. He knew what would happen next.

His hands had already started the work, were already exploring her. His body always knew.

I must not hurt her. It was probably too late. He knew that he had infected her, despite her protestations.

"You *like* me?" she said. "I *married* my husband—you never met him—and never felt more than a mild sense of 'liking.' And aside from lust in the first year or two, I never felt there was really much more coming from his side. Our marriage was more a partnership than an exploration of love. I have never felt anything very strong at all for *any* man. Much less feeling anything remotely like your love washing over me, *reverberating* in me, tonight. Think about that, Knight."

"I feel as if I'm cheating on her," Ezra said as his hands continued to move slowly over her body.

"She doesn't care about you," said Danielle. "Or love you."

Ezra did not answer that. He locked his thoughts down. He had to keep at least one secret for himself.

"I killed a man for you."

"Yes, you did," Ezra said. "But she *owns* me."

Danielle began arching under his hands, anticipating him, breathing hard, releasing small, languid moans. "So you have said. But I think that contract has been torn up." She cooed, an expert negotiator, "Let it go."

But Ezra knew he could not. Would not. Ever.

Perhaps his hands stopped moving for a moment, or perhaps his intransigence was evident to her sharp mind, for Danielle added, "If you have told me the truth, she doesn't even know you love her, only that you used your power to bring hell onto Erle and his men before they could murder her. And then she tossed you aside and remarried. Twice."

"She does what she has to."

"You won't see her. No one does."

"Perhaps I will catch a fleeting glimpse of her hair." Ezra was unsure why he clung to this point. It seemed cruel. To himself, mostly.

"You won't. It's as I said, no one outside her immediate circle sees her these days. She is a phantom, a creature of night and shadows." Danielle kissed him gently on the lips. "How did you keep from exposing your love all those years when you couldn't keep from chiming after five minutes with Rachel just because her hair reminded you of your precious Queen?"

Ezra laughed softly between more kisses. "It has not been easy. I wore my armor to contain my feelings and struggled even so. But I knew that to give myself away was to be dismissed, or worse. And in the end, after she married the Prince of Erle and he began plotting against her, I was all she had left."

He was not telling her everything, but he had said too much already. Far too much.

"It still doesn't make sense." She kissed him again, her tongue sliding against his. "You are a wreck, Sir Ezra. Too vulnerable." Another kiss, her breasts sliding like silk ecstasy against him. "Easy meat."

That statement was uncomfortable, even if she had saved his life, though he could not easily deny it. While enjoying her increasingly aggressive kisses, and simultaneously fighting guilt and pain over the Queen, Ezra considered what she had said.

"I have been away from the only one I truly love for eleven years," he began. "And the love has only gotten stronger. The need to express it more powerful. I think I would kill to see her again, even to catch only a glimpse. Or to know something—anything—about her day. What she wore, or a comb from her hair, or even to know what she ate for breakfast. A single thought from the Queen would be my heart's treasure. One moment of light from her being, one flicker from her soul, a single echo of her heartbeat, would be my Elysium. I love her, but I am starved of her and am hungry for anything *of* her."

"I can *feel* it," said Danielle wonderingly. She did not seem to be jealous. "Just on the edge of hearing." She reached between his legs and ran her hand along his hard cock.

"There is something wrong with me."

"Yes," she purred, "It is beautiful."

"The smallest detail, the smallest sign, portent, or glimpse of lost love makes my soul sing."

"I believe you, poor man," Danielle admitted sadly.

She slid down and straddled him. It had been two days, and her weight still hurt, but it did not seem likely to break open any of his wounds, not yet. The Queen had done far worse to him. "I am a practical woman," she said, sliding herself back and forth along him. "And you just *liking* me feels *very* good right now." She kissed Ezra's neck and whispered in his ear, "Close your eyes and think of *her*." Then she said one thing more, something very like a thing the Queen had once said to him. "Sing me a song with no words."

CHAPTER 7

LESSONS

"Not so wide," said Sir Marigold to Gertrude.

The eleven-year-old girl had developed early and was doing what she usually did—using her size to beat the other, smaller girls through sheer power and aggression.

"It works," Gertrude said, and took her position along the circle of sand.

Time to break this habit. Hard.

Marigold had attempted all the nice ways to no effect. They had worked for most of the class, but no technique worked for everyone. Which was part of what she needed to teach.

"It works under a very specific set of circumstances," said Marigold, waving Gertrude's smaller adversary out of the ring, taking her heavy wooden sword and her place.

"Try it on *me*."

A more intelligent student might have demurred, but aggression is not the friend of second thoughts, and Gertrude had spent too much time feeding her anger and building herself into a bully. She swung hard and wide but obvious and slow.

Marigold did not parry. She simply thrust straight, hard, and fast in a direct line to Gertrude's heart—everyone's weakest point in Marigold's experience—and thumped the big girl off her feet.

"Dead gods, damn it!" Gertrude swore and sprang to her feet, taking her place once more. She swung again, this time shouting. Marigold hit her again, but harder.

"Shouting just alerts me," Marigold said. "And if anything, it slowed you up. Try again."

Gertrude tried again. And again. On the fifth attempt, hands shaking and forehead sandy from wiping dirt onto it, the angry young girl finally tried something smarter. She thrust straight at Marigold.

But the knight barely moved. She used her wrist to redirect the blow and then poked the girl off her feet and onto her ass once more. "Brush yourself off and wrack it, Gertrude," Marigold said.

The knight called in the entire girls' class and addressed them together. "Gertrude can beat most of you through brute power. But not me. Why?"

Bethyl raised a hand, and when Marigold nodded, said, "Because you're older?"

"No. Why did she fail? Why would she have been killed if this had been a real fight?"

"Because you're better!" said Sam.

"Yes. But why?"

Ellis raised a hand. "Because you are stronger."

"Also correct," Marigold said. "I *am* stronger, and I beat Gertrude. Gertrude is stronger than you, so she beats you most of the time, Ellis. This is the way of the world, yes?"

The class was silent, except for Gertrude who was trying, unsuccessfully, not to cry.

"Your answer needs to be *no*, ladies," Sir Marigold said. "If the strongest one wins, you will die the first time you fight someone stronger than you. Most of you will die at the hands of most boys."

"Girls are just as good as boys!" shouted Sam.

Marigold gestured a finger at her. "Yes, we are, but we are not the same. No two people are the same, and the sexes are not, on average, the same. Most boys are stronger than most girls."

"That's not fair," said Bethyl.

"Seeking fairness is a waste of time," Marigold replied. "And even if you are an unusually strong woman, like Gertrude, you don't just want to beat *most* boys you fight. You want to beat *all* the boys you fight. And all the girls. How do you do that?"

The class was silent. Gertrude had stopped crying. They were all watching Marigold.

"You must be better. You must be faster, but not through strength. Don't try to mimic your enemies and compete against *their* advantage. We must find our *own* advantages. Efficiency. Ruthlessness. Strategy. Skill. Those are your paths to victory, ladies. Find your advantages, develop them, keep them close. And *maximize* them."

Be like the Queen.

"Sir Marigold?" A page had appeared in the arched doorway of the training garden. A man, this time, which was truly rare. He was holding a large, polished-silver tray in his hands.

"Go clean up, ladies," Marigold said, before approaching the page and his mirror-like platter. Besides the sealed, cream-colored envelope, she saw her own reflection in the tray as she approached. A lean, dark-haired woman in her early thirties, with just a touch of gray. A weary look about her? Perhaps.

"I apologize for interrupting, Sir Marigold. Your words were wisdom incarnate."

"Don't I know it," she returned. "But you have no idea how many times I have uttered them."

"They are still wise," said the page.

"Ha, well, it is in the nature of my order to make metaphors of our lessons, you know." She winked at him. "All the best of us do it."

"You are surely the very best."

Almost. Marigold did not want to think about *him.* Not that she really had much choice. She took the envelope. "Who is this from, then?"

"I cannot say. It was passed from trusted hands to trusted hands and finally to mine with explicit instructions to bring it directly to you," he said, bowing professionally. He spun on polished heels and marched away.

"Of course," she said to herself. His words had been nearly identical to those of all of the previous pages with all of the previous secret orders she had received over the past eleven years. They had been uttered more often even than her words to the girls about finding their advantage.

Marigold did not open the letter until she had cleaned herself in the baths and returned to her chambers. Even then, she waited a little longer before going to the locked box secreted in the wall. It was filled with dozens of the same envelopes, stacked in a neat, tidy order, each with a date added in her own hand. She removed the two most recent envelopes, opened the older one first, and unfolded its single paper. In a careful, elegant hand, it read

"Who in Province knows?"

These terse words from three months past had sent Marigold on a trip to visit Sir Ezra in his comfortable banishment once again. Nothing had changed as far as she could tell. Her old colleague was still opaque to others, dressed as he was at all times in his full armor. Even Marigold, who knew him better than almost anyone else, struggled to see his internal weariness through all that steel. The ever-widening cracks in his armor were all internal.

No one there knew that he was an Elysian Bell.

Well, that secret has left the stables. Word had come in days ago by messenger from Lady Kristen Province that three assassins from Erle had attempted to murder Sir Ezra, and that in killing them, the knight had revealed his Bell power. The word had spread quickly around the capital, and while many did not believe in Bells or any other legendary transcendental powers, except when it suited them, there was no point in worrying about Ezra's secret anymore. She looked at the second message.

"See him protected and happy while he is here."

This note was only a week old. Marigold had wondered what *happy* was supposed to mean. On all her visits to the Province estate, all those visits she had been secretly ordered to make, Ezra had never seemed "happy." He was a man who looked as if he had lost something, something that had permanently affected him, that kept him from living even half the life he should have.

How am I supposed to make him happy?

Finally, Marigold opened the newest letter. It was written in the same precise hand.

"Send him back with all haste."

Marigold sat down and stared at the three letters, pondering their meaning and how she felt about them.

What is the lesson here?

Dead gods! Lost gifts and absent wisdom, what now?

A crowd—more accurately, an ugly mob—had gathered in Leveler's Square. To a woman like Marigold, who preferred either quiet contemplation or sudden, blatant violence, a restless, murmuring mob was an ugly, worrisome knot of potentiality.

Or of truth.

How many mobs possess the truth? None.

In her imposing plate armor, Marigold pushed through the crowd easily. Her metal edges hurt the soft skin of the indolent. Her armor was as good as her tongue for running roughshod over fools.

A mob is only capable of a single thought, a naive framework on which to hang their single, indulgent sense of outrage.

The crowd began to chant, "Stop the dam! Stop the dam! Stop the dam!"

A troop of mummers on the far side of the square did not appear to like the look of the mob or the sound of the chant any more than Marigold did. A raven-haired actress in a beautiful painted dress with wide feather wings improbably sprouting out of the back and a white haired stagehand—or possibly a clown—in garishly patched pants were urgently packing up their pavilion, desperately trying to get the whole facade of a stage back into a crammed wagon. The placard advertising their play, *Saraith of the Nine Rings*, was somehow standing on its thin edge, absent any support. *Makes sense for a play about fate and chance.*

As she passed the weirdly balancing advertisement, she saw that it was on little stands painted to look like the cobbles of the square.

Even fate needs help sometimes.

A fat man in a dark hat walked right into the sign, kicking it over as he shouted, "It's not fair, it's not just!"

It sure isn't.

Shaking her head, Marigold mounted the wide stairs of an old shop on the edge of the square to see what else was not just and, if possible, figure out who was instigating the protest. She saw another figure standing on the shoulder of a stone horse, the key figurehead of the square's central fountain. It was a tall woman.

Lady Jacqueline Paron. Of course.

A good portion of the ancient Paron estate was slated to go underwater once the Queen's great Stillwater Dam project was completed. The Queen had conceived this historic civil undertaking —designed to prevent flooding and provide irrigation to some of the best underutilized land in the Queendom—and was the prime driving force behind the project. Lady Jacqueline and other landowners had been compensated, and generously, for the land they would lose to the dam, but public works projects were like privies. *Everyone wants the contents spilled onto pastures other than their own.*

Let us see what Paron has to say.

After a few more minutes of "Stop the dam" nonsense, Paron held up her hands for silence and began to address the crowd. Her message was short. In ringing tones, she said, "Our land is being drowned! Our land is being *stolen*! And all by a power-mad, husband-murdering *vampire*. The dam must be stopped. Our vampire Queen must be staked! Stop the dam, stake the Queen! Stop the dam, stake the Queen!"

The crowd took up her call at once, chanting "Stop the dam!" again, but this time adding "Stake the Queen!"

"Right," said Marigold, drawing her sword. "That's enough of that!" She had been in the capital, pacing just outside the castle walls, the night the Prince of Erle died. She had heard the terrifying sounds from within and had been at the gate when a gore-covered Sir Ezra had unlocked it, the Queen a few steps behind him, in the shadows. It required a special power to storm a castle, or clear a crowd. Marigold did not have Bell power—Ezra's former secret, now widely known thanks to the recent news out of Province—but she was not about to let a mob call for the death of the Queen.

"Clear the path and stop your lies!" Marigold roared, bounding down the stairs, holding her sword out, ready to cut the flanks of idiot from off the belly of the mob. She made eye contact with Paron, who flinched and looked alarmed. The crowd began to dissolve in confusion. The chant faltered and sputtered. A bald, red-faced man did not pick up on this or notice Marigold coming up on him, he was so intent on stopping the dam and seeing the Queen staked. She summarily struck him in the back of his head with the hilt of her sword.

He fell like a sack of wet flour.

Marigold was no wilting violet. She shouted as if she were on the field of battle, and twice as loudly as Paron, "The next idiot gets the sharp end! Disperse!"

A guardsman in Paron chain and tabard blocked her view of the now wide-eyed Lady Jacqueline. He was a big man, bigger than Ezra and bigger than Marigold by far. His sword was drawn and held high as if to strike.

Marigold did not wait for the man's next move. She feinted wide with her arms, then lunged straight for him, bringing her sword into her center-line and thrusting. She struck straight into the man's stomach, parting his chain mail and sinking the blade into flesh until it hit spine. With a yell, she twisted her sword hard with both hands, ensuring a quick death.

It slipped out easily after the twist.

"Who's next!" she cried, not asking so much as threatening. She waved her sword and scattered blood on the panicking mob, who were now falling over each other to get out of her way. Lady Jacqueline screamed, "M-murderer!" and turned to flee, her remaining guards forming around her.

That's rich coming from someone exhorting a crowd to stake the Queen!

Marigold did not bother making this retort. The weight of her armor made it hard enough to win a foot race against unarmored ladies and their more lightly armored guards without spending breath on a debate. She sprinted, closing the distance to the slowest guard, and when she got close enough, made a mighty, leaping throw of her heavy sword, which spun end over end and took the man in his legs.

He went down with a scream. Marigold leapt onto him and began to beat him in the head with her gauntleted fists. She hit him thrice for good measure after he went limp, disarmed him, and used his belt to tie his hands and feet together, all while breathing in great gasps, trying to pay off her debt of effort.

Still fighting for breath, Marigold sat on the man until the constabulary arrived.

"THAT IS some of the most awful police work I've had the pleasure of seeing," said Constable Bobby Archibald when she finished surveying the scene. She thrust a thumb back at the guardsman Marigold had disemboweled. "Is that also your fine, subtle work?"

"Indeed," said Marigold. "He drew on me."

"I gathered," said Bobby. She removed her tall constable's cap, revealing long red hair. "The sword in his cold, dead hands gives its own testimony."

"Huh. I'm surprised he didn't drop it."

"Stranger things have happened." Bobby pointed at the unmoving guardsman that Marigold was sitting on. "And what about him?"

"Another of the evildoers. Softened up for interrogation. *Probably* still alive."

"Right." Bobby put her cap back on. "Look, Sir Marigold, maybe you didn't hear me the last time I mentioned this, but the aim and goal of the constabulary is to protect the Queen's citizens, not murder them."

Marigold stood up and adjusted the gauntlets on her metal-clad hips. "Indeed. And in case you didn't hear me last time you mentioned this, I am not a constable. I am a Knight of the Queen, and my sole duty is to protect *her*."

Bobby pursed her lips and thought this over. "You may have said that." She gestured around the square. "So what exactly happened here?"

After Marigold laid it out, Bobby asked, "And . . . who handles this? Us or your knights? Either way, Lady Jacqueline is probably holed up in her palace now. Arresting her out won't be easy."

Marigold thought of the orders she had just received. **"Send him back with all haste."**

But not too hastily, perhaps? No need for hiding his secret anymore. No need to get a bunch of constables or knights killed, right?

Right.

"Have your constables surround her palace and keep watch," Marigold said with an evil smile. "I know just the person for dealing with a castle."

CHAPTER 8
TAKING ADVANTAGE

Ezra limped slowly toward the carriage, Rachel's tears helping to make every step more painful.

Telling someone you don't love them seldom feels good for anyone.

In no way did the evening with Danielle Stonehouse make up for seeing the pain in Rachel's collapsed, reddened face, or his own uncertainty about whether or not what he had done was the right thing. In fact, that supposedly guilt-free pleasure with Danielle had only made Ezra feel worse for what had been done to Rachel.

"Take my hand, sir," Pontes said, reaching down from the driver's seat.

It ended up needing both Pontes's hands to get Ezra on board, and even up on the cushioned bench beside the secretary, Ezra still hurt. But the physical pain was much less than the emotional pain from his empathy for Rachel's suffering.

I don't love you.

He did not regret saying those words, he regretted the reason that had made him say them.

It was a struggle not to turn around and see what she was doing.

Was she staring after them? Preparing to hurl a stone at the carriage? Or, worse, had she collapsed like a heap of rags onto the cobbles of the street? Ezra knew what life-changing grief felt like, and he did not wish it upon the girl.

"Perhaps we could discuss the ledgers, sir," said Pontes softly. "Our goals in this negotiation are most complex, and the Queen's advisors are notoriously difficult negotiators."

Ezra looked at the man sharply. The secretary's face betrayed no judgement. "Yes," Ezra said, "a little work would be helpful."

Driving out of town in the cool morning air, they discussed the numbers and what they might mean.

"I'm surprised Lady Kristen didn't get us a driver," Ezra remarked sometime later.

Pontes raised his face to the sun—a subtle gesture of happiness—and said, "Sometimes it feels good to drive the cart yourself, sir." He cleared his throat. "So to speak."

Ezra laughed. "Yes. When you can."

"When you can, sir."

WHEN THEY WERE ABOUT three miles from the outskirts of the capital, Ezra struggled painfully into his armor and mounted his warhorse. The metal felt heavy and constricting. Hard to breathe in.

Perhaps I am nervous too.

Considering that his problem-solving abilities appeared of late to consist mainly of lying, killing, and running away, Ezra felt that a lack of confidence was reasonable.

He had no idea whether his painful, parting conversation would help Rachel or not as time went by, let alone immediately. Ezra only knew that the lie he and Stonehouse had concocted could not stand for long. For good or ill, Rachel had deserved better than a lie and then being left alone to pine and wonder.

And dream. Dead gods, let her not dream of me.

Lady Kristen was another story. Pontes's participation in what was meant to be a clandestine escape from town suggested that Lady Kristen knew at least some version of what had happened between Rachel and him at Stonehouse's shop. *Does she know a version of events from Danielle Stonehouse or from Rachel?*

Both. Inevitably, both.

He remembered dimly that Danielle had been Kristen's co-conspirator in keeping Rachel away from him. But Stonehouse had also plied Ezra with poppy and seduced him, two acts that the knight was sure would not have been mentioned in whatever communications had passed between the two women. He did not, however, blame Danielle. He had, through carelessness and weakness, allowed her to seduce him. Even though she had seemed more than on top of the situation, in every way, what had happened was dangerous.

It was my fault.

I must do better. Be more controlled.

He could see the city in the distance. His heart swelled at the sight of it and the thought of who lived there. *I must do better.*

"Tighten these straps, would you, Pontes."

I must hold the feeling in.

"You know sir," said Pontes as he buckled Ezra's breastplate straps, "finance has rules as well."

Ezra's serious face cracked, and he chuckled. "Have you been reading my mind?"

"No, sir, I am merely observing that there can be happiness even within boundaries. If you allow yourself to find that solace. Sir."

"Hmm." Ezra had not spoken directly about his adventures with Lady Kristen and Rachel with Pontes. For days on the road, the conversation had always been about the work. Personal comments had been rare and oblique. *No one ever knows what Pontes really thinks.* The secretary was too professional for that.

"Are you disappointed that Lady Kristen did not ask you to become her seneschal, Pontes?"

"The title is not the job, sir."

Although Ezra did not know whose situation the secretary was referring to, he was once again amused. "Let us go and do our jobs, then, Pontes. At least in that we will not hurt anyone."

"Very good, sir."

Realizing that he liked Pontes, a feeling that had crept up on him over the years, Ezra rode his horse next to the carriage so he could trade observations with the man as they traversed the city.

The streets were busy. The capital had both grown and changed in the years since Ezra had set foot within it. The central road that bisected the city and led to the palace on its hill at the center was wider and paradoxically more crowded. Every balcony had something green growing on it, another striking change from the past. A few businesses also displayed signs of a political nature. This was unheard-of eleven years ago.

One street was dominated by signs reading "No to the dam."

And more creatively, "Damn the dam."

But on the next street, it was "Yes to the dam" and "Water begets water."

On other streets, there were also notices complaining about lumber, forestry, sewage, community gardens and some sort of mining project.

The grievances, misunderstandings, and passions of the people are signs of the times. I don't even need to read the posts to know all the work she has been doing.

The knight chuckled to himself, fiercely proud of his Queen, the woman who had banished him to protect her Queendom—and herself, certainly—and her ability to continue to work for her people even if they did not always appreciate her efforts.

What can I do compared to her? Glorious her. She was right to send me away.

A memory of kneeling in front of her—her arms around his shoulders while the walls shook around them and she exhorted him to "Hold it in"—returned like a flash of lightning.

And she was right about that advice too.

He held it in now, despite the feelings of love and pride rising within him.

Who am I? All my powerful memories and dreams are of her. Does that define me as hers?

Her ownership manifested in other ways too, he knew, thinking about some of his scars. His hand went to his gorget in an attempt, in vain, to touch the old cut on his neck.

If she had not done this to me, I would have regretted that more even than I have missed being near her.

In a fragile emotional equilibrium, a place of passion withheld, a place with few long-term winners and little stability, Ezra proceeded through the city.

That famous legend, "The Vampire of Sangrea," was apparently being enacted in the Ninth Square. Ezra caught a glimpse of a sign being hoisted high. His heart skipped a beat. The lead character, Serenath, was depicted as blonde, and with more than a passing resemblance to the Queen in other ways.

Less than a block later, he spotted a flag hanging from an open window. It depicted, in crude lines and rude colors, a wooden stake and a mallet. And gouts of blood. It was not an advertisement for the play.

He saw red. A tolling sound emanated from the air around him. A sound like bells and like thunder all at once. Passersby looked up at the sky for the anvil of dark air they expected to see.

"Is it about to rain, sir?" asked Pontes, craning his head out of the carriage. "Shame about the play."

How DARE they!

"Sir!"

The hint of desperation in Pontes's voice shocked Ezra back into equilibrium. And embarrassment. *What am I going to do, storm the threshold of every house and palace critical of her?*

Pontes was staring at him. "Are you all right, sir?"

"The storm has passed."

They continued riding, with Ezra only just managing to control himself as they worked their way deeper into the heart of the city.

"She has been busy, hasn't she?" Ezra said to Pontes as they pulled into the closed and cobbled square of Gunning's Inn and disembarked.

"What? Oh. Yes sir, the Queen has been tireless in her civil projects."

"Not everyone seems to—"

Ezra's comment was cut off by the clanging noise of a figure in plate armor who stepped abruptly out from under a shadowed window casing. "Can it be?" shouted Sir Marigold, "Sir Ezra alive and back in the capital?"

"Marigold!" Ezra shouted happily, not noticing the scowl that Pontes gave the other knight.

Marigold jogged loudly up to the carriage, pounded Ezra's pauldrons, and then hugged him hard, producing a flinch. "Oh, so you *were* injured by those Erlemen," Marigold said. "How many of the bastards did you remove from this dead-gods world?"

Ezra was not sure this should be a bragging matter, but he knew that Marigold's speech rarely left the jocular, sour-tough tones of the knights' baths where everything was a matter for sparring and banter. "Two."

"I heard three. There better have been, 'cause we captured three Erle merchant ships in reprisal."

"Really? What did you do with the crews?"

"Oh yeah, really. The orders came down the same day we heard the news. And the crews are fine. On their way home in rowboats." She gave him a cockeyed look and said, "You've become soft, old man, if it only took two of them to nearly put you in the ground."

"I wasn't wearing my plate. And there *were* three. Danielle Stonehouse shot one with a crossbow."

"Good for her! The stories *were* a little garbled in some of the particulars."

Her eyes shone out of her helm, fixed hard on Ezra. "One post said they had all been killed without a problem, while another said you were at death's doorway." She turned her visored head left and right and added, more quietly, "You're famous again. Good thing you don't wear a sigil and aren't otherwise memorable to look at."

"The posts?"

"Yes, you know, in the squares, information disseminated by little weaselly folks that don't otherwise produce anything useful."

No, no.

"Don't act all surprised," Marigold said, clapping his pauldrons again. "Come on, let's have a beer. Heather has set a table up for us."

"But—"

"No, don't worry, Pontes can see the unpacking done, and look, here come some of Heather's boys now."

A couple of young men in Gunning livery were indeed emerging from the stables and walking toward the carriage and a disapproving but silent Pontes. Ezra mouthed, "I'm sorry," to the secretary before being dragged away by his fellow knight and best friend.

She had always been painfully honest, he reflected, but there was a time when Marigold had been less aggressive and loud. After the Night of Erle, as it was popularly known, that had changed. Every time she visited him, the undertones of anger were just a little stronger.

"How is the Queen?" Ezra asked almost before his heavy armored butt hit the soft padded seat. A jug of suds and two steins had been waiting for them on one of the garden tables of another, private courtyard.

"Busy," said Marigold. "What else is new?"

She removed her helm, revealing dark, ringleted hair and chestnut-brown eyes. She was a pretty woman under her armor, but her face was hard, and she was not soft anywhere that Ezra had ever found.

Reluctantly, Ezra removed his own helm. "I have no doubt," he said. "But is she happy?" His heart almost stopped at the thought that brought the question.

"That I cannot speak to."

"Why not?"

"Obsess enough?" Marigold thrust her stein at him and said, "If you speak this way in front of others, they might suspect you have . . . special feelings for our lady." She put the mug down hard on the table, making little bits of foam jump. "But you *don't*, do you?"

"You are the only one I would ask."

Marigold scowled. "Gods damn you, Ezra, don't you have enough problems with your Lady Kristen asking you to take your armor off for her, not to mention her daughter skulking outside your villa every night?"

"Just tell me about the Queen, Mari."

"Don't *Mari* me, Ez."

"Would you?" It was an old joke between them.

"No! You're in love with someone you shouldn't be. Someone I won't name or talk about. Why don't you just say 'yes' to Kristen and find yourself some relief." She raised the tone of her voice, widened her knees suggestively, and crooned, "Sir Ezra, kneel at my feet. Oh, that's nice. Yes, just a little closer. Now just shuffle forward a little more yet and put your head in my lap. Now, what you do from here is—"

"Stop it!"

"*You* stop it."

"Marigold," Ezra said, feeling a sudden flood of shame. "I'm sorry, I know I'm acting like a child. You know I have no one to talk to about this. Please, just tell me about the Queen. Is she looking after herself? How has she been since Lord Shubert died?"

Marigold shook her head in mild disgust. "Shubert couldn't handle her. No one can, that woman works so hard, does everything so hard. So he got himself a consumption or some kind of bleeding disease and died. End of story, third dead husband. Probably the last one, given our superstitions."

"How does she look?"

"I haven't seen her for a month or two, but she seemed fine the last time. Tired, of course."

"Is it a month or two months?" Ezra demanded. He was shocked that Marigold had not seen the Queen recently, angry that she was not watching over her more carefully in his absence. "Who is guarding her if it isn't you?"

"Someone else."

"Who?"

Marigold narrowed her eyes. She was suddenly wary. "Tell you what, Sir Ezra, I'll find out which knights guard her door and get a report on what she ate for breakfast too, but do me a favor first."

"Whatever you want," Ezra said quickly, his anger receding.

"'Whatever I want?' Try not to be so transparent, please. People either won't take you seriously, or they'll take advantage of you." She took an aggressive, frothy sip of beer. "You sound like a naïf."

Ezra stared at her as she continued drinking.

"There is a local Baroness, Lady Jacqueline Paron. She tried to incite a crowd into *staking* the Queen today. Imagine." She put the beer mug down and added, "They would have to find her first, of course, and storm the castle, and a hundred other things that would not have worked out, but Paron has lost her mind over the Stillwater project."

Stake her? Ezra noticed that his hand was wet. His beer stein had shattered from a vibration in his hand. Rage sloshed through him from his head to his toes, and he struggled to hold it in.

"Hey! Get it under control! You just wasted most of a pint!"

Ezra did not have it under control, and he did not care about the beer. "Is that who is responsible for those flags I saw with the stakes painted on them?"

Two gauntleted hands came up, empty, and Marigold said, "I don't know. She has a lot of enemies. Erle you know about, but every project she comes up with pisses *somebody* off. You can't make a better world without upsetting those with a . . . stake in the old. But Paron I heard say it myself, so let's start with her."

Through gritted teeth, Ezra said, "Where is this Lady Paron now?"

"In her palace on the other side of town. Holed up tight."

"How many knights do we have on hand for a siege?"

"Not many, actually," said Marigold. "We have half the constabulary ringing the place to make sure she doesn't go anywhere. I was thinking that we could avoid a siege entirely now that your . . . nature . . . is public knowledge."

Ezra had assumed his secret was out. It was not his most important one, but it had been important nonetheless. And assuming and knowing were two different things. His stomach dropped. "My nature?"

"Yes, Ezra." Marigold refilled her stein and passed him the jug. "You know that I've always known, right?" She lowered her voice and said more gently, "I was just outside the door when Lilly passed. After you sent me and everyone else away. I *heard* you grieve."

Her expression—which had been soft—turned flat as she added, "Assume that I know everything else too."

No. You don't know everything, Mari. Thank the dead gods you don't.

She continued, incongruously angry now. "And I was also outside the palace walls that other awful night, *remember*? When Erle died. Just as sent away but for worse reason. I had left like the rest of everyone who mattered. Like everyone from cooks to knights. Like everyone but *you*, who wouldn't go. Her last guard."

"Are you angry with me, Mari?"

"No! Now shut up while I explain this to you. Everyone had pretty much left the area—not Kay—but I stayed close by, at the walls, in their shadow. In the shadow of my guilt at doing what I knew I shouldn't. I *heard* you. There are no *actual* bells in the palace that could make that sound, no matter what was said later. It was you. You are an Elysian Bell. Though I had already known it. I knew you used your nature to save the Queen. There's no way you could have cleared the castle on your own without that god-given power."

I wasn't alone.

"Yes, I am a Bell," Ezra admitted, not wanting to hear more of Marigold's deductions.

"Right, and now with what happened back in Province, *everyone* knows it, not just shameful old knights who let themselves get ordered away from their duty."

"And?" Ezra was aware that Marigold was telling him something important about her state of guilt, and he wanted to ask her about it, but his outrage over the talk of staking needed immediate attention.

"Just walk up to Lady Paron's palace and tell them to open up or you'll shake their whole house down."

Ezra was angry enough that he thought perhaps he would do exactly that.

CHAPTER 9

LIAR'S LESSON

Eleven years ago, Sir Marigold would never have done it, but then she had never even told a lie before that time. She had also never murdered anyone, never disposed of a body, never took secret orders, never left secret reports. Never spied on her only real friend.

Eleven years ago, I was a fool. Well, I'm no fool now. I just hate myself.

She almost hated Ezra too, because he was still a lot like she used to be.

A fool.

She almost hated him for not, like her, leaving the castle that awful night. He had stayed, and she had not. Back when she had followed orders and he did not.

He refused to be ordered out of the castle, and they eventually relented. Why argue with him when there were still others inside the castle to hear? They were just going to murder him after everyone had left, after they killed her.

Of all the strange things that happened that night, of all the things she had learned about the Queen then and since, and about Ezra, about bad people too, and about herself, she had never fully understood why Ezra had been banished afterward. The Queen was an excellent liar. All Queens had to be. Why had she not come up with a lie that would have kept her truest, strongest knight by her side?

The image of her secret box of orders flashed across Marigold's mind.

Now I'm a liar too, and I am going to use him. And lie to him.

Who's the fool now?

Lady Paron's palace consisted of a large, stone central building and wall connecting other smaller but similarly styled stone buildings. The effect, together with a thick iron gate, created the illusion that it was all one massive structure. The protected square, fountain, and stables could be discerned only if one put an eye up against the gate. Which Marigold would not do, since there were soldiers inside armed with crossbows and scorpions waiting to try a knight's armor from close range. In its design, the complex was not unlike Gunning's Inn, except that it was locked up tight from the inside and surrounded by about eighty constables and twenty Knights of the Queen.

"Well, are you ready to give it a try?" asked Constable Bobby Archibald.

Marigold looked up at the sky for the ninth time. There was a cloud hanging there, dark and potentially useful, and she had an idea of how to take advantage of it. "Almost," she replied.

"Try not to kill *everyone*, please," said Archibald.

"This is just intimidation."

Archibald snorted. "Just remember we don't know how many civilians are in there beside the lady and her guards, so keep this under control."

"That's the plan," said Marigold easily. *I think the timing is about right*

She looked up at the cloud again. *Now.* "Let me speak to our siege weapon one more time."

In his armor, Ezra did indeed look more like a machine than a human being. A thing to be used, a thing she *would* use in the Queen's service. His bright eyes were barely visible from the shadow of his helm, and his face not at all. His humanity was well hidden under all those layers of metal plate, chain mail, and padded underlayers.

She was one of the few who had seen that armor off. Many times, early in their training, and most tellingly that night after he cleared the castle. She remembered his pale skin as she sewed him up, the barely contained vibrations that a careless observer might have mistaken for trembling from shock. She remembered flinching from the odd, errant feeling that shot up from his skin through her needle and fingers. She remembered nearly letting him bleed out from fear of what the wrong resonant emotion might do to her. Those memories did not make her nearly hate him. They only made her hate herself, for she had decided to treat him in the way he appeared in his armor rather than the way that he was inside.

Fool.

She looked up at the cloud one more time before approaching her friend. "Security is ready. Are you, Knight?"

Marigold realized that she had been wrong about something. She could see now that his eyes were big and angry. He was furious. Someone had threatened his Queen, and the castle-clearing Ezra of old had returned.

"Yes!" he said, his voice larger even than his person, making goose-bumps spread, improbably, across Marigold's skin despite all the layers she herself wore to protect her.

No armor protects what is most important.

As Ezra marched toward the gate, a feeling of dismay crept over Marigold. She wondered if she should, or could, call this off, call *him* back now that she had primed the situation so well. Pulled inexorably by her doubts, she followed Ezra and took a position close on his flank.

"Open the gate!" he called in a new voice, in a sound like thunder.

The heavy iron shook, and Marigold was washed over by goose bumps again. The sky abruptly darkened, too, an event that she had waited for, that cloud and her timing paying off now in an extra degree of intimidation. Waves of dark sound emanated from Ezra like a hundred-foot gong hammered by a giant. They manifested from him but also from the air around him, from the ground below and the sky above. The waves rippled through Marigold, filling her with foreboding.

"*Open the gate, you who would harm my Queen,*" Ezra roared with the voice of a legion, his rage manifesting in another, stronger wave of foreboding and a low pealing sound, a sound eloquent of death and destruction.

"Sir Marigold!" came a voice almost pressed to her helm against the awful sounds keening in the air. "Sir Marigold!"

She turned to find Sir Jennifer Shryke at her shoulder. Shryke was pulling on her arm—Marigold had not even noticed the other knight's presence from within the emotional and physical maelstrom that Ezra was creating—trying to lead her away.

As Marigold resisted the tugging, she saw Lady Jacqueline Paron press herself up against the iron gate, her mouth moving, entreating something of Ezra. Marigold tried to read what the woman might be saying. Was it, "Wait! Hold, Knight, let me speak!" Whatever it was, Paron kept repeating it.

Ezra must have understood her, for he said, "*Speak, then!*" and the keening lowered.

"You must come now!" Shryke roared, her lips against Marigold's helm. "Now!"

"You need to know the truth!" came the shouted whisper from Paron, now just audible to Marigold. She wanted desperately to stay and hear what the lady would say, but tall Shryke pulled her away from Ezra and the gates. Even as he listened to Paron, Ezra's deep, heavy sounds remained powerful, and their throbbing rhythm followed Marigold and Shryke like the heartbeat of a titan as they passed the lines of constables and knights, many of whom crouched and leaned forward as if fighting to stay upright against a colossal wind.

"He sounds like a god," said Shryke once they were far enough away that they could speak without straining their voices to the utmost. She waved to a page who stood not far away, flinching at the pressure carried by the air.

"It's powerful, not a doubt about it," said Marigold. Shryke was too young to have been there on the night that Erle died. She had never even seen Sir Ezra before, let alone heard him. Goosebumps continued to ripple across Marigold's skin, out of sight but not feeling.

What would it feel like to touch him now? What if it was love and not destruction being sung? How would that feel? Would I collapse, swooning like a gormless schoolgirl, or even come, affected by some endless reverberating orgasm of love, instantly addicted to the feeling?

A page's approach interrupted her restless curiosity and her discomfort. She held a silver platter and repeated the familiar words about trusted hands, words that Marigold could scarcely make out over the throbbing heartbeat of Ezra's anger. On that platter, shaking in the unstable air, was a cream-colored envelope. *Now?*

Marigold took the envelope. "Take three steps back, Jennifer," she shouted, and opened it. In neat, black script, she read,

"Do not allow Lady Paron to speak to him."

"Dead gods damn it!" Marigold stuffed the letter into the sleeve of her gauntlet and charged back across the lines toward Sir Ezra—past constables now huddled on hands and knees or turtling with arms around their heads—around whom the storm appeared to have suddenly gotten louder and darker.

"*LIAR!*" came the booming roar, followed by a pressure wave like a colossal slap.

Marigold's eyes squinted half-shut against the wind, but she saw the scorpion bolt meant for Ezra pushed abruptly off course and slam to the cobbles in front of the gate.

"*See your house fall down!*" Ezra roared and raised his arms.

It is not possible, normally, to *see* sound, but enough particulates now hung in the air that the long, heavy wavelengths were horrendously visible. A half-spherical bellows of power rolled in a blink of dark dust and broken stone toward the gate. And shattered it.

Even before the gate fell teetering and resonating to the cobbles,

Ezra had turned to the stones of the main building, and they too had begun to crumble.

Marigold passed Constable Bobby Archibald, who was stuck motionless against the wind, but trying to reach Ezra as well. She saw Bobby's lips, vibrating like liquid against the pulsating air, mouth the words, "Stop him!"

"Ezra, stop!" shouted Marigold, "we don't know who else is in there!" But she may as well have tried pissing into the wind. Even for women, this is not advisable when the wind is strong enough. But at least you got some relief even if the piss blew all over you. In this case, it was as if Marigold's words had never been spoken, they were so swallowed up into the vast physical and emotional tide of Ezra's fury.

Her regret over recruiting Ezra, manipulating his emotions, and then thinking she could ride the maelstrom was intense. She forced herself on against a pressure both psychological and physical, one halting step at a time, toward her friend. She left Archibald behind. And Shryke. A step closer and then another against the pain and foreboding. Against the realization of her error.

Eleven years, and he kept his complaints to himself. And now he is close, so close to the one he killed so many people for . . . and now, so close to her again, thinking maybe, just maybe, he will see her, when he is at his most hopeful and yet in his greatest despair, I gave him someone to hate, someone who said the Queen should be murdered.

This is the worst thing I have ever done.

She was only a step away now, leaning in against the gale. She imagined her armor being stripped away by the wind. Pieces of metal plate, then chain, then padded underlayers, flying off, her sense of self being flayed like the skins of an onion, being scoured by rage and the impulse of destruction. An instant before grabbing him, perhaps attempting to tackle her friend, Marigold reconsidered.

If I touch him, what will happen? Will these feelings of destruction go into me? Will it be like the legends of love say about Elysian Bells? Except that instead of being in love with him, I will forever be transformed by his awful rage?

She drew her sword carefully, using both hands, turning it slowly until she had it by the blade and swung it hard, striking Ezra in the head with the heavy hilt.

He staggered and clutched his head. The storm abruptly ended, debris hit the ground, and the emotional pressure popped, an instant vacuum that made Marigold also stumble.

"Mari, *why*?" Ezra said, confused, still angry, yet some part of him trusting her.

"There could be children in there. I'm all for crushing Paron, but not the entire household."

Ezra staggered a second time. He clutched at his helm and flung it off. The heavy metal fell with a clang and bounced amid the debris from the palace. "Oh gods! Oh, Mari, what have I done?" he shouted, heartsick now, his rage turning in on itself.

Shryke and some of the constables ran by into the compound. Marigold was tempted to follow them, but she could not leave her friend there alone. He had sunk to his knees, weeping. She stepped in front of him ignoring the sound of scattered fighting and shouts.

Is he safe to touch?

Marigold felt such a coward. Much like she had on the night that Erle had tried to kill the Queen, when she had followed orders that she knew she should not have.

Damn it. She wrapped her arms around him.

"I'm no good, Mari," he said, still weeping. "No good for anyone. Did I kill any children?"

The feelings rolling off him made no sound, not quite, but Marigold could feel them nevertheless. Powerful and pure, deeply, genuinely sad but with a hint, a hint of a hint, of love.

"I am not sure you managed to kill anyone," Marigold said, still holding him. "You're really just a blowhard." When he kept on crying, she added, "Stop your crying now, you baby."

"*You're* the baby."

"No, *you* are."

"Thank you for saving me, Marigold," he whispered to her, breaking her heart.

A powerful feeling began to flow into her from him. It could only be love. Marigold spasmed, the powerful feeling lifting her heart and soul effortlessly and irresistibly, like a high surging tide. In an instant of panic, she stepped away from him, almost crying out.

THERE WERE, in fact, very few casualties. With the gates broken and morale shattered by Sir Ezra's assault, most of the guards surrendered without a fight. One was killed for not releasing his loaded crossbow, and three more had to be beaten into submission by the constabulary, but they were alive. The lack of bloodshed was a miracle for a palace siege.

Paron was the exception. She was found dead beneath the ruins of the gate, her head cleaved from her body. Sir Marigold had been attending to her misused siege weapon and missed the discovery of Paron's remains.

Her death is no great loss. A plus on the whole. But on whose orders was she killed?

The note that she had received—too late, it had turned out—came to mind. A chilling thought occurred to her.

The Queen did not want her talking to anyone in a trial.

Ezra had eventually recovered his wits, put his helm back on, and after going on and on about what a good friend Marigold was, headed back to Gunning's Inn on his own. Watching him go, Marigold examined her feelings once more.

I know why I almost hate him, why I almost hate myself. Why I sometimes hate her. We lesser people are ruined for her. For her greater purpose.

I have participated in it. I have ruined myself for that purpose.

And we have ruined something beautiful in this man. His passions fall across sound like a chorus from heaven, and yet are sent away. Or used for destruction instead of love.

CHAPTER 10

NEGOTIATIONS

Deep, deep under the ocean, down where the last flickering perception is bathed in half-imagined indigo, along the cold edge of hard ice, where the pressure could squeeze a chest full of air into a space no larger than a heart and could smother the last dream from the dying, there is a room. It is encased in clear crystal and lit by a soft golden hue from the treasure within.

A woman lies there, naked, on a bed of two-inch-long thorns, her tawny blonde hair spread about her like a lion's mane. That great fan of gentle gossamer delight provides the only light in the room. It reflects darkly off the fat drops of blood that well at the end of each of a thousand thorns.

She is a woman of lean limbs and jewellike breasts, of perfect hips and flat stomach. She is strong and beautiful and neither moves nor utters a sound of complaint despite the thorns she rests upon.

Her eyes are closed, but upon her face is an expression of terrifying, still intensity.

Approaching the castle filled Ezra with conflicting feelings, tightened his stomach, and set his mind racing. It was like going home only to step off a cliff. He was terrified but excited.

Still your mind.

They had been *her* words.

He took a slow, deep breath, struggling to avoid falling down the bottomless well of memory and passion. He fought against thinking of her, or of the night the Prince of Erle had died, or of his last night with her before being banished.

Having Pontes beside him helped. The steady, calm, infallibly polite professional acted as if nothing was amiss in Ezra, even though he could surely see that his knight and possible future seneschal was in a desperate state of anxiety.

"Sir, could you kindly carry the ledgers for me? My hand is hurting again."

Pontes had a mild affliction of the nerves in his hands that sometimes turned acute. Ezra took the books from him just as they stepped under the shadow of the castle. The ledgers were large, with heavy wood and leather covers and a locking strap that held them securely closed.

It was early, and the broad cobbled square was empty of the usual crowds. This made reaching the castle easy but it also made not obsessing about who dwelled inside it all the more difficult.

With every step, the vast stone edifice seemed to grow taller. Ezra looked up and up toward the tower where her private chambers were. Many people, perhaps most, would feel envious of the person living in such a castle, surveying the city from its highest tower, but Ezra knew the soul-crushing, solitary work of being Queen. He knew the complaints, the exhaustion, the inevitability of betrayal. And the terrible, unremitting loneliness.

It is so easy to envy the powerful, so difficult to appreciate their burden.

As they reached the castle entrance, Ezra was unsure whether he was more frightened for himself and his fragile equilibrium, or frightened for her, having endured eleven more years in that awful role. His armor, for once, seemed lighter than air.

"I do hope the . . . situation was not too frightening," said Lady Jayne Orton across her ten-foot-wide, polished-oak desk. Her face was poise itself, despite her words. She was perhaps forty years old, quite short, of medium build and exceptional posture. She reminded Ezra of Pontes.

"I rather think that it was not Sir Ezra who was afraid," said Pontes dryly, taking the ledger from her.

Sir Ezra did not speak. He was in his armor once more and preferred to keep his helm on and his feelings to himself. Here in the palace it was doubly important that this be so. While he would gladly have spoken about the night with Marigold, and had touched on the major events of it with Pontes, it did not seem correct to engage in small talk about it with strangers.

"How do the terms look?" he asked Pontes, keeping his eyes on Lady Jayne. She smiled coolly under his scrutiny as Pontes flipped through the pages of the heavy-backed tome.

"We believe that you will find the terms quite generous," offered Jayne, her expression betraying nothing, dispassionate and polite as always.

Pontes clucked and nodded to himself as he scanned through the book. "Ten percent of gross to go toward the town's new reservoir, cisterns, aqueduct system, or other public works? That is . . . unexpected."

"To be held in trust until required for qualified projects, of course." Jayne's half smile turned full for an instant before subsiding to its normal cool detachment before she added, "The Queen believes in planning for the future, as you know."

"Legendarily," replied Pontes. He turned to Ezra. "They have given us good terms—better ones, in fact, than I expected."

Jayne was quick to interject, "To account for the ten percent."

Pontes looked at Ezra expectantly. He said, "I am not the seneschal yet. If you think Lady Kristen will agree, I will trust you."

"Excellent," said Lady Jayne. As if by magic, she produced a feather pen from somewhere behind her. "Shall we execute, then?"

Hmmm.

Acting on instinct, Ezra said, "Tomorrow? After our more thorough review."

"Tomorrow, then," said Jayne urbanely, after blinking once, "and may I say that we in the palace are all very pleased that the traitor was dealt with so quickly and easily. Now we can put Lady Paron and her madness behind us. Please accept our thanks."

Is that why these negotiations have gone so well?

Pontes had told him he expected the negotiation to last days, perhaps a week, but Lady Jayne Orton had given them more than they wanted before they had even made their case.

The Queen's senior treasurer nodded to Ezra. "Thank you for your visit, gentlemen. Shall we say tomorrow morning at the same time to execute?" She stood up. "Now if you'll excuse me, I must be off. Another important meeting."

Ezra also stood and, just as quickly despite all the metal around him, asked, "Is the Queen in residence today?"

"I'm sure I don't know."

Was that a flinch?

"Who is the knight in charge of her security?" he asked as the small woman scurried past him.

"I believe that is your friend Sir Marigold, sir," Lady Jayne Orton said, rushing out the door.

"Marigold is not in the castle today," Ezra said to Pontes. "And she has not personally guarded the Queen in weeks."

"What does it mean?" Pontes asked.

Good question.

"Let us go ask for the Knight Captain on duty."

THE KNIGHT CAPTAIN was Sir Roger Corning, whom Ezra had vaguely known before being banished. Corning did not wear plate or helm, only a rich blue tabard over chain mail.

"So where is she?" Ezra asked, irritated that the man could not seem to give him a straight answer.

A bead of sweat ran down the side of Corning's face, catching in his long gray sideburns. "T-the Queen keeps her own schedule, Sir Ezra," he said.

Ridiculous. "What do you mean, her own schedule? You have to organize a guard for her, surely."

Corning put his hands up placatingly. "The Queen operates differently from back when you were here. She does not always include the guard in her planning, and even when she remembers to give us a schedule, we have no idea, really, where she is, except by chance or custom."

"Really? By *chance*?" Ezra's voice involuntarily grew with each word. "Why are you even here, then?"

"We do what we can, when we can, how we can." Corning said defensively. He then said in a whisper, "In truth, sir, no one can keep up with her. She is almost . . . inhuman."

"Careful with your words," said Ezra ominously. He did not want to remember Lady Jacqueline Paron's shocking words at the gate the night before, her claim of murder in particular. It was a claim he had refused to speak or think about since then.

Pontes stepped between the two men and the building tension. "Perhaps we should retire for the moment, sir, and review these ledgers." He looked tiny compared to the two big men with metal piled on top of them.

"When does she hear petitions next?" Ezra asked, looking past the secretary.

"This afternoon, perhaps," Corning said. "And tomorrow morning, certainly."

Ezra gave him a tight, hard-eyed nod. "Then I'll be back this afternoon."

As they exited the palace gates, Pontes said, "Perhaps we can refrain from knocking the castle over until after we ratify our new deal for Lady Kristen."

Ezra laughed at that. The sunlight was warm and welcome on his helm. "Let's find a tavern with a clean table and hearty fare. There used to be a spot called The Queen's Lance just off the square."

"It is still there, sir."

"Sir Ezra! Sir Ezra!" A young woman in a cheap, low-cut dress was yelling and jumping—flouncing— up and down a few yards away. When Ezra looked over at her, she shouted. "Elysian Bell! Come give us a touch!"

For dead gods' sake!

Her eyes were chestnut brown, but they burned with the light of thoughtless zealotry and enthusiastic unreason.

"Just *one*," she entreated him, stepping closer.

"No, thank you," Ezra said. He grabbed one of the ledgers from Pontes and tried to block the woman with it, but a hand snaked around and swatted his armored butt.

He thought the encounter would be over after that. She had got her touch, but his next steps took him right into the equally grabby arms of a rapidly gathering mob. They were accoutered in every mode of dress imaginable, from peasants' sackcloth to wealthy merchants' velvet jackets to the long robes of two scholars. One of whom, Ezra noted with alarm, carried a covered birdcage.

I know those two! But before he could react, the mob was on him with a chaotic bouquet of demands.

"Elysian Bell, bless my baby!

"Elysian Bell, save my baby!"

"Elysian Bell, make a baby with me!"

"Gods-damned murderer!!"

"Tell us the words of god!"

"Save the Queen!"

"Save us *from* the Queen!"

"Say hello to my bird, will you?" This request, perhaps the strangest to come from the knot of zealots, was accompanied by the covered birdcage being thrust almost under Ezra's nose.

"Squawk!" said the bird from its hidden perch, likely agitated from the jostling and the noise of the crowd. "Squawk! Squawk!"

Why on earth a bird?

Pontes hunched protectively around the ledger he still held. "They don't seem to be of one same mind about you, sir."

"That is likely a very good thing, Pontes. Get behind me. I'm pushing through." Ezra considered applying his armored shoulder to the lot of them. *I must not draw my sword.* Frustration washed over him. He held it in, under his armor, as he knew he must.

But what is the point as things stand now?

He realized there could be an advantage in releasing his anger temporarily. He allowed a low, deep keening to manifest in the air around him.

The crowd spasmed in a kind of shock and parted while Ezra marched himself and Pontes through as people shielded their head with their arms, turned away, or crouched on the cobbles. He was unsure how long the effect would last, remembering that many of the Knights of Erle had fought him quite capably that evening eleven years past, so he moved quickly. He did not pull the anger back until they were well past the recoiling mob and the squawking bird.

Ezra narrowly avoided shouting over his shoulder, "Isn't that what you wanted?" But he knew that would have been foolish. They all wanted different things from him, as people did when they made other human beings into objects.

The two men turned and passed through a clothier's shop to confuse anyone from the mob before entering the Queen's Lance by a side door and finding a dimly lit corner booth. Someone's hand made glancing contact with Ezra's butt as they passed through the darkened room.

"What is it with the ass grabbing!" Ezra said as he took his seat, still shedding the last of his summoned rage.

Pontes did not meet his eyes. "I expect it is the legends, sir."

"Legends?" *Oh.* Memories of his final night under Danielle Stonehouse's care returned.

"Do I need to say, sir?"

"Forget it." Ezra motioned for beer from a serving lady. "Though if people on the streets and taverns are starting to recognize me, perhaps I should consider a disguise."

Pontes did not reply. He knew Ezra was never going to wear anything but armor. He met his companion's eyes and asked, "How *are* you, sir? Really."

Ezra hesitated, unsure how much to confide.

"I keep having the same dream. It is quite . . . affecting."

"About what?"

"I am swimming. In an ocean."

"There is a port here, sir."

"And there is an iceberg," *A beautiful iceberg.*

"Not in this port," Pontes said dryly.

"It reminds me of something *she* said once..." *About floating on a vast sea.*

Ezra struggled to remember the fading details of the dream. *Was that her on the bed of thorns?*

"Who?"

"The Queen." *I keep dreaming about the Queen, except in the dream, she is an iceberg.*

Pontes seemed about to say something, probably something banal and sympathetic. To forestall him, Ezra said, "Let's look over the ledgers again."

It did not take long to confirm that the crown had indeed made them an excellent offer. *Suspiciously good.*

"We could take this back today, Sir," Pontes said diffidently.

"No, we could *not*."

Pontes cradled his beer, keeping it well away from the ledgers. Then, as if having second thoughts, he folded the books up and placed them behind him on the bench, leaned forward, and said, "Sir. Lady Kristen admires you. Perhaps we should accept our victory quickly and go home. To *her*."

Victory? All I did was knock down a gate.

"Not yet."

"Is it the Queen, sir? You want, perhaps, to see her?" Pontes seemed to summon some new courage. "Why, sir?"

"Why?" Ezra looked at the man, took in his gentle sincerity. Trying to decide if he could trust him and add a third confidante to his list besides Marigold and Danielle.

"She did, uh, send you away, sir," Pontes said, softly. "After you saved her."

Pontes's manner decided the question for Ezra. "Because sometimes you find your reason, Pontes."

"Reason?"

"Reason for living," Ezra said, his voice unconsciously resonating. Somewhere in the distance, a bird began to trill a beautiful melody. "I found my reason for being. It was her inexhaustible dedication and appetite for work that caught my eye at first, you know. She is amazing, like Kristen, but ten times more so. She never stops. She is driven. She gives *everything*, Pontes, but no one understands what that is like. What sacrifices it requires. To lead. To know that if you don't get it right, no one will, and people will suffer. To lead is to be watched all the time, judged all the time, especially by the people she is trying to help."

He studied Pontes's face for a moment, then added, "But under it all is a woman. And when I fell in love with her soul, I also fell in love with her smooth, strong voice, and her hair, her tears, even her anger when it erupted. I fell in love with everything about her, even the parts of her that doomed me. And I cannot fall out of that love, man."

He downed a painfully large gulp of beer. The tavern was quiet. Somewhere, a chorus of melodious bells rang softly. A bird sang in tune with them, but Ezra did not notice, even though he was the bell.

"And now it feels as if something strange is going on. As if I am being lied to and no one is guarding her. Where is she?" He put the stein down and held Pontes's gaze. "We aren't leaving until I know she is safe."

The chiming faded.

Pontes nodded as if all this made sense. "Very well, sir," he said. "Let us find your Queen and ensure her safety. Then we shall go home."

The birdsong was close. Ezra looked up and saw the two scholars from the square—and from Lady Kristen's hall—in their robes with their covered bird cage. The smaller one, a slim red-haired woman, the one not holding the birdcage, raised both hands in surrender and said, "It's okay, Sir Ezra, we just want to talk." She sighed theatrically and added, "We have been trying to speak with you for some time."

"Must you?" said Pontes, showing Ezra a new, less diffident side.

"Who are you?" added Ezra.

"Simple scholars, Sir Knight," replied the woman, as if her academic robe and its rosebush-and-puma crest did not speak for her. "From the Pyracantha Institute. I am Professor Olivia. And this is Adjunct Parsons."

"We study the heaven-sent," said the somewhat younger, bald man with her. Parsons was lean and frail-looking but had a pronounced pot belly. He seemed to struggle to hold the cage up.

"The rare *humans*," corrected Professor Olivia, "with an extraordinary, uh, talent." She kept her eyes on Ezra. "You, sir, are the only one we have been able to get close to. There may be another, but . . ." She exchanged a look with her colleague.

They better not try grabbing my ass.

"What do you want?"

"To study you," said Olivia. "At the Institute."

"It is really quite important," chipped in Parsons. "*Vital.*"

Pontes stared at the two scholars as if they were bothersome street mummers. "We are really quite busy. Now if the two of you and your bird could just—"

"Excuse me, Sir Ezra," said a new voice. A tall, dark-haired female page shouldered her way between the scholars, jostling the bird cage and ending the song from it. A small squawk escaped the covering. "I have a message for you. Passed from trusted hands to trusted hands and finally to mine."

With a flourish, she produced a cream-colored envelope.

When Ezra took it, the page announced, "You others must step aside so the Knight of the Queen can read his message privately."

"These two were just leaving," said Pontes as he carefully exited his seat. He took both ledgers with him.

"But—" said Professor Olivia.

"Have you read *The Last Tolling*?" asked Parsons, desperately.

Ezra ignored them. Their graceless argument with the page and Pontes held no interest for him now.

This is from her.

He opened the letter. In neat dark letters, it said,

"Return home. I do not need you."

CHAPTER II

DISCOURAGEMENT

I t hurt like a steel mallet to the gut. **"I do not need you."** From *her*. Sir Ezra sat in the booth and stared at the message for a long time. He was only vaguely aware that the scholars had been chased off by Pontes and the page, who now watched him from a distance as Ezra sat and stared at the cream-colored paper and its dark, painful words.

"Return home."

It might not *have been written by her. Even if it sounds like something she would say. Even if the writing is exactly like hers.*

Who has seen her lately?

The Queen had always valued her independence. Had always said that leading was her task, and hers alone. Her duty. Ezra knew that. He respected it. He had always been happy merely to protect her while she did what she had to do. He had even guarded her when she had married the Prince of Erle in exchange for financial assistance. And had refused to go when Erle had supplanted her in her own Queendom, lying, bribing, and winning over so many of the nobles. Tricking others. Scheming in the shadows while she worked on affairs of state late into the night. And finally ordering her guard away, making ready to murder her. She had been so young then, so preoccupied and overworked, and had neither seen what was coming nor defended herself in time.

She would not make that mistake twice. In the end, she had outlived not just Erle, but two more husbands, and her limitless capacity for work had enriched and strengthened the once-destitute Queendom. Even in distant Province, Ezra had known that.

But she is more alone than ever now. He thought about Lady Jacquelin Paron's claims, claims he hoped that only he had heard.

"She murdered a young man, only days after you saved her and were banished, Sir Ezra," Paron had said. "A *lover*," she had added, "A young actor—hardly more than a *child*. She is a *vampire*, Ezra. She must be stopped. She will consume the Queendom if she is not."

Underneath his armor, an old scar on his neck began to itch. Ezra had exploded, called Paron a liar and destroyed her gate in a transcendent rage.

So alone.

"Page!" Ezra called. When the woman approached, he said, "Thank you for the message. Please take back my reply: I go nowhere until I am satisfied."

The page's expression was unreadable. Without a word, she disappeared into the crowd.

"What was the message, sir?" Pontes asked, approaching diffidently.

"We have been ordered home." Ezra produced a few copper coins and dropped them on the table.

Pontes looked at the amount, smiled, and added two more coins. His widow's peak was wet with sweat. "We aren't going, are we, sir?"

"No."

The other tavern patrons parted for them as they exited.

Ezra avoided the square, leading Pontes around the port side of the castle down to the water gate, the stone and gravel canyon between seawall and castle wall, where a contingent of guards waited. He stopped at the intersection where the gravel way that Ezra and Pontes had taken connected with the route that led to the docks. The fist-sized rocks that lined the seashore were dry. The tide was out, but Ezra noticed a few wet tracks. Leading the guards was a helmless but plate-armored Sir Jennifer Shryke.

She looked surprised to see them. He guessed that few in full armor or carrying ledgers used the water gate. "Sir Ezra!" she called after recovering herself. "The death of castle gates and doom of Erle. What are you doing down here?"

"Avoiding the mob."

"Oh? In the square? Well, you *are* twice famous."

Ezra noticed something odd among the stones of the path. He crouched to pick it up.

A two-inch-long thorn. It was brown and sharp enough to cut a corner.

Was she here? Coming or going? A thrill rolled through the knight, which he urgently tried to suppress.

"May we pass?" Ezra asked, deciding not to ask Shryke the question that the thorn had pricked.

She smiled. "Can't stop you, can I?"

"Let's not find out."

Shryke laughed, pounded on the gates behind her, and called for them to be opened. A ratchetted portcullis went noisily up, then a raised iron door. Ezra led the way up the ramp, past the high-water mark, stepping over flakes of rust and across the threshold, leaving Shryke gazing after him with a lingering smile.

"Sir?" Pontes said as he was led through the secret and less secret ways of the castle. Ezra remembered intersections and corners where he had killed men once. A tight spot where he had been forced to drop his sword and use gauntleted hands.

Places where she had been.

As they walked, Ezra repeatedly thought he saw her. A flicker of long blonde hair and she was gone. Each image brought a sharp pain not unlike the gut punch of her letter.

"You want to know why, don't you, Pontes?" he said, trying to resist the siren distraction and control his reaction to it.

"If she ordered us home . . ."

They reached the top of a set of stairs, opened a hidden—nearly invisible—door and entered a viewing gallery set above the Queen's audience chamber like a balcony. It looked down twenty feet or more onto the long, empty hall of the chamber, which was filled with uncomfortable-looking wooden chairs in neat rows. Hundreds of them. Empty.

"Because she said she doesn't need me."

Pontes only stared at him, so Ezra continued. "She has isolated herself in her work again."

"I am rather confused."

Ezra looked further down the chamber, toward where she would sit, but was shocked to see that the dais was covered over with a fine wire barrier—a kind of screen—separating and darkening the space where the Queen would sit. That space was all in shadow. He knew she was not there now, was sure he would sense her, but an audience would only know by the sound of her voice.

No wonder some are calling her a vampire.

A few had always called her that because she worked so late, but he had always assumed it was intended as a metaphor, even a kind of joke. And she had said it herself, for reasons that Ezra had come to understand were more complex. Paron, though, had said it in earnest.

"She doesn't need me," Ezra replied. "But she *is* human." *Not a vampire.* "We missed her today, Pontes. Let's go." Ezra walked to the back of the balcony and pushed open another unmarked, almost invisible door. "This is the quick way down."

As he led Pontes out the main gate into the busy square bathed in afternoon sunshine, Ezra's mood changed again. At a magnificent fountain done up in the style of the nine dead gods—those nine inchoate, colorless, vague forms—he paused to drink, holding the ledgers for Pontes and then passing his helm to the secretary so he could drink as well.

"Simple pleasures," Ezra said, accepting the warm sun's rays on his face. "Is this happiness, do you suppose?"

"Sir?"

"Pass me my helm." Ezra saw several groups of people approaching. "Quickly!"

"It's him!" someone shouted from a roughly attired group of seven or eight, mostly on the poor side of the cloth. "The Elysian Bell!"

They scrambled forward, eyes dead bright, both men and women, looking more than a little wretched but also feverish. *More in need of the fountain than I am.*

"Bless us, bl—"

It was a second group that had caught Ezra's attention and caused him to ask for his helm. A tougher-looking group. Several big, hefty men and one tall woman. They marched carelessly and belligerently through the first group, scattering the motley collection of petitioners.

Ezra's hand went to his sword and stayed on the hilt.

"Bless—" A dirty-faced woman missing her front teeth was knocked roughly to the ground by a huge, thick-bodied man in a long, heavy cloak. The sound of the collision had a hint of metal in it.

Instant anger erupted from Ezra's soul into the space around him. It split the air like the cracking of a Herculean whip.

"You!" he thundered, drawing his sword. "Apologize to that woman."

The colossal man stopped. He was as big as Sir Gregory Whall, champion swordsman and the only person ever to fight Ezra to a standstill. In a sparring match once. This man's short, brutally square blond haircut perfectly matched his antagonistic demeanor. He pulled his cloak back in a quick movement, his hand going to a sword of dark metal on his left hip. Ezra noted chain mail under the cloak and a dark, long-sleeved shirt.

The air rumbled ominously around Ezra. Townsfolk, including

some of the ones who had been rudely shoved aside, scrambled, trying to flee. The second group—six of them, Ezra counted now—did not flee. At least one of them had the look of Erle on his brow. They kept coming. Hands on hips. On weapons.

"Castel!" shouted the woman among them. She was also blonde. "Let's go."

The man seethed, his blue eyes hard, and with a jerking motion like the precise start or end of a child's tantrum, he released his hilt. "Dark notes won't stop darker steel," he said cryptically. "Next time." He wheeled and marched toward the castle with the rest of his group.

"Perhaps you could get us both killed at another time, sir," Pontes said, panting. "May I ask why you drew on him?"

"He should not have knocked that woman down," Ezra said, releasing his anger and sheathing his sword to find a nearly empty square and a sudden silence. "Let me help you, lady," he said to the woman, who was still huddled on the ground where she fell.

Her eyes went wide in a kind of shock, and she slumped mutely away, presumably having had enough experience of an Elysian Bell for one day.

"That sounds like a sufficient and necessary reason for death," Pontes said, voice hoarse.

Ezra smiled wryly at him. "The day was also too hot for all those layers. Not without a good reason." *I have mine. What is theirs?*

"You were ready to fight them out of curiosity, sir?"

"But they didn't fight, Pontes. That is what is curious."

"THERE ARE questions that need answering, Mari," Ezra said with more than a hint of anger in his voice.

Marigold did not like it. She could not tell if the dark feeling came from her own reaction to the situation or from a subtle push from Ezra's nature. A new message had barely beat Ezra to the practice ring where Marigold, unarmored, was in the middle of teaching her girls' class. The girls had scarcely been moved to the outer rings, the page had just vacated the yard, and Marigold had only just finished reading the message when her friend arrived with his upright, silent secretary. Her hasty disposal of the note left her feeling flushed and guilty, which she also did not like.

Pontes was looking at her disapprovingly, as always, but this time Marigold wondered if he truly saw through her. He was far too unreadable in his silences. *And why is he acting as if he is Ezra's squire? That does not fit either.*

Ezra's rant was not over. "And I did *not* like the look of those fuckers from the square either."

Ezra hardly ever swore, but there it was.

"Something is going on," he added.

Marigold had been sitting on one of the benches, twirling a heavy wooden practice sword. She leaned back now and said, "There's always fuckers, and there's always something going on." Then she added nonchalantly, "What are you going to do?"

"Stay here until I'm satisfied the Queen is safe."

"You aren't wanted."

It hurt to say that, but Marigold was getting more used to hurting Ezra, and herself, all the time. "That's what the note said, isn't it?"

"Yes."

"Just go home, then. Leave things to me."

Ezra pointed at the girls' class practicing in the rings adjacent to theirs. "You're busy. And there is just one of you."

"I am pretty awesome."

"Did you know that no one is guarding the Queen? Lady Jayne Orton thought it was *you*. So who, if anyone, *is*?" Ezra picked up a heavy wooden practice sword from the blade barrel.

"We have this under control, Knight."

"Horseshit you do, Mari. *She* isn't letting you. She has to do it all herself."

"This is getting boring," Marigold said, not enjoying the shape of the words. "The Queen is quite capable."

"Everyone needs help, Mari. Everyone."

Marigold stood up, practice sword in hand. "Oh. And it's just *got* to be you, Ezra? The rest of us aren't good enough?"

"That's not what I meant, I—"

"Sure it is." Marigold stepped away from the bench. "That's exactly what you meant." She turned from her friend and raised her voice to the girls. "Gather around, ladies. A lesson is about to be taught."

"Perhaps we should leave now, sir," she heard Pontes say, standing behind his own bench. "Sir Marigold has to teach her class."

He has never liked me.

Marigold winked at the secretary, knowing he would hate this, and squared off against Ezra. "We are going to spar, Sir Ezra. If I win, you admit that I—and *all* the other knights—can do our jobs and guard the Queen."

"And when I win?" he asked, smiling just a little.

This was exactly the way Marigold liked Ezra. When he was smiling just a little. She said, "In the unlikely event that you prevail, I come with you tomorrow, and we go find the Queen together."

"Deal."

"But take that armor off. Especially that steel block you've attached to your left vambrace."

"Mari—"

"I want you to feel the touch."

"Balance the ledger, sir!" Pontes shouted. Well, for him it was a shout. Most of the little girls were louder. A lot louder.

I guess that's his version of "kick her ass." Marigold found herself respecting the secretary just a little more.

Getting the armor off Ezra took some time, though not as much as getting it on, Marigold knew that too well.

"Shirt off too," she said.

"You're being gratuitous."

Maybe. "I want the ladies here to—" She raised her voice, "Ladies! This is Sir Ezra. He has killed more men than drunken horse racing. I'm going to show you how to beat him." She grinned at Ezra. "Shirt. Off."

"Fine," he grumbled, "but this is as far as it goes. We aren't recruits in training anymore."

He peeled his last top layer off. Some of the bolder girls whistled—though they were too young to know what they meant. The rest cringed. Ezra had the body for a whistle, that was certain. Or a tear. He was lean and raw-boned, wrapped in wiry muscle and spidery vascularity. But he was also covered in hideous scars, more than a few of which were purple. Recent ones.

Mari remembered where he had earned some of them. Some in training. Some in border skirmishes against neighbors. Most of them on that night when he had cleared a castle by himself. Mari remembered sewing those wounds up. She waved her sword around to hide her own reaction to the history written on her friend's skin.

"How do we win, ladies?"

The girls were silent. Loud when not called on to speak, shy when called.

"Well? How do we win?"

"Strategy!" shouted Ellis.

"Efficiency," yelled Sam.

"Hit him first!" hollered Gertrude, making Marigold smile.

"You are all correct," replied Marigold. She motioned Ezra to the center of the sand with the tip of her wooden sword.

They faced off. Saluted. The duel began.

Marigold knew that it was not a fight. Ezra would have killed her quickly in a real fight, unless she somehow stabbed him surgically and by surprise in the first seconds, or by accident or a gross turn of luck. But this was not a real fight, and she knew that Ezra would hold back. He wanted to win, certainly, but not through her pain or injury.

The way he was coming on, not quickly committing, also told her that he did not even wish to embarrass her.

This was a duel, and Marigold knew her advantages. *The harder I fight, the harder it will be for him to protect me.* She growled and came on hard, stabbing straight and fast.

Ezra was no Gertrude, and he knew how to use his wrists. He

blocked each thrust quickly and countered, but not very hard. He pressed the attack, but Marigold saw each blow coming.

Perhaps he is out of practice.

She changed her timing suddenly and came on in a new series of quicker, more efficient strikes. Ezra caught them all easily.

Not so out of practice.

Marigold made another decision. She pressed close and thrust straight and fast. Ezra twisted over her blade and countered. She countered back. They engaged in tight with each other and began a blurringly fast game of sticky swords, their blades rolling over each other.

A master could do this with her eyes closed—it was a technique that Marigold taught her girls, and she was a master—feeling the rotation of the swords, the balance, and their weight. They moved as if arms and swords were twisting springs, back and forth and around and back and forth, again and again, rising and falling in power and speed in a beautiful martial harmony.

This could have been sex if he had ever fallen in love with her.

Instead of being distracted by this errant fantasy, Marigold dove in deeper, matching Ezra's footwork, moving in synchronicity with him, her feet and shins nearly touching his, taking the duel to the level of a dance, closer to sex than anything she had ever experienced with a weapon before.

They moved more and more quickly as if to some new, unconsciously agreed tempo. They turned and spun as if each segment of their bodies was made of springs in tension and in contact with each other, not fighting so much as exchanging energy, information, feeling. Creating, together, a joint effect.

He's not trying to hit me.

An almost inaudible chiming filled the practice ring. It could easily have been missed, but it rose and fell with their movements, to the song they were creating with arms, bodies, and weapons.

She looked at his face. He was smiling at her.

Marigold abruptly broke harmony and viciously kicked his knee, then thrust her sword hard and fast, the tip just hitting his chest. She held it there in victory.

"I won't leave, Mari," Ezra said, unhurt. His voice was firm, but with a new tone, not love—not quite—but not destruction either. "And you know I love you, though not like I love *her*. I would never hurt you, Marigold."

The chiming sound grew, and Marigold saw that his arms had grown blurry. "Striking you was never how I planned to win this duel." He brought his arms sharply across Marigold's sword from both directions at once, blurring in vibration.

Her strong wooden blade sheared neatly in half.

~

After Ezra and Pontes had left and she had dismissed her class, Marigold produced the letter she had received earlier and dropped into the blade barrel before they had seen it.

"Discourage him."

"Well, that didn't work." Marigold shook her head. *Some people* cannot *be discouraged.*

She was not sure if she was thinking more of Ezra or of the Queen.

CHAPTER 12

AUDIENCE

Lady Jayne Orton had been joined by Lord Seltser, the Queen's Secretary, for the signing, in a new and even more impressive meeting room than Orton's office. They were both dressed immaculately, though Seltser's back was hunched and his voice weak. Pontes was impressed with them and signed the agreements with a happiness just observable to the untrained eye. To Ezra's eyes, his lean, careful companion was practically jumping for joy at being served by both the Queen's Senior Treasurer and her Secretary, though merely smiling and lifting his head just a little higher than usual.

"You should sign as well, Sir Ezra, as Seneschal to Lady Kristen," stated Lady Jayne with her now familiar sense of decorum.

Ezra exchanged a look with Pontes. He had told the secretary about the cream-colored envelope he had observed in the sword barrel at Marigold's practice yard. And he was pretty certain that Lady Jayne and Lord Seltser had received cream-colored envelopes of their own.

Everyone seems to be receiving secret orders.

He hoped this was the Queen's doing. But despite his mind's constant conjuring of her blonde hair, he had yet to see the woman he had thought about every day for eleven years.

She is like some mythical creature. Or a god, inscrutable, acting every-where, subtly, with effect but never seen.

But Ezra knew she was a woman, not a god or a myth, and he was worried.

"Certainly," he said. "I will sign on behalf of Lady Kristen along with Pontes. And then I believe I shall go witness the Queen's general audience."

I will hear her voice.

Lady Jayne smiled in her urbane way. "They won't let you into the audience chamber with your sword. Not even you."

Ezra took charge of one ledger, locked it carefully, and handed the other to Pontes, making sure the secretary felt equal ownership of their victory. "Indeed. Shall we, Pontes?"

"Yes sir."

~

Something is wrong.

She was late.

"I'm not surprised, sir," Pontes said. Marigold was supposed to have met them outside the Knight Captain's office near the main gates. A great many people had come and gone, but none of them had been Marigold, who would have been unmistakable in her plate armor.

"Sir Corning!" Ezra called to the captain himself, who was rushing down the hallway, clutching something in his left hand. "Have you seen Sir Marigold?"

Corning looked harried as he marched—almost ran—quickly by, jingling in his chain mail. He seemed to hesitate, stutter stepping, then stopped. "No, I haven't se— no, that's wrong. She came through about a quarter hour ago. Maybe longer."

"Going where?"

Corning hesitated. His head shook subtly from side to side. An unconscious gesture of futility. "No one tells me anything, they just expect everything and expect it immediately. I have to go. *Now.*"

Ezra saw the edge of a cream-colored envelope in Corning's left hand and followed the Knight Captain, motioning for Pontes to come along.

"Somewhat improper of him," mused Pontes, breathing hard. "Complaining."

"Not everyone has your sense of propriety, Pontes." said Ezra. He saw that they were taking the straight route to the audience chamber. "Let's take the back route up to the viewing gallery I showed you yesterday."

I'm not giving up my sword.

"Sir?"

"That balcony we were on." *Something is about to happen.*

Ezra both wanted something to happen and feared what it might be. He wanted an excuse to do more than listen to her voice through a dark screen across a long hallway. Yet instinct told him that something was amiss and that his personal desires were suddenly unimportant. He converted his plate-armored trot into a heavy, clattering run. Pages and courtiers scattered out of his way. Guardswomen and men grabbed hilts and listened in alarm, either to the jangling of his massive, plate-metal carapace or, more likely, to another low sound, just on the edge of consciousness, that began to rise off him.

He hit the concealed door and pushed it roughly open, still holding a ledger under one arm and balancing the hilt of his sword with the other, saying, "Come on, Pontes!"

Sweat was streaming off the scrawny secretary, slicking edges of the sharp widow's peak of his fine hair, but he made no complaint. Instinct strumming his heartbeat to a higher rhythm, Ezra sprinted up the winding staircase three steps at a time, narrowly avoiding tripping on his sword. With each leaping step, he feared he was too late, that he had been too patient, that they should not have waited for Marigold as long as they had. He burst open the balcony door, hitting something hard with it—a spectator to the Queen's audience who had been leaning unwittingly against it.

"Aaahhh!" cried the man, sprawling.

"Sorry," said Ezra, not even seeing what the fellow looked like. The shouts rising from the hall below had his full attention.

"The Queen is a murderer! A vampire!" shrieked a frenzied voice that Ezra did not recognize.

"Shut your mouth and put up that sword!"

The second voice was Marigold's. It was mixed with cries of dismay and grunting noises out of sight. Even on the viewing gallery, well-dressed nobles, merchants, and humble peasants alike were shouting and pointing. Some were screaming. An old man in a black cape was weeping.

Ezra sprinted, winding between panicked observers, people quick to gesticulate but capable of no executive action. "Get out of his way!" a lady in a yellow dress screamed.

The sound of metal clashed below. *How did someone get a sword in here?*

Ezra slid to the rail and looked down. The hall below was in chaotic disarray. The hectic mix of aggressive antagonists and panicking bystanders made any quick identification of the principals impossible, though he spotted Sir Marigold immediately. She faced off against a richly dressed man and three soldiers—their chain mail showing around the edges of their cloaks. Long, dark cloaks like the assassins of Erle wore. Behind her, under Ezra and closer to the main doors, Sir Corning and four Knights of the Queen faced ten or more adversaries all alike in cloak and chain. Ezra recognized the tall blonde woman from the square among them.

Where is the big man?

There!

Castel was crouching, concealed behind cringing lords and ladies of the audience chamber, doing something with a sword and a chair. Sharpening a wooden stake from one of the chair legs.

"Kill her," commanded the man facing Marigold. He then turned and faced the cowering members of the audience, people of every description, nobles included, some of whom were piteously scrambling toward the walls and corners of the room.

"Our Queen murdered a man eleven years ago," he declared. "An actor named Brayden Fellows. She sucked his blood and had his body hidden in a stone monument somewhere in the Queen's Cemetery. She is a vampire!" As his soldiers feinted with Marigold, he gestured toward the dark screen. "See how she hides in the dark! No one has seen her in the light for years. This ends now."

Without warning, Marigold moved like a spring, using the strike she had attempted on Ezra the day before, and put her narrow sword into the wide neck of one of the men facing her. Before the blood finished spraying over her sword, another adversary struck her in the left grieve with a clang, making her stagger, and the other soldier—a man—barged her off her feet. The man who had struck her leg raised his sword to deliver a devastating blow on the downed woman.

Marigold!

A deep, thunderous blast shook the room, and Ezra threw the heavy ledger he had been carrying as hard as he could. It rotated, end over end, held tight by its lock, missed the man with the sword and hit his companion, who had been recovering his balance, in the face.

"Gaahhh!" The soldier's feet came up, his arms recoiled wide, uselessly, and he fell violently onto his back.

"Good shot, sir!" said Pontes, words Ezra never expected to hear out of him over a thrown book, and tossed him the other ledger. Ezra hurled this tome at the other swordsman, the one who had been about to hit Marigold.

Without waiting to see if he had hit the man or not, Ezra leapt off the balcony, right hand on the hilt of his sword to keep from impaling himself, and hit the ground with hair-raising speed to the awful sound of tortured metal. He rolled expertly to protect himself, then rotated right into a man who had been crouching over a chair, sprawling him onto the stone floor.

"AAAAhhh!" someone shrieked. The man he had collided with.

Up! Struggling for air, unsure what had been broken or damaged, Ezra surged to his feet, drew his sword, and chimed death. Marigold had also regained her feet and was facing someone. The same man who had been about to kill her? Ezra could not tell.

He sprinted toward them on split, protesting grieves and jambeaux, and with all his rage, swung his sword down on the man's head, parting it to the neck in a heavy splash of blood and brains. With a brutal grunt, he pulled his sword back, sawing though the man's parted skull, and turned to search for the next person to kill.

"Stay out of this, Sir Ezra!" shouted the noble who had called for the Queen's murder. With ferocious speed, Ezra picked up a chair with his left hand and hurled it at the man, who disappeared in an explosion of wood.

Ezra did not care in the least who the man was. Thunder continued to roll off him. Some of the trapped audience members were screaming, but their cries were barely audible over the low-pitched keening.

The tall woman sprinted past Ezra with a sharpened wooden stake in her right hand. He leapt after her, tackling her and landing on top.

The stake scraped over his helm. She was aiming for his eye. Ezra reared up and struck her mercilessly in the face with his steel gauntlets. Once, twice. Her hands went limp, and she fell back against the floor. He grabbed the stake her slack hands had dropped and slammed it through her right eye into her brain. Her legs spasmed once, hard, levitating off the ground for that long moment of which only the worst memories are made.

"Eaton!" a loud voice called in distress, loud enough to penetrate Ezra's thunder.

A tremendous blow to Ezra's side—just on the left edge of his breastplate—swept him off the woman. Gasping for air, the wind knocked out of him, Ezra staggered and groped for his sword. He had lost it. He saw the next horrendous strike coming just in time to raise his left vambrace—the one with the steel block welded to it—and catch the impact where his armor could hold it. The blow nearly broke his forearm, cracking the side of the vambrace opposite the steel block.

Ezra scrambled backward, struggling for air, knew he had been cut by the first blow, that perhaps one or more ribs had been broken. He looked up and recognized his attacker. It was the big man from the square, the bully, Sir Castel. The stake sharpener.

The blond man's lips were moving, but Ezra could not hear him over the sound rolling off him, nor did he care what Castel had to say. Ezra leapt away from the enormous man and snatched a wooden chair in each hand, then leapt back and brought both chairs up and around, faster than thought, to hit the man from both sides at once.

Castel tried to protect his right side with his sword but was stunned by the kinetic detonation of wood. Ezra looked again for his own sword but still could not see it. He did see a cloaked female soldier cut a pair of lips through Sir Corning's nose. Ezra sprinted forward and struck her over the top of the head with his left vambrace block. As she fell, he snatched her sword out of the air.

He turned in time to take a new strike on his breastplate. The blow cracked the metal right down the middle and made his heart skip a beat. He saw lightning and caught himself before he hit the ground—a flash knockout—then twisted and caught the sword he had momentarily released and brought it up just in time to block Castel's next blow.

With a chime of pure hatred, Ezra counterattacked, twisting into Carried by the Cyclone, turning and smiting Castel's sword, then his chest and his arm, again and again, turning and striking in the nine manifold revolutions of the form, unleashing rage and frustration—eleven years of anxiety and worry over the woman who he loved—onto the colossal man and the hateful rumor he represented.

The whole chamber reverberated to the maneuver. Chairs jumped and bounced like toys. Those who had not yet fled fell to their knees and covered their heads in terror.

When he stopped spinning, Ezra saw that only a foot of blade was left of his broken sword and that Castel's arm had been hacked into three pieces held together only by the few remaining unbroken rings of chain mail on his sleeve. His face had been obliterated and his blond hair was orange now. Castel's head looked like a crushed and mangled grapefruit draped in orange fuzz.

Without pausing, Ezra hurled the fragment of sword at the soldier facing Marigold across the room, then retrieved Castel's badly notched blade.

A blow to his helm added a new ringing to the air. Ezra staggered. Another blow on his right pauldron—from the other side—almost made him drop Castel's sword. A further blow came from behind. Ezra picked one opponent, spun, and struck with everything he had left, cutting through the man's mail and halfway through his lung. A vomit of blood splashed from his mouth as if thrown from a bucket. Without pausing, Ezra stepped in tight to the next closest soldier—a wide-lipped, wider-eyed man—grabbed the man's sword arm with his left hand and smashed the hilt of his own sword into the man's jaw. As the attacker fell backward, Ezra released his arm and cut ruthlessly across his neck, opening the throat.

Someone tackled Ezra from behind, forcing him into the remains of a broken chair. Another blow struck his helm, and he found himself on his back staring up at a long-bladed knife coming straight for his eyes. Instinctively, he intercepted the knife-wielding wrist with his left hand. And vibrated.

There was a scream as the blade fell away. Ezra regained both his feet and Castel's sword and continued spinning and laying about as if more than his life was at stake.

"Ezra! Ezra!"

The voice was Sir Marigold's. Hands wiped blood from Ezra's eyes. He staggered, but she caught him. Held him. He found himself patting her back. There was a moment of euphoric peace in her arms.

Blood began pooling into his eyes again. He released Marigold and found that he had nothing to wipe the blood away with.

"Here," she handed him something. A handkerchief. He wiped his eyes and surveyed the carnage.

Bodies lay everywhere. He counted twenty dead before giving up.

They were mostly in long, dark cloaks, but a few were Knights of the Queen. Sir Corning was crying piteously, clutching at his face. Many of the other innocent witnesses—people who had only come to make their pleas to the Queen—were also crying or groaning. At least a dozen of these were bleeding or staunching some injury that had been inflicted accidentally during the battle. All four of the knights who had stood at Sir Corning's side were down—dead most likely.

Marigold's armor was dented and gashed. Her helm was gone, and bloody hair fell about her shoulders, painting a red image on her gorget and pauldrons. She looked like a blood-red goddess of war.

"I'm glad you're . . . on your feet," Ezra said to her.

She shrugged in a poor performance of nonchalance, but Ezra could see she was on the verge of collapse.

"I look better than you," she said. "At least my armor's in one piece. You should stop blocking swords with your helm."

Ezra took a few ringlets of her bloody hair in his fingers and said, "*You* stop."

"No, *you*." She managed a smile.

A pounding sounded on the doors at the back of the room, interrupting their self-consciously childish patter.

So how did this happen? How did she end up in here ahead of me?

Ezra pointed at dead, cloaked bodies. "You spotted some of them early on."

"Yes," Marigold said. "They looked like they might be of Erle . . . and that Castel fellow fit your description from yesterday too well."

"And so you decided to follow them instead of meeting us."

"Had to. I figured you would sort it out and know what to do." She gestured at Corning and the downed Knights of the Queen. "They barricaded the door as soon as Sir Corning entered."

"He had a message," Ezra said. "An envelope."

"The Queen knew."

"Huh." *Almost too late.*

How did they get all these swords in here?

Just then, Ezra saw a rope fall from the balcony and looked up to see Pontes help a knight climb over the rail and lower herself down.

"Open the doors," he said to her as her feet touched the ground. "And get the surgeons in here."

The noble who had called for the Queen's death was struggling to his knees.

"Who is he?" Ezra asked, limping over to him.

Marigold came with him, limping even worse, and put a hand roughly through the man's white hair. "This is Lord Ronald Paron, cousin to the late but unlamented Lady Jacqueline."

There was a sudden rush of knights, servants, and nobles through the doors, though they quickly came to a halt, aghast at the violence that had been wreaked upon the room and many of those who had been trapped within it.

"She's a *vampire*," Paron hissed weakly. "Do you think you're a hero protecting her? She killed a young man—"

"Shut up!" Marigold said, striking him with her gauntlet.

"Look at the shadows she hides in!" Paron whined, trying to shield his head, trying to appeal to the crowd pressing into the room. He pointed a shaking finger at the dais.

Ezra considered how it must look. The dais was only ten strides away. The dark screen had been constructed with a thin, dark, perforated cloth and spanned from floor to ceiling. Even as close as he stood, he could not see through it.

Why?

A flash of the Queen, her long blonde hair and her longer nights of work, came to his mind. And he *knew*.

"You fool," Ezra said in loud, ringing tones. Disregarding his injuries and exhaustion, he grabbed the front of Paron's tunic and dragged him bodily to the dais, up the stairs, and right up to the perforated blind. He turned to address the crowd and the remaining witnesses on the balcony. "***The Queen is not a vampire,***" he roared, chiming as he shouted.

Releasing Paron to slump where he had been dragged, Ezra thrust his fingers through the screen and began pulled it apart, ripping a seam. Marigold joined him with a sharp dagger and together they tore down the screen so everyone could see what Ezra had guessed.

Several chairs had been arranged behind the cloth barrier and around a table. On the table were feather pens, ink bottles, ledgers, and files.

"The Queen sits behind a screen so that she can keep on working while you make your appeals!" Ezra shouted. "She was not hiding from the light like a vampire. She was stealing time like a Queen devoted to your welfare!"

She just didn't want you to know she was doing two things at once.

A door at the back of the dais stood ajar. Ezra knew that he had just missed seeing her.

CHAPTER 13
DISCOVERY

"**D**iscover yourself."

That is what was written in the cream-colored letter that had been left on the thin white sheet covering Ezra's chest. He tried to sit up, and for the second time in just a few weeks, found himself too weak. Rereading the note, he muttered, "Who am I?"

"Kind of an idiot," replied Sir Marigold from a padded leather chair beside his bed.

For an instant, he mistook her for Danielle Stonehouse, the situation was so eerily similar. Except Danielle had not had a white cloth bandage wrapped around her head.

"That's what the message says, Mari. More or less."

Marigold shook her head. "She isn't big on long explanations."

"Are these notes really from her?"

Marigold shrugged.

Ezra tried once more to prop himself up. But Marigold jumped up and pushed him down—again reminding him of Stonehouse. "You have two broken ribs, fool, and you just about bled out under your armor before you collapsed in front of the princess. No one here is quite sure why you're still alive. At some point during the night you

115

suddenly got . . . better. At least that's what we think. I slept through it, I'm afraid. Right *here*, fool." She gestured at the chair behind her. Seemingly replete on calling him names, she patted Ezra's chest affectionately. "Just stay still for a minute, would you? Let the stitches hold you together because I think your stubbornness is finally exhausted."

"Where's Pontes?"

Marigold, still standing over Ezra, shook her head again. "Drink this first," she said, holding out a big stein of pungent fluid.

Ezra did what he could with it, trying not to spill the sharp stuff onto the very nice cloth of the sheet. "Where are we?"

"Private room in the castle infirmary."

"Huh." Ezra had never merited a private room in the castle before. "And Pontes?"

"Sick of *me* is where he is," Marigold laughed. "I sent him back to your inn to rest. He'll bring you some fresh, non-blood-soaked clothes later."

"Are *you* okay, Mari?"

She rolled her eyes. "I'm tougher than you, didn't you know?"

"And smarter?"

"Oh yes!" she said happily. "And also, they seemed to hate you more. A *lot* more."

"Oh." Ezra vaguely remembered being hit from every side at once. "Where is my armor?"

"We threw it away, it was so beat up."

Seeing the look on his face at this news, Marigold added, "Okay, I think it is being repaired. But don't look for it anytime soon."

Damn it. I'm supposed to lie here naked and think about who I am? The idea was singularly unappealing.

"Did you say princess?"

"Yes." Marigold looked away. "You finally met the Queen's daughter. Don't you remember?"

~

"Let's go, Marigold," Ezra said, marching noisily toward the door at the back of the dais in his cracked, dented, now barely functional armor. He could barely move in it.

Is that the broken armor or me?

He looked down at his feet. Blood was leaking out of his sabatons. More blood was rolling down his face, making it difficult to see properly. He was also struggling to breathe.

But his sense of anxiety over the Queen rose like a tide once more, lifting him into action.

How did they get so many swords in here?

Marigold had been handing Lord Ronald Paron off to another knight. Now she limped toward Ezra, saying, "Perhaps we should look at your wounds first. And mine." She gestured at the chaotic mix of surgeons, pages, knights, and functionaries scattered about the room, busy with the survivors now that the fight was over. "Let me get someone."

Ezra knew that if he sat down, he would not soon get back up. "Stay here, then," he said. "I have to know."

Marigold grumbled, "She won't be any safer with you dead," but she limped after him into the passageway. "You need to turn left at the second landing," she called to him.

Ezra did not reply. He did not have the energy to spare, and his heart was filled with fear and anticipation. The basic structure of the castle and its secret ways to the Queen's chambers would surely not have changed during his absence. The passageway was narrow and lit only by tiny rectangular vents built into it. He leaned into the wall and pushed upward when he found the stairs, his friend somewhere behind him, breathing loudly, complaining a little less loudly.

Ezra found the landing, crossed the sky bridge that few knew about, and entered the Queen's Tower. Then began an endless-seeming climb up yet another narrow stairway. There were other stairways, all of them heavily guarded, but this was the one *she* would have taken. He did not think her habits would have changed. This was the most direct route, if one knew of it. He climbed in dark isolation, passing from all the death that had been left below in search of the one life he hoped to find above.

An eternity of slow steps later, there was a prolonged and ugly crashing sound below like the noise of every copper pot in the castle kitchens falling from some high and unwise stack. He turned laboriously.

But he could not see Marigold.

"Mari?" he called.

"No, I will *not* marry you," she said from around a corner below, her voice strange.

Ezra painfully retraced his steps until he found her sprawled out on the stairs. He reached an arm out to her. "Marigold, let me—"

She swatted at his hand with her gauntlet. "You dead-gods idiot, I just slipped down four of these stairs because they are slicked with *your* blood! You have to *stop*."

She was crying.

This felt worse than any blow. Like that time with the Queen, but more familiar.

Ezra could not think what to say. He froze, one hand still reaching down to her. He was stuck, fixed in place between concern for his friend and fear for the Queen. After a time, he said, "I have to see her, Marigold."

"I know," she said.

He turned around and resumed climbing. Ezra knew that repeating his offer to help would only lead to further violence and cursing. Or worse, more tears.

"You better not say anything about this later," he heard Marigold say.

"You mean if I don't die in this stone tube?"

"That's right. 'Cause I'll kill you if I hear *one* story. One dead gods-damned word of it."

Ezra started to laugh. The sound echoed down the stairs.

"What?"

"We're there." He pushed open the door. Sir Jennifer Shryke stood in the hallway on the other side, not three paces distant. Her sword was drawn.

Ezra sensed that there were more guards further down the hallway. His laughter had dried up, and his vision was beginning to narrow from his increasingly tenuous grip on consciousness.

He held up a hand, listlessly, almost feebly, at a loss for words, but when Marigold emerged behind, she said, "There's no need for that, Shryke, we've been bludgeoned plenty already.

"Oh?" Shryke retorted, "so you're in the nearly dead, foolish phase?"

"It's a phase for me," Marigold said. She thrust a trembling thumb at Ezra and said, "But that's his normal state of being."

"I'm getting that."

Ezra caught himself from nearly falling. His vision seemed to be going gray. "Let us just make sure the Queen is safe and we'll be good."

Shryke pursed her lips. "A page told me you two killed them all."

"All that we know of. But someone helped them get those weapons into the audience chamber," said Ezra. "I'm worried they may have agents in the castle."

"Sir Corning will have to investigate," said Shryke. "He has certainly let us down."

"He won't be investigating anything for a while," said Marigold.

"Oh?"

"He took one to the face."

"Dead gods! The pages didn't mention that."

"Oh yeah," said Marigold. "I think we will need a new Knight Captain."

Ezra had no patience for small talk, which he was barely following anyway. He said, "I need to see her."

"You can't," said Shryke, sheathing her sword. "She's gone already."

"What?" said Marigold, skeptical. "Where?"

"Conferences, meetings, work. The usual."

Ezra pushed past Shryke. "I need to see."

But it sounded like her. Only the Queen would survive an assassination attempt and head to her next conference without pause. *She would die for her schedule.*

"She's not there," said Jennifer. "But try the next door down. You might find someone familiar."

Right. Better than nothing. He could barely hear anything now except the rapid, fluttery beating of his own heart.

Ezra felt a tug on his left pauldron. The force of it started to turn him until the pauldron failed and came off. "Stop, Ezra," said Marigold, tossing the bent, heavy hunk of steel to a noisy destination somewhere down the hall. "You heard Jennifer. The Queen isn't here. You'll bloody bleed to death in her apartments."

He trudged on, passing the four other guards he had barely even noticed.

"Ezra!"

"What the hell, Shryke? He should not be here."

"*You* brought him."

Ezra barely heard them. The blood pounding in his ears percussed more and more softly with every beat. By the time he reached the door, he could barely hear the sound of his life at all.

It opened easily enough—possibly because Ezra had to lean into it to keep his balance—and he stumbled halfway into a child's bedroom. On the floor, twenty feet away, writing carefully in a small leather book, was a little girl in a long purple dress. She had shoulder-length blonde hair. Ezra's knees almost gave way at the shock of seeing her. She looked *exactly* like a tiny version of the Queen.

"You're Sir Ezra!" said the little girl without hesitation. She snapped the book closed and locked it with a broad leather thong much like the ones that bound the ledgers that Ezra had used as weapons downstairs not long before. Pushing the book aside, the girl took up something new. A foot-tall brass figurine of a knight in plate armor.

"Come in, there's a draught," she said, holding the toy knight out to him in her right hand.

He walked carefully toward her, leaving a red trail behind him.

"You are Princess Eryka."

"Obviously." She produced a hardwood mallet and struck the figurine. It rang and held its high, pure note for an impossibly long moment.

"Is that me?"

She gazed at him steadily. "Doesn't it sound like you?"

Ezra blinked. "I don't know."

"I felt you downstairs," she said.

Ezra frowned. "That's not possible."

"You *were* pretty loud, Ezra," said Marigold from the door. "Come on now, stop bothering the princess, and let's go see a surgeon. Or a gravedigger. You are *done*."

Eryka dropped the figurine and mallet on the polished floor and jumped up. "I heard you yesterday too. In the square."

"How——?"

"Hello, Mari," said Eryka, too fast for Ezra's ponderously forming question.

"Your Royal Highness," Marigold said, bowing.

Ezra's mind was working very slowly now. He could not think what to say to this little girl. That the Queen had had a child by the late Prince of Erle, he knew, but it was not a subject he and Marigold—or he and anyone—had spoken of much. Yet here she was, painfully reminding him of her mother and seeming every bit as intelligent and focused. At last, he came up with, "This has been a pleasure, Princess. I never thought to meet you."

"And I thought you'd be smarter," said Eryka.

Ezra started chuckling at this but never got to his next question. He dropped unconscious straight onto the little girl's brass figurine. It chimed loudly as he landed on it.

～

"You might find someone familiar."

Ezra lay back, thinking about what Sir Shryke had said. Among all the unanswered questions and all the things that had seemed wrong about the day before, that statement was most on his mind. More than the horrifying idea that they really had meant to stake the Queen. More than the way that female soldier's—Eaton's—legs had spasmed when he had driven the stake through her eye. What Shryke had said was not horrifying at all, it just stuck out. She had said it just moments before he had met Princess Eryka.

Sharp little girl. Sharp as her mother.

Strange figurine.

Ten years old.

"Marigold!" Ezra shouted.

"What?" Marigold said, alarm in her voice.

She was there, was still right there, had stayed by his side while he remembered, just as she had been the only one to visit him in the eleven years of his banishment.

My only true friend.

Marigold was the only one, besides the Queen, who had known all these years that he was an Elysian Bell and that he loved the Queen. She was his sole connection to a past he had harbored and preserved in his mind as if under glass. Marigold was the one friend who had stayed a friend, a rock of trust, of familiarity and strength. Through her regular visits, she had helped him keep despair at bay all those long years.

Visits he now suspected had been made under orders.

"Why?" he asked, some part of him hoping it was not true.

"Why what?" she answered, an unfamiliar edge of emotional uncertainty in her voice.

"I expect *her* to do what she has to do," Ezra said. "But I never thought you would hurt me."

Marigold's face turned white. "I didn't—"

As upset as he was, trembling under the thin sheet, holding in an awful keening of betrayal, Ezra would not say the words aloud. He could not. They were too dangerous. A Princess of Erle growing up in the Queendom must have been an essential diplomatic shield in negotiations with that rich but backward nation, perhaps the only reason for peace after their prince's violent death. Ezra was not going to utter so much as a whisper to endanger the little girl or her mother. But he could still ask Marigold about her role.

"Were you ever really my friend?"

"Ezra..."

"I'm supposed to discover myself," he said wearily. He trailed off into a whisper. "I don't know what this says about me. But about *you*. And *her* . . ."

Marigold covered her mouth with her right hand. She seemed to be choking.

I have a daughter.

"What else haven't you told me?"

CHAPTER 14

AGENT

"There is a point in your life when you must decide if you are the waves or the rocks, ladies," Sir Marigold told her class. "Are you the worker or the worked, the changer or the changed, the agent or the stooge"

"To win, you must be the agent. You must strike first, hard and without remorse. You must do what you must, no matter what."

"Why are you so angry, Sir Marigold?" Ellis asked in her squeaky, little-girl voice.

"Who did you fight?" asked Sam.

"Are you hurt?" asked Bethyl.

"You look hurt," said Gertrude, awe on her face. Her oversized hand went to her own face.

Am I so obviously bruised? Marigold had tried to forget her own injuries in the aftermath of the fight, Ezra's near death, and his discovery of her betrayal.

Ezra.

Marigold crushed her anger and regret and waved the interrogation away. She had a lesson to teach, not a conscience to explore. On most days, Marigold enjoyed teaching. But not today. Not on the days when she was reminded that in life a person can never choose to be just the cause or the effect.

"You can't hesitate, no matter what. When the time comes, you must know it, and you must act." Marigold looked at their rapt faces and wondered if any of them would have done as she had done.

I walked away once when I shouldn't have.

I lied when I shouldn't have.

The realization belied her simplistic lesson that one could always know when to act and how to act. No. Any action could both keep faith and betray at once. Loyalty to the Queen, betrayal of her friend.

I cannot lie to him again.

This felt like releasing a weight. With her confidence at least somewhat renewed, Marigold continued the lesson. "Initiative and commitment win more fights than any other factor. Do not allow yourself to be the acted upon, to become the changed, the victim. Be the agent, the actor, the changer."

"Whatever it costs," she added, her voice faltering.

She heard the page enter the practice area before she saw her. And she knew without looking what was on the polished tray. The message was another matter. That could never be predicted.

"Square off, ladies," she said, readying her troubled soul to receive new orders. She would not tell the girls that even the agent is affected by her actions. She never said it all in a lesson, for a lesson can only be about one thing. "It is time for an exercise to prove my point."

The things we do change us too.

"We missed her again, sir," said Pontes.

How does she move so quickly?

Ezra looked up into the sunlight, wondering how Lord Paron thought his vampire claim was going to convince anyone. The Queen did not just work through the long hours of the night. She worked all day too. *And I cannot seem to move quickly enough to catch up to her.*

Pontes was giving him a side-eyed look. Ezra knew the faithful secretary was far from happy about chasing after the phantom Queen all over the capital. "Perhaps we should just find her in the palace tonight, sir."

Ezra felt naked without his armor, but at least no one recognized him without it. He felt lighter too, and freer in his soft leather boots, loose-fitting pants, and the rich, belted tunic that Danielle Stonehouse had tailored for him. "There is no guarantee of that, Pontes. She may not go back to her chambers at all."

Especially if she is avoiding me. Ezra almost laughed at the thought. She had used all her power to forcibly avoid him for eleven years. *Why did she change her mind? And if she did, why continue discouraging me?*

But he did not laugh. It hurt too much. He had felt like a man adrift in an endless sea of love and despair before, but now that he had met Eryka, the pain was worse. Much worse.

She has a figurine of me. She knows my name. She knows me.

"Is she still the reason?" Pontes asked quietly, almost hesitantly.

"Yes," Ezra answered, though suddenly the Queen was not the *only* reason. "But she isn't *your* reason, my friend. Why don't you take the ledgers back to Lady Kristen? Dead-gods only know how long it will be before I am satisfied." *If ever.*

"I think I'll stay, sir, nonetheless." The secretary adjusted the short sword he now wore, reluctantly, on his hip. "Until you find her."

"Everyone has a reason." *Though I don't precisely know yours.*

"Yes, sir. Indeed." One of the ledgers had exploded from Ezra's use of it as a missile, but its pages and binding had been meticulously reassembled. While surgeons had worked to save the injured bystanders and hideously wounded knights after the Battle of the Audience Chamber, Pontes had labored tirelessly to gather the scattered pages amid all that carnage and recreate his precious record of inputs and outputs.

"Look sir, a bench. Perhaps a brief rest is in order?"

"Perhaps not all the gods are dead," Ezra muttered as he crossed the wide square and sat wearily down. He had been sewed up for the second time in a few weeks, but his broken ribs hurt with every breath, and the little strength he had was soon exhausted.

No wonder I can't catch her.

He knew the Queen would slow down for nothing and no one. They had been to the lumber grounds, the fresh fish market, the south corrals, even to the miners' guild in hopes of intercepting her, using the loose schedule that Sir Shryke had given them. Shryke had not lied, Ezra was sure of that, because the Queen had been seen at each of those locations, just not when they were there. Ezra felt tight and shrunken, drawn in on himself. He made himself open his eyes as wide as he could and said, "We are in the square of the Pyracantha Institute, you know."

Pontes said nothing.

"Where those scholars came from. You remember those two, Pontes, don't you? You really got on with them." The lean man said nothing, which Ezra found odd. "What's wrong?"

Pontes frowned at him. "Why is Sir Marigold not here with us, Sir?"

"I thought you hated her."

Pontes smiled wryly. "Not hate, sir. No."

"Noted, but you definitely don't love her."

"But you *do*, sir." Pontes hesitated for a moment before adding. "Not like the Queen, of course—that is a special case—but like you love the other women. She is your friend. And she fought with you in the hall. I didn't." His hand went to the hilt of the sword sitting so awkwardly on his hip. His weak and often painful hands were made for the feather pen, not the iron hilt. "Do you know how horrific it was to watch that battle unfold? But she was there with you. Three times—no four—you took blows to help her. She did the same for you at least once too. And now she isn't here."

Oh, dead gods.

Marigold had been there with him. She was the third weight drowning him in his endless, empty sea. Did it matter that she had kept Eryka a secret from him? He knew why she had done so. The Queen had made a decision, and what was Marigold to do? Cause Ezra years of pain? Bring danger on everyone? She was in an untenable position, caught between conflicting loyalties.

I have lied often enough myself, directly to others and through omission to Marigold. He recalled her fighting, risking her life with him, then, badly injured, following him up the stairs to the Queen's chamber. And to Eryka.

How stricken she was.

He felt a new vibration stir the air around him, a soft, muted, elegiac flutter. As if answering it, a birdcall sounded from somewhere nearby.

Poor Marigold, caught between friendship and the Queen.

He remembered Marigold back when they were in training together, and then when they were accepted as Knights of the Queen, how tough she was and how she never put up with foolishness from anyone. He also remembered her after the night the Prince of Erle had died. She had been unusually quiet.

Ashamed?

The soft ringing rose gently. The birdcall met it, a little louder too, more beautiful than before.

He understood certain things he had not understood before. He recalled Marigold's increasing truculence in recent days. That, and meeting Eryka, put other memories into perspective. The look on Marigold's face when Ezra's banishment had been announced was even worse than on the Night of Erle, he recalled. He realized that she had known something was wrong, had wanted to fight for her friend, but there was no one to fight. Obviously, Marigold could hardly criticize or oppose the Queen's decisions after she herself had abandoned the castle that night.

Just as she has had to keep following orders from the Queen for all these years even when they went against our friendship. Oh, Marigold!

"Oh, Sir Ezra?" came a soft voice.

It was the female professor. *Olivia?* She stood about five paces away, hands palm out as if dealing with a skittish horse.

Ten paces farther away, almost behind her, stood the other professor, Parsons, with the bird cage and his pot belly jutting unattractively out of his thin frame. The birdsong—which had been teasing the air for some time, Ezra noted, had slowly faded away.

"Please don't leave," Olivia said, still in a low, calming voice. "We know we approached you . . . inopportunely . . . before, and we're sorry. Please stay and speak with us."

"You should not talk with them, sir," said Pontes, more boldly than usual. "They cannot be trusted."

Ezra frowned at him, not in disapproval, but with a subtle apprehension once again that there was more going on than he knew.

"What do you want to talk about?" he asked, turning to Olivia. "And what's with the bird anyway?"

"The bird knows!" blurted Parsons, lowering the cage to the cobbles and shaking out his hand. "It sings to the heaven-sent."

Pontes snorted with scorn. "I thought you said you were professors. You're talking religion. And putting animals above scientific discernment."

A strange, cold feeling swept through Ezra's gut. "What does any human know about heaven?" he asked.

Olivia ventured a step closer, her bright eyes making a sunset of her red hair. "Only a few, we think. Only a very, very few. But not heaven," she scowled at Parsons. "May I sit?" she said, pointing at the bench.

Pontes moved aside with an ill grace. She sat down gingerly, arranged her robes primly, and said, "Adjunct Parsons believes that there are a few, a very few people in the world—the heaven-sent—who can touch the worlds of Elysium and . . . access special powers from that realm. He believes that they carry an aspect of the nine dead gods within them, and that some of their powers are outlined in ancient stories such as *The Last Tolling*."

Ezra put a hand on Pontes's arm before the secretary could express his scorn again. He said, "And what do *you* think?"

Olivia allowed herself a tight smile. "There are no gods. Never were. But there have always been a few rare humans who could access a . . . higher level of reality. What the Church of Nine calls Elysium is in truth a realm of ideas, of essences, of pure energy and thought. Some philosophers call it *Eydos*. We—I and Adjunct Parsons—we think you are connected to Eydos in some way that no one understands. As yet. This is why you ring, why you are an Elysian Bell, as the vulgar call it. It is why your emotions have a power either to proclaim and nourish love or to visit destruction. We think that, under the right conditions, you may even be able to travel to Eydos."

An image of long blonde hair—of her—lying on a bed of thorns, deep under the ice flashed across Ezra's mind. He dismissed it.

There is a heaven on earth, but I cannot find her. Why would I go looking somewhere else?

Instead of saying this, he looked past her at Parsons who remained where he had stopped. Some prearranged position, Ezra guessed. "And you, what else do you have to say?"

"Only sir, that you and the people like you are all that is left of god," the pot-bellied professor replied.

The metaphor surprised Ezra. It was almost poetic. He had not thought that Parsons was capable of a non-egoistic statement. He considered Pontes, who looked like a man who had just realized that he had left his jacket behind as a storm approached.

Ezra glanced at the bird cage. "What is it exactly that you want from me?"

"We think we can answer the question of what you are, Sir Ezra," said Olivia. "You and the people like you." When Ezra stared at her, she added, "Through experimentation."

"Fantasization," said Parsons. "In front of the bird. And other things."

Olivia pursed her lips. "Direct empirical study."

Pontes rolled his eyes. "Empirical study, my left foot."

"Empirical study," repeated Olivia, still looking at Ezra. "Purposeful and planned experimentation. Mostly in the form of mental exercises, Sir Ezra, with you as our subject. This would include simulated feelings under observation, reading tests, being shown images while tracking your responses. We have been working on a protocol for years, but with no willing test subjects, well . . ."

Pontes sprang to his feet. If the storm had arrived, it was in his face. "Sir Ezra is not a *thing* to be poked and prodded by the likes of you!" He wheeled to face Parsons and spat. "Fantasizing in front of a *bird*? Really! Can't you see that some mysteries should be left alone? With their dignity intact!"

Olivia's eyes widened as she fixed them on Pontes now—the skinny secretary with the sharp widow's peak of receding hair and a trembling hand on his sword hilt. Ezra stood up, more slowly than his companion had, and said gently, "Pontes is right. It would feel wrong to push feelings in such a contrived manner. Whatever it is that I have, that I *am*, such a thing should not be manipulated. Or stripped bare."

"But Sir Ez—" began Parsons, only to be interrupted by the knight.

"Come, Pontes. I can think of two *rare* humans that we need to find."

"IT IS hard to obey all her notes, isn't it?" said Ezra.

Marigold's heart leapt at the sound of his voice. The feeling irritated her, but irritation lost out to relief that he was talking to her again. For a tiny sliver of a second, she did not know what to say, caught uncomfortably in the combat between these feelings. She surprised herself by admitting, "If you can even figure out what she really wants."

Ezra crossed the space between them and joined her in the sand of the dueling circle. He gazed at Marigold silently.

Relief poured over her at seeing him alive and on his feet, walking around somehow despite his injuries, pale as white snow without his armor. Relieved even more that he had come to her again. He was here despite her lies. Despite Eryka. She felt something hot in the back of her throat, and to head it off, she said, her voice trembling slightly, "Her notes are so damned terse."

In the next moment, Ezra's arms were around her. He was warm. Marigold did something she never did unless she was asleep. She closed her eyes.

When the shaking started, Marigold did not know if it was Ezra— there was a faint, gentle chime on the air—or if she was crying again. "That's enough of that!" she declared, pushing him away and turning away to hide her stinging eyes. "I have a reputation to consider."

"The children," said Ezra in a gentle voice.

"Yes!" she declared, smiling, euphoric, relieved, feeling somehow more complete. "We can't undo all my hard-taught lessons by letting them see us . . . carrying on."

A tremor ran through him, not a chime, just his physical weakness. Images of the fight in the audience chamber flashed across Marigold's mind. Ezra like a god of war, scattering their enemies, saving her with just the hilt of a sword he had destroyed from swinging it so incredibly hard. But also Ezra being hit again and again until his armor was a ruin, his blood everywhere, the horror of her slipping on it while climbing the stairs behind him.

He found a bench beside the sword rack and sat down very carefully. "I can't seem to catch up with her," he said.

"She's busy."

Seeing Ezra out of his armor was almost shocking. His boots and tunic looked rich and well made even if the fragility of the man underneath was all too apparent. Marigold realized vividly how protective she was feeling toward him. Here he was, in her domain, hurting, without his armor. And forgiving her. Her heart almost broke over it.

Which made her angry. Really angry. Emotions were supposed to be positive and when not positive, dispensed with quickly and decisively.

"I'm sorry," she growled. "For keeping things from you."

Smiling at her discomfort, Ezra replied, "I kept things from you too."

Responding with an edgy smile of her own, Marigold said, "We met a product of that deception yesterday."

His pale face reddened. "We did."

Marigold sat down beside him and put an arm, casually she hoped, around his shoulders. "So . . . secrets from everyone else, just not from each other, then?"

"Right."

"I've been made the Knight Captain, effective as soon as I can wrap things up here." Marigold announced. "I guess all my deceit is being rewarded."

"We both know that's not why."

Another weight lifted. "What do you need, Ezra?" she asked, balanced now, giving him all of her attention rather than fighting her own feelings.

"I need to find her. I *have* to talk to her." He looked around the practice area. "I needed to before, but now . . . with Eryka . . . I—"

"Right," said Marigold. "I see that. No need to beat it out with a hammer."

And safer if you don't say straight out that you're Eryka's father. That you were banished so that the Kingdom of Erle would think Eryka was the daughter of their dead prince. To keep the peace.

Marigold had wondered about Ezra's banishment often enough before this. She had wondered why the Queen had not recalled him sooner. But when she saw Ezra with Eryka, she had known at once. Anyone would who saw them together. As much as Eryka resembled the Queen, she also looked like her father.

It was a secret that could not be kept. It had lasted about five seconds, even to Ezra, who had been dying at the time.

Ezra, however, had not quite died. He interrupted her thoughts. "Have you seen her?"

"The Queen?" scoffed Marigold. "Of course."

"Lately?"

"Well . . . not lately. Not *really*."

"When *was* the last time you saw her?"

"A week ag—" Marigold stopped herself from automatically lying and thought about it. *When was the last time?* "More than a month." She narrowed her eyes at him. "What are you getting at?"

"What if something has happened to her?" His hands clenched, and Marigold could feel a new vibration emanating subaudibly from his body. "Pontes and I have been running all over the capital looking for her. We keep on just missing her. Or so we are told."

"You're not exactly moving quickly, Ezra. And Pontes is hardly a paragon of physical prowess. And let's not forget, just because you're obsessively running everywhere doesn't mean your running is called for, or . . . wanted."

"All we have seen are these messages from her," Ezra said, undeterred. "What if the person behind the screen was not the Queen but someone else? What if she has been . . . replaced?"

"Are you crazy?" Marigold wondered if the blood loss might have affected her old friend's brain. She knew it could do that. "You're all over the place, and I'm not just talking about your panicky charging all over town. Leave the conspiracy theories to people better suited for them. Replaced? You. Are. Insane."

"Am I?" Ezra said, not budging.

It made no sense. Well, Ezra obsessing over the Queen made sense. His replacement theory did not. Marigold fixed him with a withering glare. "Who do you think is sending these notes? Who is organizing the pages? And Shryke is there. She's unquestionably loyal, I can tell you. And wouldn't your daugh— wouldn't Eryka have said something to you?"

Ezra sat there for a moment, staring at her, then suddenly started chuckling. "Okay, you're right. It's a crazy idea. And the notes certainly look like the Queen's handwriting. Sound like her, too. Two-word instructions that could mean anything, she's so damned busy."

"Yah. It's her. She's fine," said Marigold, her voice trailing off into silence. She felt good, having her arm around him, calling him names, feeling him so close, even if they were talking about another woman the entire time. That was just the way it was with the Queen. Rarely seen, but always at the center of things.

"The thing is," said Ezra, working himself up again, "this is a lot like what happened with Erle. She got so busy that she didn't look after herself. She went from *almost* no sleep, to *literally* no sleep, to marrying an evil, woman-hating cad, to missing the poison he was spewing to her own people, and finally, nearly getting murdered. And now all this vampire talk and another assassination attempt. By paying just a little more attention, she could have seen it coming."

"So you're going to find her and help her," Marigold said.

"I have to."

"You sure she needs your help?"

"Probably not, most of the time. But Mari," Ezra said, lowering his voice almost to a whisper, "I don't think we are done with the Queen's enemies. The conspiracy goes beyond the Parons. It took some doing to get all those weapons into the audience hall, and I haven't heard that the mystery of that has been unraveled yet. We may not fully understand it, but we are in an existential crisis."

"An *existential* crisis now, is it?" But there was no sting in her words.

Ezra looked up, as if visualizing something vast. "No one sees it all at once when it's happening, but this *is* an existential crisis. It will only get worse. This is not just me panicking and trying to give myself a reason for staying here. It may take all of us to get through it."

Still enjoying his closeness, Marigold replied, "I hope you're wrong."

They heard Pontes coming before they saw him. He scowled at Marigold when he saw her sitting so close to Ezra. This only made her snuggle closer, a move she would never have performed in front of anyone else. "What now, Secretary of Disapproval?" she said sardonically.

Pontes put on an air of cool superiority. "The Queen has left abruptly to look in on the Stillwater Dam project," he said.

Ezra did not hesitate. "I'm off to the desert, then."

Stupidly, Marigold thought. Of course Ezra was going after the Queen. He had no choice but to follow his nature, and his nature was to protect her even if—perhaps—she did not really need him. It was frustrating. The Queen was out of her mind to go to the desert while her court was in such an uproar. She should have waited until she had managed the nobles, rooted out the conspiracy—if there was one—tamped down the upset over Lady Jacqueline's beheading, and dealt with the man she had sacrificed for so long.

But the Queen was a lot like Ezra. Neither of them would stop once they had a goal in mind.

"Without your armor, Sir?" asked Pontes, registering his disapproval obliquely.

Marigold made up her mind. *Oh well. Nothing to it but do it.*

Squeezing Ezra's shoulders one last time, she met Pontes's gaze. "He doesn't need it. I'm coming along and that will keep his virtue safe."

As Pontes and Ezra stared at her in disbelief, she added, "My latest orders from the Queen were **'Protect him'**."

CHAPTER 15

ICEBERG'S TIP

A man alone, thirsty, falls asleep.

"WHERE AM I?" asks the man. He seems to be bobbing high in clear aquamarine water. All he can see is a vast expanse of ocean and a clear crystalline structure that floats nearby. Something seems familiar. He had been in a desert, travelling with friends, but now he swims upon an endless ocean.

"Have I been here before?" he asks. The tug of oceanic currents and the endless blue horizon pull on some memory . . . something important.

"You are in the sea of Eydos," says the crystalline structure. It has been floating toward him, quietly, its approach, until then, unnoticed.

"And you are an iceberg," the man says, smiling, unconcerned, unsurprised by the nearness of the mountainous structure. He does not know what Eydos is, but he thinks he may recognize this vast icy creature. Something tells him that he may have seen *her* before, though his memory is as difficult to make out as words written on water.

The iceberg shakes from side to side, creating little ripples and dancing waves. "I suppose that I am."

"Your sides are so smooth," says the man. "I like you."

The iceberg shakes again and glides right up beside the man. He floats high enough in the water that her ripples of laughter do not threaten to drown him. "You are brave, aren't you?"

"I am not afraid to look upon that which I like. And say so."

"Look down then, man, and tell me what you see."

The man dives down a few body lengths, searching. When he resurfaces, he is smiling even more widely than before. "You go down and down, out of sight, beyond light and reckoning." He shakes his head at her. "Most of you is down below, unknowable. How vast are you?"

"Never ask a lady her size," the iceberg says, creating even bigger waves as she shakes the waters, laughing. "My size is my depth, and my depth is my size."

"Well, I like it. I am just a man. Not vast or mysterious like an iceberg."

"An amusing man, I think," replies the berg.

The man asks, "Where are you going?"

"On currents that are my own, on purposes that are my own, for reasons that are my own."

"I don't know what I am doing here or where I am going," says the man.

"Typical," replies the iceberg lightly. "Most do not."

The man, swimming hard beside her, says, "You are certainly moving fast through this ocean."

"Indeed," says the iceberg. "I am an agent of my own destiny." After a moment, she adds, "If you come around back and swim in my eddy, you will be pulled along. You can rest while we talk."

The man looks at the smooth surface of the iceberg. "Can I not just slide up onto you and rest there?"

"No!" says the iceberg, firm. "I am hard and cold. I would burn you. If you touch me, you will be undone." Her voice softens as she adds, "It is nice in my eddy. Swim there, man."

He shrugs and does as she says.

"Oh, this is nice," says the man. "I can look at you and talk at the same time."

"Glad to help you do two things at once," giggles the iceberg, making tears of water jiggle and parade.

And they talk on through the day, the man endlessly curious about the magnificent creature of the waters.

"I love you, iceberg," declares the man.

"That's nice, but you don't even know a tenth of me."

"Good point," laughs the man. "I need to dive deeper." He takes a deep breath and dives into the dark again.

Missing completely the iceberg's cry of "No!"

The water starts at a clear color, or is it green? Then it turns light blue, and then to deeper and darker shades. The man pushes and kicks, fighting his buoyancy, feeling the weight of water build and build, following the clean lines of ice down into oblivion.

Heavy, crushing pressure begins to squeeze him. It is like the weight of memory, everywhere pushing, everywhere trying to change and deform him from his human shape, trying to make his courage fail and shatter his hope. But he loves the iceberg and he needs to follow her down.

At the utmost point of indigo darkness, he finds a new light. It shines from a clear chamber in the ice where a figure waits. Lungs bursting, he pushes deeper, drawing level to the translucent walls and the woman who lies inside.

She is naked but for her long, tawny hair. Like a lion's mane, it frames her long, pure face and spills over her delicate, perfect shoulders. She looks at peace. Her eyes are closed, but she is smiling.

This is the heart of the iceberg, the man thinks, in the crushing pressure of the deep. So beautiful.

Then he sees that she rests upon a bed of long, sharp thorns.

"Oh no, oh no, oh no," the man sputters between desperate inhalations. "She is being tortured. *You* are being tortured."

The iceberg pulls them both through the endless sea. She has been silent since he returned from the deep.

"Someone put the heart of you on a bed of thorns." The man floats in her eddy, gazing upon her perfection, baffled. "Why?"

Her voice is flat, like an unmoving glacier. "You should not have dived so deep, man."

"Of course I should have. I must know all of you if I can."

"Should you?"

The man's mind races, thinking about what to do. "I must dive back down and break through the chamber walls, pull her—pull you— off those spikes."

"You will drown if you try. Or if not, you will die from the pain of your first touch. You cannot succeed, man. What one of us does in Eydos, another cannot undo."

"Who did this to you?"

The iceberg shook once more, creating a thin froth on the clear water. "How little you understand. *I* did this. Be not concerned, my little friend."

The man is silent for a long time, perplexed. "Why, though? Do the jagged thorns mean pain and betrayal?" He thrashes wildly in the water, looking around for enemies. "Who betrayed you? Point them out to me."

"Hmmm . . ." says the iceberg. "Much of my ice has calved and fallen away. I have been betrayed, lied to, abandoned. I no longer trust or allow other ideas near me without long consideration. Too many heartbreaking, terrible things have happened. But those disappointments are not what the bed of thorns represents. The liars and betrayers are long gone from thought and idea. Do not bother yourself looking for them."

The man slumps in her current, not knowing what to do. "What does it mean, then?" he asks after a while.

"It is love," says the iceberg. "Everyone who has loved me is a little spike there in my bed. There are many of them, and they hold me up comfortably."

"No," the man breathes.

"Yes. You will be one too, since you say you love me. And if you leave me, or if any of the others leave me, I will be fine because the other thorns will still be there."

The man shakes his head like a bull, confused. "That is wrong. It's too melancholy. It's the reverse of what love should be."

"Stop!" shouts the iceberg, rotating hard and fast, moving violently in the deep, creating a surge that drenches the man. "I rest on the bed *I* choose. I choose my course in Eydos. I create my space and give myself purpose. I am content. Fulfilled and happy. Who are you to say what bed I should lie on?"

"I'm sorry," says the man. "I just think you deserve better."

The iceberg moves violently on the deep once more and, in a voice like calving glaciers, says, "You must not pity me."

The man cannot answer for a time. He has swallowed too much water. "I do not pity you. I love you."

"Even though you know my heart now?"

"*Because* I know your heart now," replies the man. "I know that it is beautiful. I just don't want to be someone who hurts you." He keeps his hopes of better things for her to himself, searching for some eloquence he has so far lacked with which to convince her. But none comes.

The iceberg seems to consider him for a moment before saying, "Then stay in my eddy and be my friend."

∼

Pulled along in her eddy, the man spends the day enjoying the cool, perfect beauty of the iceberg and thinking of the woman she keeps down in the deeps on a bed of thorns. Everything about the woman and the iceberg—they are one and the same, he knows—is sublime. He has never known such a wonderful creature or been more in love. Her every clear, icy curve is a plane of heaven for him. And even though he knows he has seen but an infinitesimal fraction of her great crystalline body—that almost the entirety of her true self lies out of sight in the deep—he is in raptures over her.

She tells him of her work with little things—human people and their transient struggles—and the man is amused.

"Why do you laugh?" she asks.

"I am amazed," he replies. "You are such a colossal creature, so vast and great, and yet you work for the tiny."

"The smallest change can make the biggest difference," the iceberg responds solemnly.

They float on together in silence through sunsets and sunrises. Eventually, she says, "What have you brought with you to this place?"

The man rotates away from gazing down into the depths and looks up at the light reflecting off the iceberg's highest peak and says, "I don't know. I can't remember much. I think I lived in a desert." He ponders harder, rising a few inches in the water, and remembers, "It is so dry there. The flowers have not bloomed in years."

"Perhaps that is why we are in an ocean now," says the iceberg wryly.

The man laughs, gliding along behind her, weightless, in love.

As the days go by, the man frolics all around the iceberg, making up stories since he has so little memory, and listening to her ideas, which are manifold and deep.

Just as she is, the man thinks. And he remembers what it is that lies down in the deeps. The heart of her. A woman on a bed of thorns. The iceberg seems happy, but that heart tells him there is something more going on, something he does not understand. He is ecstatic swimming in her eddy, but every time he remembers the woman and the bed of thorns, he becomes distraught.

She is in pain, he thinks. I must try, he decides.

And down he dives again, swimming, thrusting himself deeper. Repeating his past mistakes. Through clear light to light blue, to dark indigo, he descends. His ears and chest feel the crushing weight of memory. He approaches the deep places where her greatest beauty and most appalling melancholy dwell, but can only glimpse the iceberg's outline continuing on down out of sight. There is still more to her, at depths that would crush his last idea. Finally, he sees the woman in her clear chamber, lying naked on the bed of thorns.

There are many thorns, he sees, long and sharp and uncaring. Made to puncture an idea. To perforate and rip happiness from experience, comfort from rest, and love from memory. Hope from tomorrow.

He swims closer to the woman, reaching out, but a sudden, great upwelling of current thrusts him away before he can touch the clear crystal wall that separates her from him. He is caught in a percolating bubble net, hurtling upward toward the light. He struggles against it, but his will is nothing against these buoyant forces. He broaches the surface, gasping and floundering in the cascade of spume that has carried him up out of the dark.

"What happened?" he asks between labored breaths.

"You were about to interfere," says the iceberg. "You must not pity me."

"I do not," the man says, "but thorns make a poor mattress and a worse reminder of the past."

The iceberg shakes ruefully on the vast sea, creating a dancing standing wave, admonishing the man. "In my heart and in this place, *I* decide. This has been explained."

It is true, he knows. It is up to her, he whispers to himself. And she seems to manage the pain so well. But then he thinks again on the bed of thorns, and he cannot help himself. It is as if they pierced *his* heart when he saw that they pricked *her* skin.

"I must reach you!" the man says, overcome by love of the iceberg and the woman inside, made reckless by a desire to replace the thorns with himself. He extends his hand toward her clear icy surface.

"You must neither pity me nor touch me," says the iceberg firmly. She has told him before.

He kicks against the heavy water of Eydos and reaches for her.

"I will burn you."

He arrives at her flawless, smooth surface.

"Ahhhh!" he cries, recoiling, his right hand frozen in instant agony, burning and freezing at once.

"You will recover," says the iceberg. "Eventually."

He clutches his hand to his chest, floating on his back, trying to take the pain inside, to lock it in its own clear room.

When he opens his eyes, the iceberg has floated away from him. They have never been so far apart, and the distance grows with every gasping breath he takes. "Where are you going?" he calls to her.

"I am following my current, complete and happy," replies the iceberg.

The man tries to swim after her, but he has lost her eddy and his right hand—still pierced with her cold—will not unclutch. He falls farther away from his beloved iceberg and the woman inside.

"I can't keep up!" he shouts.

"I know," she sighs, even as she floats still farther away. "I will add another thorn to the bed in memory of you."

"No!" shouts the man. "Please do not do that," he calls out desperately. He can barely see the tip of the iceberg on the horizon now. He roars to her as she nears the vanishing point, "Not a thorn!" He pleads, "Please let me be something else. A flowering rose! That would be better. Flowers can also hold you up. I cannot bear to hurt you."

He can just see her tip merging with the horizon as he shouts, "I'm not the only one! Others will love you."

She is gone.

He sobs, sorry for himself, hopeful for her. "Please let me be a flower, not a thorn." He can barely hear himself through the dreadful misery of his heart.

In a moment more, he is not even sure in what direction she has floated away.

"Where did the love go?" he asks the vast, uncaring sea.

THE MAN AWAKES, alone. Spikes of pain pin his confused mind to his right hand. It is impaled on a cactus. He extricates the injured limb and removes the spines. As the throbbing pain recedes, he looks more closely at the cactus and sees that it is in rare form. It is flowering a brilliant pink in the morning light.

He remembers the dream.

And his thirst.

CHAPTER 16

FRUSTRATION

"Have a nice dream, did we?" said Marigold acidly as Ezra wrung out his hand. The desert was supposed to be cold at night, but he had warmed it up with his chiming. He had also cried out at the end. What was it he had said? *Something about a rose.* Whatever it was, the sound and feel of the whole experience seemed to have powerfully aroused Marigold. Pontes, too, was sitting up in his blankets, knees to his chest, looking just as ill-used by the emotional waves that Ezra had unconsciously broadcast.

Hot, wet, and with nothing constructive to do with her arousal, Marigold decided to chide Ezra further. "I mean, can't you just keep it to yourself, man? All this, 'Don't leave me! I'm sorry!'" She put her hands on her hips, still painfully aroused but needing to trick herself into thinking it was rage. "Dead gods, when are you going to learn to let things go?"

"I don't think I can, Mari," said Ezra.

Hearing him call her "Mari" always made Marigold's heart skip a beat, and now, as sexually frustrated as she was, the insane thought of just marching over, straddling him, and grinding him into Elysium rose in her mind. Perhaps if Pontes had not been there, staring at her, also looking miserable, she would have. "Don't Mari me," she muttered instead of taking her aching frustration out on his cock. "I have a life outside of you, don't you know? Students to teach, knights to captain. The Queen to guard."

Ezra just nodded, unruffled, and was about to get up when Marigold found herself extending the harangue. "What are *you* sorry for, anyway? You're the only one of us that did it *all* right, *all* the time. *You* didn't leave. Not for Erle, not for anyone. Except for *her*."

Ezra looked slowly to the left, then the right, and seemed about to say something when Marigold interrupted him. "And another thing: *we* don't all revolve around *you*. We aren't your little moons. Life has gone on just fine without you." She paused and added, "*So there.*"

But she still wanted him, wanted release so badly.

It was abundantly clear that Ezra did not know which way to go with this. Twice, Marigold could see, he had almost started saying something, making the kind of little preparatory motions a man does when he wants to deescalate a situation with his wife. But he had stopped himself each time. Perhaps he remembered that they were not married and never would be as long as he could not forget his insane love for the Queen. Or perhaps he knew that a man should not even try to deescalate a row, should just shut the hell up and listen.

It was Pontes who spoke first, or started to. "I say," he began, on his feet now, but with the blanket still wrapped around him as if to conceal something. "That really was uncalled for, Sir Marigold. What has Sir Ezra ever done to you? It was you that betrayed him—"

Marigold's hands came up in front of her face and made twin fists. "Oh, that's rich," she retorted. "You're a liar too, if I ever saw one. Following Ezra around everywhere when you should have taken your precious deal back to Province a long time ago. What—you think this squire act is fooling anyone? You're no squire. If anyone is up to something, it's *you*, Pontes. Whose creature are you, exactly? Lady Kristen's? Or even the Queen's herself?"

Ezra sprang up out of his blankets, perhaps worried Marigold and Pontes would be at fisticuffs next. He moved easily, too easily, having healed twice—maybe four times—as fast as another man would have. His body was a rainbow of bruises and cuts, but he still looked like a man fifteen years younger, half-hard and in his underwear.

Marigold backed away, or tried to, her arousal seeming to pull her hips toward him as fast as her non-destructive side pushed her head away.

"Everyone just calm down," Ezra said. "We are all in the Queen's orbit. *All* of us in some way."

"*You* calm down," Marigold said, still trying unsuccessfully to step backward.

"No, *you*," Ezra said, playing at their old patter, oblivious to her throbbing, relentless arousal. He stepped toward Marigold, but she managed to take a half-step away and turn toward her saddle and the laid-out pieces of her plate.

"Stay back, maniac," she squeaked.

I need to get this armor on.

Three horny, angry people around a campfire aren't going to get up to anything constructive.

～

"I'T'S JUST A TRICKLE," said Ezra, looking at the stream.

"Well, you know," said Marigold, suited up in steel and held in check by something approaching her usual iron resolve, "grandiose things, little beginnings. Give it a few seasons, and this will all be under water."

They had passed the headwall of the dam some time ago and were now in the large, flat bowl that would be the first Queen-made reservoir in history. Proof against drought and flood both. Water to the desert. That was the theory at least.

A wagon train of farmers appeared out of the dry haze in the distance.

All this flat space had been scrubby pasture and farmland before, and all those farmers were having to move. Their lords too, which

Marigold suspected was a big part of the motivation for the attempted assassination of the Queen just days before.

As they drew closer, Marigold was shocked at the mixed collection of wagons, horses, cattle, donkeys, outriders, walkers, a few children clutching dolls, and parents clutching at the straws of a relocation offer. Most of them looked exhausted, red eyed, and filthy faced. They did not fit in well with the big wagons—eight wheelers driven by men and women in the clean tabards of the Queen.

This is how it is, moving so many people.

"Why aren't you with the Queen?" a broad-faced, balding driver called out, noting Marigold's armor.

Ezra, crazy for the Queen as he was, jumped at that, cutting off Marigold's brown horse with his oversized monster—proof that Lady Kristen kept him in good stead, the horse must have cost a small fortune—and asked the man, "We're trying to catch her up. Where did you see her last?"

"Try'n to convince some folk to git out before the water raises itself up over their houses." He pointed vaguely back along their trail.

Marigold almost laughed out loud at Ezra—he was so transparent to her—as he looked incredulously at the shallow, slow-moving body of water to his left.

It doesn't have to go over their roofs before it ruins their houses, idiot.

He had a mind for philosophy, and a heart frighteningly filled with love, but he could be awfully simple at times. But she remembered that the water would get deeper as they worked their way into the heart of the desert.

"Thank you," said Ezra, polite and happy, and clucked his monster into a trot, then a canter as he passed the end of the wagon train, following their trail toward the object of his obsessive love.

"Is she worth all that?" asked Pontes, watching after him and the cloud of dust he stirred in his passing.

"She has an effect on men," said Marigold with a shrug, mildly surprised that the secretary was talking to her. *Perhaps we will become friends yet.*

Pontes gave an uncharacteristic snort. "Is it as big as *his* effect on everyone?"

Never thought of it that way. "It's different." A thought occurred to Marigold, and she looked at Pontes in a new way. He had told her something she had not guessed about his relationship to her. And to Ezra.

We will not be friends after all.

"You love him too, don't you?" she said, starting down a road with only one destination.

Pontes's face turned instantly scarlet. He fumbled his reins, hands clumsy with upset. "Don't be absurd. *You* love him. That's been as obvious as sunrise for eleven years."

Marigold laughed. "You can't embarrass me, *secretary*. He's been my friend forever. We trained together. I held his hand when his wife died, fought beside him, faced pee-myself ridiculousness and shit-yourself danger by his side. I'm practically married to him, Pontes." She laughed again. "I've sewed him up with enough thread to make my wedding dress. And like any good wife, I've called him an idiot more times than there are days in the year and marveled at his vast, pure, ingenious simplicity just as often. Whatever I feel, I can own. But can you?"

She looked him up and down. Somehow, he turned one more shade darker, a kind of burgundy, and would not meet her eyes. "And here I thought you had orders from Lady Kristen, secret orders. Maybe some from the Queen too. But that's not it at all."

She laughed, but hated herself as she did so, for exposing Pontes also exposed—and unleashed—the feelings she did *not* truly own, the deep pool of love she had never dived fully into. "When did it happen?" she asked herself, remembering the first time she had seen Ezra nearly naked after training, lean and primal, exhausted and happy. He had glowed, and she had felt an ignition somewhere hidden, had denied to herself that deep inside her a fire burned.

"Were you outside his lonely, isolated villa one night," she asked Pontes, "and happened by lucky chance to feel one of his dreams for the Queen? Is that why you so readily shared your accounting projects with him? You discovered he was a Bell, and knew why Lady Kristen had housed him so far from everyone else. You knew why she coveted him. She felt he was *her* gift, but you found out his secret and made a little of that gift *yours*."

She had certainly felt it this morning, the thing she had worked so hard to avoid all this time, the *power* of it. A hundred times deeper than the hints she had accidently brushed up against a few times over the years. This was not just the fleeting platonic caress she had felt from Ezra at those times, but something far deeper, far more intense, and more complete, full of pain and love, an infinite cup of desire. It had turned her secret, simmering fire hot and blazing. She had burned with it, instantly wet and aroused, her skin boiling hot, and with no outlet for the passion he had blanketed her with. Of a love she had never felt before, stronger than gravity, more uplifting than a tide. And she *still* felt it, felt it surging up again despite her plate armor, could not let it go, could not stop bludgeoning Pontes with her frustration over it.

"Were you leaning up against the stone of that forlorn little building every night, soaking up all that feeling—shaking with it— with arms around yourself, wanting to be in his?" she demanded, ignoring Pontes's obvious shame.

She imagined mounting Ezra, taking him hard and deep into herself, owning her passion. Owning *him*, and receiving that feeling of love even deeper inside her. And never giving it up. "Are you following him because you've grown addicted to the feeling of love he throws off like light from the sun or ripples on a pond?"

Pontes's face closed in a sneer. He shot back, "Must you cheapen everything? Not everyone is driven by lust. Why you—"

Something seemed to snap inside him, and he froze, staring at Marigold. A second later, he abruptly pulled his horse in front of hers, and with a rising dignity, managed to look her in the eyes. "Your manner of speaking just changed, Marigold," he said, his eyes wet. "Quite remarkably. Suddenly you're speaking poetry, and that isn't like you at all." He smiled bitterly. "Who wouldn't follow someone who makes their rough and literal soul sing so? You, *sir*, are no better than I."

With that riposte firmly landed, Pontes put his heels to his horse and galloped off to catch up with the object of Marigold's desire. And of his own.

THE WATER WAS DEEPER NOW. A hundred to two hundred yards wide and brown with silt. They had already passed three old shacks with water lapping at the lowest boards, turning them black, making them sag like sad old hats.

On the sides of the long depression, in the distance at the edge of sight, they could see laborers for the Queen. Tree planters. Here and there a woven hose extended from the brown water up that shallow slope. Sometimes they waved.

"It's a huge project all right," said Marigold.

"Enormous," Ezra replied.

"Prodigious," added Pontes.

Pontes and Marigold had caught up with their friend eventually. Had fallen in beside him. And had not spoken about their ugly argument, both trying, Marigold imagined, not to think about it anymore.

Marigold had thought Ezra's mind was only on catching up with the Queen—though what he would do if he succeeded, he could not know—when he surprised her with a question. "How many of the assassins turned out to be men of Erle?" he asked.

"Huh" she snorted, "they don't exactly wear tattoos like the Skellish tribesmen, do they? And long robes alone don't prove anything."

Ezra's eyes bored into her. She snorted. "We could not account for nine of the assassins from Paron's estate records or descriptions," she said.

"Nine," said Pontes. "Nine for the dead gods. A holy number. It sounds like something the Lords of Erle might do. They sent three for Sir Ezra. Now nine for the Queen."

"What's next?" asked Ezra.

"Who can know?" said Marigold. The question frustrated her. "We can't guess at everyone's motivations." *Mine are cloudier by the day, split like dust in the air by love of friend and loyalty to Queen. When Lo—*

Marigold stopped herself mid-thought. *I'm starting to think in verse.* She gripped her reins harder, felt the hard armor that protected her. *Is this* his *life, every day, holding it in, struggling with frustrated potential, unexpressed feelings, unrealized love?* Biting down on tears of frustration, she breathed deep, reaching for calm.

"Something has changed," said Ezra, unable to see through Marigold's helm or know her pain. For which she was thankful.

"Erle has been quiet now for years," he continued. "Why strike now? What has happened? Who has been helping them? How can we get ahead of this?"

"Perhaps," said Pontes, "We could—"

Faint shouts not too far down the broad bowl cut across whatever Pontes had been about to suggest. Three sets of ears strained to hear what the wind carried. It was the sour and exigent sounds of fighting, yelling, cursing.

As ugly as those sounds were, they brought relief to Marigold.

"Let's go," she shouted, loosening her sword in its scabbard, happy to be in motion and to leave unwanted poetry and frustrated desire in the dust. Spurs to her horse, she galloped along the water's edge ahead of Ezra, back in charge of him and, perhaps, herself.

No more damned verse.

A crew of tree planters, three women and two men, faces plastered in dried mud, a mix of black and white as it dried, faced off against about a dozen men and women on the smudged and muddy boundary of the water. Farmers by their checkered wool jackets, leather ankle boots, and suspenders. The whole mass of people were staring intently at one big, black-bearded fellow who stood with one boot on a hose and one hand on the long handle of a scythe.

"Git yer hoses and yer water-gulpin' weepin' willows off our land! That's a damned stupid tree to plant in the desert," he bellowed at the planters, drops of spittle flying out of his mouth and spraying the face of the short woman he was roaring at.

"Right!" shouted Marigold, swinging a leg over her horse even before it was fully reined in. Stepping down, she tossed her reins to a little girl who couldn't help but accept them and strode right into the midst of crowd. "That's enough of that. I could see you bathing the lady with your bad manners even from a distance." Marigold gestured at the hose. "Step off the Queen's equipment and let's talk this over."

Talk was what Marigold genuinely wanted, but she kept a hand on the hilt of her sword. *Don't feel like getting a haircut with that scythe.* And she noted other weapons in the crowd. Pole arms. A short sword on someone's hip.

Out of the corner of her eye, she saw Ezra reign in on the back edge of the scrum, then felt him take her side close to the water's edge. She was not sure where Pontes had gone to, but he was about as useful in a confrontation as a harmonica in a riot.

With a grunt and a graceless expression, the bearded fellow took his boot off the hose, creating real art out of the contradiction between action and meaning by making the stepping off look aggressive and defiant. "They're trespassers!" he shouted at Marigold. "This is *our* land!"

Oh kay. Marigold pointed at the hose. "That bit of embroidery causing you a big problem?"

"It's our land!" someone behind the bearded fellow yelled.

Marigold turned to the short woman who seemed to be in charge of the Queen's laborers. "And you?"

She held her hands out, palms up, and said, "We're just doing what we were told. Pumping up to the trees yonder." She pointed up the side slope, but Marigold knew. She'd known what was going on before she reined in.

Everyone has got to have their say. There can't be any peace until then.

She stopped herself, noting that her newfound poeticism had stopped for the moment, and allowed herself a smile.

"Okay, then," Marigold said. "Just everyone step away from each other. We're all fellow citizens here. We can be polite." No one moved. "Come on now," she said. "Just give each other a little space. You're all hard-working folk, you have that in common too."

There was some grunting from the farmers, but as soon as the Queen's people took a step away, they made some space, two or three grudging steps making up one good pace.

Marigold nodded. She could somehow feel Ezra's approval beside her. Turning to Beard, she asked, "Were you compensated for your land?"

"We didn't agree," he said, though he involuntarily nodded. He turned to the angry clan arrayed behind him. "This has been our land for fourteen generations. We don't have to do nothin' we don't want to with it."

"Tried to give it back," said a stick-thin, bent-nosed woman in a long coat behind him. Marigold frowned. The coat was out of place.

"And look," shouted some other fellow, pointing at a crooked wooden fence taking a walk into the rising water and rotting oblivion. "Our pens are under water."

"Where are your cattle?" asked Ezra.

"Had to move 'em up slope," said the woman. *She seems genuine, but where did she get that coat?*

"Grass ain't so good up there," said someone else.

No shit? It's practically a desert here.

Marigold couldn't see the cattle, but she believed the story. She squinted, and in the distance, she thought she could make out a collection of buildings that had to have been their homestead. Right at the edge of the rising water now.

"Did no one come to help move you?" Marigold asked. "Drovers, wagons, and such?"

"Sent 'em packin'!" came a shout from the crowd.

Marigold looked at Ezra. He was calm, his face seeming to say they would sort it out.

"Which way did they get to?" Marigold asked. *Maybe I can send Pontes to fetch them.*

"Down that way." Beard pointed further down the valley with his scythe.

"We can help you," said Ezra.

"We ain't goin'," said Beard, but quieter now.

"Look," said Marigold. "We know you didn't ask for this." She pointed at the muddy water. "But the water's rising. Like it or not, this is happening."

Some of them started nodding.

"I'm told the land that's been parceled out for you is good land."

More nods.

"It won't have the history of this land, but you can make it yours."

I have them! Marigold could see raised shoulders relaxing.

"Let us lend a hand," Marigold continued. "And we will get the Queen's drovers and Queen's wagons here to help you out. Then we ca—"

"The Queen? We hate that bitch!"

The curse seemed to come out of nowhere. *Damn it.* Marigold had forgotten that the Queen's name had become a trigger for some people. It had been going on for weeks now. It was bad enough in the city, but where people were being displaced, feelings could only be even more volatile.

"To hell with that!" shouted Beard just a heartbeat behind. "The Queen can shove it up her ass!"

"What?" said Ezra, as the air began to shake and the sun seemed to darken, the temperature perceptibly dropping.

Marigold reached for Ezra, but her gauntlet somehow slipped off his shoulder.

"Vampire!" shouted the stick woman. "The Queen's a vampire. We saw her hiding out in her tent during the day."

"Stake her!" Beard or Beard's friend shouted.

"You will not *touch* her!" roared Ezra, a deep, almost subaudible sound filling the space around, felt more in the bones and body rather than heard. The woman who had been representing the Queen's laborers ran out of the way in sudden fright as Ezra stepped toward Beard.

Most of the farmers stumbled back, scared but confused too. Some looking up at the sky for the anvil head of a thunderstorm that was not there. But Beard did not. He squinted and seemed to lean toward Ezra as if pushing against a wind, but he didn't back down.

"Who's she think she is tellin' us what to do! We ain't goin'. Fuck you and fuck *her*."

Ezra's face darkened as the subaudible thumping crept more and more into hearing, low like the deepest part of thunder, ominous. Marigold felt it rumble across her skin.

A horseshoe abruptly appeared in the air, thrown by someone on the edge of the crowd, and Ezra twisted aside, stepping back, both feet in the water. Beard came at him, swinging his scythe like a staff, maybe forgetting about the long blade on the end of it, maybe not.

Marigold shouted, "That's enough!" and drew her sword. A memory of the Queen's audience chamber came to mind, of Ezra laying waste to armed and armored men. It was impossible not to cringe thinking of the nightmare of slaughtered farmers that seemed to be in the offing. *There'd be no explaining that to Bobby.*

Ezra, in the few seconds in between, had gotten two hands on the scythe, and he and Beard drunk-danced four or five paces into the muddy water, up to their knees now.

Beard put some ultimate effort into getting his scythe out of Ezra's hands, but in a crack like lightning amid a sound of thunder, it shattered into two pieces. Both remained in Ezra's hands. Beard stumbled backward, farther into the water, eyes wide.

"Jed!" came the call, and a short sword followed it, spinning crazily through the air, almost hitting Beard in the groin. He made an abortive attempt to grab it out of the air, realized he was going to lose hand or cock, and stepped frantically aside. Beard—Jed—fished around in the mud, water up way past his elbows, and came up with all his fingers and one wet sword.

"This is going into the Queen after it goes into you," shouted Jed—suicidally, Marigold was now convinced—over the deep ringing that rose from Ezra.

"NO!" howled Ezra, incensed by the stupid boast, triggered by eleven years and more of frustrated love.

Jed's about to get obliterated.

Having felt the full power of that frustration, though in a very different context, earlier that morning, Marigold understood. She resigned herself to a massacre.

But Ezra did not draw his sword. He raised his hands. The deep, painful roaring increased from him, and Jed leaned forward comically, like a man levitating in a mummer's show. Droplets of muddy water took to the air and hurtled toward the farmer. A few, then a few more, then a lot more. The air was vibrating painfully, but in an instant it became a furious wind.

Marigold's ears popped agonizingly.

A reverberating, twisting cone of water corkscrewed into Beard, engulfing him, sending him flying backward, abruptly and horrifically, in a deluge of brown, out of sight.

And quicker than it rose, it stopped. Ezra dropped his hands, the pressure in the air popped, and he stood where he was, frozen.

Not as frozen as the silence that followed. No one took a step.

Then some of the farmers walked cautiously and slowly into the reservoir, giving Ezra a wide berth, and helped pull Jed to his feet. He was soaked through, muddy, half drowned, his beard caked with brown soil and his eyes blinking painfully.

The sword was gone.

They said nothing as they dragged him away, walking dejectedly back toward their farmhouses in the distance. Drenched as much in humiliation and powerlessness as in mud.

"Sir Ezra," said Pontes, "take this."

The secretary had fished a clean white towel from one of his saddlebags.

~

THEY DID NOT SAY much after cleaning themselves off and making camp high up on the bank with the Queen's tree planters. But Marigold could see the curiosity in the planters' faces. A Bell was an attractive thing, an object of curiosity and fascination, but unlike the raw sexual power that she and Pontes had been drowned in that morning, the arborists had seen only fury.

They were as afraid of him as they were attracted. Perhaps, Marigold suspected, a healthier state than either she or Pontes were in.

A horse appeared out of the dusk. One of the Queen's pages, coming from deeper in the desert.

The arborists stirred, excited again.

The page dropped lightly off her horse.

She has not ridden far.

"Sir Ezra?" she asked in a crisp, young voice.

She held out a cream-colored envelope, and when Ezra rose to take it, she said, "This message is for you. Passed from trusted hands to trusted hands and finally to mine." As soon as Ezra had taken it, she bowed, turned, mounted her horse, and rode briskly away.

Ezra watched her go. Marigold noted that the page had not waited to record his reaction as they sometimes did. *She knows. The Queen knows what he will do.*

"What does it say?" Marigold asked after Ezra had stared at it silently for a moment.

Wordlessly, he handed the message to her.

On the clean white paper was written, **"Help them."**

THE SECOND NOTE

Marigold slept farther away from her friend that night. One day's aching sexual frustration had been more than enough. She also made sure that both Pontes and the tree planters were farther off too.

No need for an orgy.

She slept better, avoiding for the most part her fantasies of sneaking over to Ezra's bedroll. During the night, she felt perhaps one brief vibration on the air, a piercing call that arched her back, but it was attenuated by distance and passed quickly. When she woke, she found Ezra dismounting from his warhorse. It was already a hot day.

"Where have you been?" she asked, jealous that he had gone off without her, irritated by her jealousy. *This isn't like me.*

She did not want to admit to herself that some secret part of her had been cracked open on the previous morning. It made her feel weak and needed to be denied.

"I found the drovers. They'll be coming back this way to help."

"Not to help cart off a bunch of dead farmers, I hope" Marigold said.

"I . . ." Ezra trailed off.

"It is the humiliation sir," interjected Pontes.

Marigold remembered that. *Nothing like being caught in a cyclone of muddy water and tossed like a child by a god.* "Perhaps we should try *not* to say the Queen's name this time," she said. "Moving wasn't their idea. They have a reason to resent her."

Ezra unpacked his brush and began attending to his horse's mane. He said, "Someone helped stir them up."

"This is part of Lady Paron's barony, is it not?" said Pontes. "The enmity seems consistent throughout her family. And perhaps across all the lands that owe the family fealty."

Marigold nodded. "But it still might be more than that. Did you see that rake-thin woman? With the long coat. No need for such a coat in this weather, surely."

"I thought a coat alone meant little," said Pontes pointedly.

"She didn't fit in," said Marigold. "Not one bit."

"We aren't fitting the picture of it together at all," said Ezra. "First, they try to assassinate me in Province. Then Lady Paron and Lord Ronald Paron stir up rebellion in the capital, and Ronald, with several agents of Erle—nine, maybe—make their attempt on the life of the Queen. And now we suspect more agents have been *here*. Where else might they have been?"

"The answer could be in the numbers," suggested Pontes.

Marigold looked at him quizzically. "In your ledgers?"

"It is possible," replied Pontes. "We know that Lord Ronald had nine agents. We surmise that at least one agent has been here. Perhaps there are clues in our transaction records. If we can identify the dead, find out when they entered the Queendom, track their finances, look for clues in the numbers, we may even be able to determine who helped them bring weapons into the audience chamber."

That'll take a while. Maybe as long as forever.

"You should try," said Marigold, meaning it, but a second later wondering if perhaps some part of her had been waiting for an excuse to send Pontes away so that she could be alone with Ezra. *No.* Another part of her was ashamed and annoyed by the whole idea, which was even more annoying, because not so long ago she would never have been so confused about her motivations. She had never *had* any secret motivations. Even her guilt over lying to Ezra, over carrying away that body so long ago, could be blamed on loyalty to the Queen, not some possibly imaginary traitor inside herself.

"Another page is coming," announced Ezra, unfolding his field glass, leaving the brush sitting on the middle of his horse's back. "But from the direction of the capital."

"That's damned odd," said Marigold, still feeling guilty that a small, traitorous part of her might still be thinking about . . . just maybe . . . one day . . . straddling her oldest and best friend. And how to best get into a situation where that could, just maybe . . . happen. *Just take the initiative, as I've taught so many girls in class. Listen carefully, girls. "Send the scrawny secretary away, then fuck your best friend into next week. Be the agent of your destiny."*

And then more guilty.

The page trotted up, this one a short, thin girl who looked hardly more than fifteen, and was clearly a lot more travel-worn than the last one. "Any bets on who this message is for?" asked Marigold flippantly, moving past her internal conflict for the moment.

The girl rode right through the Queen's tree planters, who were taking turns working a hand pump to haul water up the long, shallow slope to the trees they were installing along the ridge.

She stopped in front of Ezra, Pontes, and Marigold, dismounted stiffly, and said, "Sir Ezra? I have an urgent message for you. Passed from trusted hands to trusted hands and finally to mine."

With an unexpected precision for someone looking so tired, she bowed and handed the familiar cream-colored envelope to Ezra. He took it with a puzzled expression. The page did not move while he opened it.

"This is . . ." he hesitated, "interesting." He folded up the letter and said to Pontes, "Pass me yesterday's letter, will you?"

When Pontes produced it, Ezra held both of the letters up for

Marigold to see. They were both on the same thick paper in identical bold, black handwriting. The older note read,

"Help them."

The new set of orders,

"Come back to me."

"That is oddly contradictory," said Pontes unnecessarily.

"You think?" sneered Marigold. But her stomach clenched. *This is too strange.*

Neither the page nor Ezra said a word. Marigold's mind raced. She snatched up both letters and held them up to the sun. *Perhaps more light will reveal the imposter.*

They looked exactly the same. Except for the contents and, more puzzlingly still, the direction that they had apparently come from.

Still no one spoke. No hint came from the page. Finally Marigold said, "And coming from the other direction. The Queen is fast, but no one is that fast." *What in the dead god's realm is going on?* Ezra's insane ramblings about replacement and imposters now seemed not so preposterous. *I thought he was joking!* A morbid joke, certainly, but it did not seem like a joke now.

She stepped into the page's face. "Who gave you this?"

Unfazed, the girl replied coolly and professionally, "From trusted hands to trust—"

Marigold put her hand up, almost touching the page's face, "Yah, ya, blah blah blah blah, I've heard that before. So you really don't know?" She looked at Ezra incredulously and hissed, "Maybe something really *is* going on."

Ezra did not respond. He seemed dazed. At a loss. *He's shocked.*

Then, abruptly, he started laughing, big belly laughs. Not one or two, but an unending, full-stomached supply of them. He leaned back and laughed to the sky. The Queen's laborers, twenty paces away, stopped working and stared.

His mind has come apart.

Ezra kept laughing.

All that dreaming and pining has finally done for him. Everyone has a limit.

Ezra laughed some more, then suddenly began crying.

He thinks they've killed her.

Marigold had no idea who "they" might, but absent any solid information, "they" would have to do.

He has *lost it.*

Finally the tearful sounds of a tragically broken mind trailed off, and Ezra wiped his eyes with his hands. He pulled Marigold gently out of the page's space and told the girl, "Inform her majesty that I will be along as soon as I can. Send that along to your trusted hands." He started turning away, then stopped. "You're heading back now, aren't you?"

The page nodded.

"Can you take my man Pontes with you? He has work to do in the capital."

"THIS IS SERIOUS. You know that, don't you?"

"Yes."

He did not look serious. Ezra appeared unconcerned for the first time in . . . ever. That worried Marigold. Outside of her girls' class, she preferred to be the unconcerned one—or at least appear unconcerned. Marigold liked to act, and act decisively, not worry. But he was leaving her nowhere to go, *forcing* her to be the worrier. And that was the least of it. The Ezra she knew was a deeply caring man. Also an obsessive fool. He was the kind of person who would climb hundreds of stairs while bleeding out just to be sure someone else was safe, or chase around the city the day after nearly being killed, again just to be sure. But here he was, a big, stupid smile on his face, and no trace of worry in sight.

Someone has got to think this through. But why does it have to be me?

"So why aren't you charging off to find out who is sending you these notes," she said, pointing deeper into the desert, "out there or," she pointed back toward the capital, "back there?"

Ezra chuckled, "I can't catch her, Mari. She is too fast. She has always outworked and outmaneuvered everyone. I bet she has groups of pages—shifts of them—just to keep up with her."

"So you're giving up?" Marigold didn't believe that for a second.

"No." He mounted his warhorse. "I'm going to do what the Queen asked me to. Come on."

"I'm getting seriously angry with you."

"I know. You like to be in charge." He urged his mount into a canter. "All the women I know do. That's one of the things that makes each of them great. They—you, even if you won't admit it—want to make a better world. You can't sit on your laurels waiting."

None of this happy talk made Marigold feel any better. At least one person was pretending to be the Queen, and Ezra had just decided to play along. He was acting the fool again.

He deserves better.

"Why are you doing this, Ezra?" she asked, throat hot, eyes hotter. "Following the orders of anyone who can write a note?"

Damn it!

Then the vitriol started flowing out of her. "Why are you still chasing after her? She sent you away for eleven years! She doesn't care about you." She took a breath and let more of her anger loose on the air. "Do you know how much I hated seeing you sent away? I hated it, I fucking *hated* it!" Spit was flying now. Marigold knew she was starting to make no sense in her rage, that somewhere her concern over the two sources of orders and her frustrations for the last decade and more had gotten mixed up, but she could not seem to stop. "Why did you go? Why did you come *back*?"

Ezra reined in, blocking her horse. "You know why."

She nodded fiercely, "I do." *She bit your neck once and now you're in thrall to her forever.*

Or she bit something else.

Ezra did not move. He held still for a long moment, regarding

Marigold. She felt like he was peering into her. It was uncomfortable, but it was nice too. Her anger began to fade.

Eventually he smiled softly and said, "I have dreamt about her every night for eleven years, Mari. I dreamt about her most nights before then too."

"You are truly pathetic." She snorted louder than her horse, almost laughing now. "Ever consider giving yourself a break? That's crazy."

Ezra's brows shot up, but mildly. "Maybe it is," he said. "Lately I've been dreaming of her in some ocean. She's an iceberg there." His face turned beatific. "Vast. Powerful. Calm. Beautiful."

Now Marigold did start laughing, or something close to it. "Wait a dead-gods minute," she said when she could breathe again. "You've been dreaming about the Queen as a what? An iceberg? That erotic dream you had two nights back that drove both Pontes and me crazy was you fucking an iceberg? What is *wrong* with you?"

"There's a woman inside," he said with a straight face that Marigold wanted to punch.

"Really? Inside?"

"Down under the ice. On a bed. Of thorns."

"On a bed of thorns in the middle of an iceberg." Marigold pursed her lips. "I find my anger curiously sated." And indeed it was. The hot taste of tears had disappeared from the back of her throat. The cathartic laughter had also rolled up its tent and departed. "Forget my outburst. I take it back. You, Sir Ezra, are an idiot."

"Possibly," he said, seeming not to mind the insult.

What had kept him from getting literally punched in the face during this exchange was the fact that he had never tried at any point to hug Marigold. His calm lack of defenses was exactly what she needed. Marigold realized that, for all his strangeness, Ezra was a rock. A rock, moreover, that knew better than to patronize her when she went off.

"Two academics came to speak to me about this," Ezra said.

She backed her horse up and went around his, waited until he caught up, then asked, "And they are the ones who put this iceberg-fucking idea into your head?"

"No, I met the iceberg first." A cluster of farmhouses was coming into sight. "They said that people like me can travel to a world of ideas."

"Oh, you're in your own world of ideas, all right."

"They called it Eydos." Ezra frowned. "Actually *she* called it that too. Before I knew the word."

"Who?"

"The iceberg."

"The Queen?"

"Yes." He gestured ahead to the farmhouses and the people spilling out of them. "Let me try to fix this."

"Oh, this is on your head, mighty mud typhoon."

"But you know what that means?" Ezra asked, eyes suddenly bright.

No, I don't.

Wait.

A thought formed.

"You think you aren't just *dreaming* about her," she said, feeling for where his obsession was taking him. "You think she's actually in there with you." Marigold tapped her helm with one gauntleted finger. "In your head."

"It means that the Queen is like me."

Marigold felt a cold dagger in her gut. Maybe it was true. *She is a vampire.* But she said, "A Bell?"

"Not a Bell, but something like one."

Marigold did not know what to think, whether Ezra was insane, obsessed, or if perhaps he might be right. There was no denying his power, after all. And really, she knew he was not insane.

Probably not.

The farmers had gathered ahead of them near the steps of the largest house, a well-constructed place with a wide front stoop. The edge of the water was only a pace away from the steps, drinking the ground up hungrily, coming for the house. The farmers did not look happy. They looked as much like a swarm of angry bees as people could. Looking at them, Marigold felt relieved.

Who would have thought a swarm of angry bees would make a welcome distraction?

"What do you want now?" said the stick-thin woman in the Erle coat.

Ezra dismounted and walked slowly up to the scowling knot of protesters. Jed pushed up next to Sticks. Two small children, maybe four or five years old, pushed through the crowd and latched onto Sticks' legs. Marigold was surprised they didn't knock her over.

"Good day," said Ezra in a loud but relaxed voice, apparently unconcerned about the hostility rolling his way. "I'm sorry about yesterday. My name is Ezra."

"Ezra?" said Sticks. "Ezra? Who is Ezra? Why do I know him?"

Ezra seemed to think better of trying to answer that.

"It's the guy," someone said.

"What guy?'

"The *guy*."

"Which?"

"That killed all the foreigners."

"Foreigners?"

"In the castle."

This all happened in a garbled jumble that Ezra ignored. Finally, Sticks exclaimed, "Sir Ezra! He killed 'em all. Dead gods, Jed, that's Sir Ezra! The killer!"

I guess Sticks isn't an agent for Erle after all. But the skinny woman had still gotten that coat from somewhere. Had some agitator from Erle passed through?

Jed looked a little sick now, but he plucked up enough courage to ask, "Did you murder Lady Jacqueline last week?"

"No," Ezra replied. "But I did kill some foreigners in the Queen's audience chamber. Assassins from Erle."

I wonder if Jed is going to curse out the Queen now and be needlessly slaughtered?

It had been an emotional week, to say the least, and Marigold found herself wondering if Ezra's use of his reputation was going to come to a productive or a slaughterous end.

"I'm sorry about yesterday," Ezra said. He looked directly at Jed. "What is your name, sir?"

Ezra knew of course, but being asked had an effect. "Jed Fenner," he replied with something like pride. "We're the Fenners. Been here a long time."

Ezra nodded. "I understand." In one smooth motion, he drew his sword. It cleared his scabbard like lightning and rung with a loud clear note that rode high on the morning air.

Everyone jumped, even Marigold. Almost. Almost Marigold.

The blade continued humming, holding the glorious note far longer than it should have. It felt like magic.

Marigold knew that it was.

As the beautiful, clear sound trailed off into infinity, Ezra abruptly flipped the shining clean blade around, held the hilt out to Jed, one hand on the cross-guard and the other careful under the blade. "You lost your sword, Jed. Take mine."

Jed and the rest stared, open mouthed at this. Ezra let their mouths hang open for another moment before explaining. "I know this is awful. You Fenners have been here for generations. And now you are being asked to leave, to go somewhere new. Everyone tells you it's going to be a wonderful place, that it's a fair exchange. But it isn't fair because you didn't choose it yourself. You're being ordered. I'm sorry." He gestured with the sword again. "Take it. Please. I know how you feel. Eleven years ago those foreigners, men of Erle, tried to kill my Queen."

Then Ezra shouted, "I didn't let them!" He let those words hang ringing in the air before lowering his voice again and saying, "And then I was forced to leave, to go away to a place I was told would be nice. That it would be . . . if not exactly fair, as fair as it could be under the circumstances. I, too, had to leave everything I loved behind." He turned and glanced at Marigold. "Everything."

Marigold's throat was hot again, but her armor hid her feelings.

"I can't take your sword," said Jed, awed now. "You may need it."

Ezra spun the sword around, and sheathed the steel as fast as he had drawn it, leaving another sweet, pure note hanging impossibly long, fading slower than thought, teasing the mind that maybe it was still there just on the edge of hearing. "Then take my help." He paused. "I will call the drovers back. Please go with them."

"I can't believe that worked," said Marigold as they made camp. "You had them eating out of your hand like that monster you ride."

Ezra had the grace to look sincerely confused. And he *was* confused, Marigold was sure of it. *He meant every word.* He was a true rarity, and not just for being a Bell. He was intelligent in so many ways and not at all hesitant to use what he knew, and yet he kept his sincerity.

She fixed her eyes on him while he prepared camp. Tied the horses, built the fire. Then he got his bedroll ready. Marigold felt an uncomfortable arousal flooding over her. She knew he would close his eyes and dream about *her*. Again. Maybe in some otherworldly reality, maybe just in his mind. But Marigold knew she would be alone while all that emotion rolled over her.

Getting aroused by him is wrong. It was the most beautiful wrong thing she had ever experienced.

Thinking about her friend so sexually was vile. She knew that.

He's not an object.

But his dreaming also had a real physical and emotional effect on her. And she hated knowing that. Hated thinking about what might happen when he dreamt. *Am I going to have to run off? Hide somewhere out there, arms around my knees rocking in the misery of needing release from the feelings he gives me? Or am I going to follow up on the opportunity and take him while he's dreaming?*

It was so ugly and so arousing that Marigold felt vomit rising.

"Mari?"

"What?" she snapped, miserable, which was no way for Marigold to be. It was not her. She turned away from him.

Arms came around her. "Don't run away," he said.

"Are you able to read my mind?"

"I'm sorry, Mari."

"Don't 'Mari' me."

He put his lips next to her right ear and whispered, "There is nothing you can do that will hurt me, Mari. Don't go off into the night. Alone. Don't."

Mari thought about the problem while she laid out her own bedroll. Next to his.

We will see what kind of friends we really are.

CHAPTER 18

GARDEN

The man awakes, alone. Spikes of pain pin his confused mind to his right hand. It is impaled on a wild rosebush. He extricates the injured limb and removes the thorns. The throbbing pain recedes. He looks closer at the rose and sees that it is flowering—flowering a brilliant red in the morning light.

He remembers his dream of a vast and mighty iceberg and a beautiful woman at its heart.

Despite having been on an endless sea, he is thirsty in a way he has never experienced before.

Looking about, he finds himself in a garden. There is a small stream and some rusted gardening tools nearby in the verdant grass. He finds a can and fills it to water the rose.

"You look thirsty," purrs a voice from the bushes. It is female, but deep, and the sound thrills the man's soul. Hearing it is like drinking cool milk on a hot day. "Why are you watering that rose instead of drinking yourself?"

The man peers into the bushes, looking for the speaker. "Because I love an iceberg."

The voice growls. Or is it laughing? "What does an iceberg need of a rose?"

"It is for her bed."

The voice growled again. "Icebergs do not sleep, silly man. They go about their business, floating on currents of their own making."

"Yes, that's true," says the man, still trying to locate this new creature. He can hear her moving about in the underbrush, thinks he spies two bright blue eyes flashing through branches and brambles. Sees a tail flash in the shadows.

He wonders what amazing creature could be lurking there, and how dangerous it might be. But he keeps his voice steady. "She is busy enough, follows her own purposes, and sleeps little. But even so wonderful, vast, and driven a creature as my iceberg sometimes sleeps. And when she does, it is naked, alone, and she rests upon a bed of bare thorns."

"You have seen this?"

"Oh yes. She had long, tawny hair, like a lion's mane, and she was so beautiful and seemed so alone that I almost drowned at the sight of her."

Now the growl is harder and deeper, more threatening. "You pitied her aloneness?"

"No!" exclaims the man. "In that moment, I saw her entirely and loved her. I wanted to touch her and relieve both our loneliness." He looks off into the green depths of the garden. "But now it feels as if I haven't seen her in years."

"Perhaps it is you who are lonely."

"Undoubtedly. But I do not think that I saw into her heart, and she did not also see into mine."

"You should save some water for yourself, man. You seem to lack an instinct of self-preservation."

He held out the watering can. "I will drink a little if you come out of those bushes and share the water with me."

"I do not need your help."

"Of course, but I have it right here."

The bushes shake then, and a sleek, enormous puma steps gracefully out onto the green grass. She is long and lean and moves with a sensuous poise. She is visibly powerful also, with taut limbs and rippling muscles. Her fur is tan and brown, and frames a heart-shaped face. When she stretches, her claws and teeth shine in the light.

The man wonders if she might eat him. She is powerful and fast, and could take him down with ease, but he feels curiously unafraid. *Why?* he wonders. And the answer comes. "You are too beautiful for me to waste my feelings on fear," he says, speaking his realization aloud.

"Get me a bowl, man, and I will not devour you today," says the puma, enjoying the man's reaction to her power.

THE PUMA DOES NOT COME BACK the next day or the day after that. The man searches the garden thoroughly but cannot find her. He waters his rose bush alone and, without assistance, helps it grow.

At night he dreams himself into Eydos and the great ocean there, searching for the iceberg. He swims and swims without finding her. There are other, smaller chunks of ice here and there in the vastness of the idea, but none of them are her. Many of them are lost: calved and sundered from a greater whole. But lost is not a word that could ever be used to describe *his* iceberg.

She has simply gone on her own business.

The man waters the roses and sighs.

"If you are so sad, perhaps I should devour you and end your suffering," comes the smooth voice of the puma from somewhere in the garden.

She is so beautiful and so powerful that she could devour me. And there is something about her. Something familiar, and he knows he could never fight the big cat. *I might let her devour me.* He also knows he should not share this thought, for the puma has not become such a magnificent animal by passing up meals. Instead he says, "Now that you're here, I find life sweet, Puma. Why don't I entertain you with a story, and then you can decide whether to devour me or not afterward?"

"Fetch me water first," says the puma.

Sitting by the flower bed as the puma absently chews on one of the roses, the man tells her the story of the iceberg and the colossal beauty and grandeur of her. He speaks about her depth and tells how her presence continues down below where the water turns indigo and black and how she swims on currents of her own making. He speaks of her calmness and tells the puma that her vast size is a reflection of how much ideas matter to her. In Eydos, the iceberg is a giant.

"But the greatest secret she holds, puma, is the inner woman on her bed of bare thorns."

"Why do you fixate on her?" the puma growls. "I think you simply lust after this naked woman."

The man laughs, feeling powerful because he knows the truth. "Oh, wonderful cat that you are, know this: I lust for her because I love her, not the other way around."

The puma blows a petal into the air, then spears it on the end of one long claw. "Tell me why you love her."

"Well, mighty puma, there is a riddle to this iceberg. She is such a powerful, grounded, self-aware being. She has magnitude and idea and drive like few others. She needs neither pity nor love nor marriage. Her cup is full. And yet, puma, and yet . . ."

"And yet?" growls the puma.

The man smiles. "That is a story for next time, my voracious feline friend. Come to me tomorrow—"

"I am hunting tomorrow," the puma snaps.

"Come to me the next time you can, and I will tell you of the beautiful contradiction of the iceberg."

And so the man is not, that day, devoured.

~

Time passes, and the man dreams every night of searching Eydos for the iceberg. And every day, in the garden, he listens for the puma. He finds neither, but he waters his roses every day, and they spread and grow.

One day the man is shaping his flower bed. It is just about right, almost perfect. He hears a twig snap behind him and knows he is being stalked.

"Have you come to devour me?" he asks, his back to the creature.

"Perhaps," comes the low, sultry growl.

"I thought we were friends."

"That just brings your danger closer," she replies.

The man turns slowly, smiling. "I accept that, oh mighty one. But come out of the bushes, I know you are there. Come and hear about the iceberg and her beautiful secret."

The puma pads gracefully out of the dark and approaches the man. "Nice flowers," she says and crouches in the center of the flower bed. "Now tell me this secret."

"The iceberg, the naked woman at its center . . . she needs nothing."

The puma growls, heart-shaped face resting on her great paws, "You have said this."

"Yes, I did. Well, she does need nothing, puma. But she is lonely still. She has lost friends to calving, family to warmer conditions. She has been betrayed, lied to, tricked, overlooked, not appreciated."

"But you said she was mighty!" the puma replies with a deep, threatening yowl.

"She is," says the man, holding his hands up in surrender. "But no woman is *born* so vast and mighty. The iceberg has *made herself* these things. She was always brave and took chances for the sake of happiness. Tried to please, perhaps, a few times. She has trusted, and that takes strength, even if afterward she may have felt she knew better."

The man sighs. "It always seems that way afterward, but trust is trust and knowing better afterward is the contradiction inherent in such precious qualities. It is a priceless thing that is sometimes placed in the wrong people."

"I thought she was independent," says the puma.

"Like you?" the man said, "A lone hunter, powerful, lustrous, and quiet?"

The puma yawns, showing her great, razor-sharp white teeth. "Indeed."

"She is all those things, though in service to something greater. And she won't be tricked or betrayed now. She is beyond and above that."

"Hmmm. Good."

"But therein lies the contradiction, puma. She lies on a bed of bare thorns, but that is her way of managing and overcoming the betrayals, deaths, and lost loves. She harbors no ill will. She has accepted with a glad heart how all the events of her life have made her a great and wonderful woman. A colossus."

The puma growls thoughtfully, roses gathered in claws that could rip six-inch-thick tree branches in two. "This is good. A puma hunts alone, needs no help, and mourns not loneliness."

The man places a cut rose behind the puma's ear. "Yes, it is good. I have only respect and compassion for the iceberg and her bed of thorns. So many have loved her, and she has managed it so well that it does not hurt her. But there is a cost. She can leave . . . love ... easily. And that, sometimes, is sad."

The puma growls in quiet laughter. "Because she left you, *you're* sad, you mean!"

"Certainly," the man says.

"I think I shall devour you now," says the puma. "You have convinced me of nothing much, and you are not so different after all." She rises up out of the flower bed, petals raining off her like filmy pieces of heaven. Her mouth opens to reveal her teeth. And one by one, each claw extends from her paws.

It should have been terrifying to see her long teeth and claws in that rain of red petals, but as before he realizes that the experience of her power is too gorgeous and precious to be compromised by fear. She saunters up to the man, who stands very still, and rubs up against him. Her tan fur is hot against his side. "Are you ready?" she purrs.

The man smiles and holds up one finger. "Wait. I must tell you one thing more. Come back tomorrow, or after your next hunt, and I will tell you the last part of the story."

And so the man survives for one more day.

⌇

THE PUMA DID NOT COME the next day or the day after that. The man works diligently on his flower bed in the time he has left.

More time passes. He wonders what has become of the puma, where she has gone, what hunts she has performed. Although she is powerful, he worries for her.

One morning he finds her lying in the flower bed, asleep. He lies down on his back, among the roses next to her, and closes his eyes.

"I told you of the iceberg's beauty, puma, and of the hidden woman on her bed of thorns," he whispers. "And of her ability to turn past pain and losses into something positive. I also spoke of her drive. And I lamented that, despite her great strength, leaving love behind— treating it like a bed of thorns—was sometimes a melancholy thing. For me also, puma. You were right about that."

The puma lay very close to him. Heat pouring off her smooth tan hide.

"And so I wanted to be a flower—perhaps the sole flower in her bed. To be something soft, not weak but comforting for her. The one love that would never leave her or that she would have to leave."

"But didn't she leave you, man?" the puma asks.

"I believe that I will see her again."

"Perhaps you will, if I have not devoured you by that time."

The man puts his hand on the puma, a very dangerous thing to do, but he knows something now. "It doesn't matter if she comes back or not," he says. "I will still love her. No matter what. No matter what value she places on me or where she must go. I have seen her, down in that deep, clear chamber, naked. And knowing her, I am helpless. I cannot but love her always."

"Always?" comes the low growl.

"Yes. And so *I* am a flower in her bed." He caressed the long flank of the puma. "But as you now know, I have decided that a single flower in her bed is not enough. This flower bed is her bed of flowers, and it is here anytime she wants it. It too is filled with thorns, but the red petals will protect her."

"Why?"

"Love, puma." The man puts both his arms around her now and rests his face against her breast. "I cannot know what challenges and heartaches are out there for her. What long hours, new betrayals, or burdens may come from the ever-calving ice flows. But she will always have only love and comfort from me."

"Why tell *me* this?" the puma purrs.

"Because even the most powerful, loving, wisest animal needs a bed of flowers. Even you need love, puma, no matter your completeness." He kisses her fur and says, "And also, I know who you are."

CHAPTER 19
MOMENT IN A BOTTLE

Marigold awoke, her body shuddering in a long, rolling orgasm. Lightning lit the back of her eyelids as she arched and spasmed with it. She gasped, shocked back into unconsciousness, still shuddering. Her mind was bathed in liquid pleasure, and she let the dream and the euphoric feelings spread her legs in languid ecstasy, slowly but inexorably rocking her pelvis, folding her, unresisting, in its soft, powerful, petals.

When she awoke fully, Ezra's arms were around her.

"I dreamt I was a large hunting cat," she said, uttering words she never would have guessed that she would ever speak. "On a bed of roses."

"You rode on her tide," Ezra said gently, "feeling what she felt."

The Queen again! But Marigold was in no mood to break free of his arms. She knew they might never be alone like this again. She wanted time and memory to dilate and stretch until there was only this single moment. She did not care that what had just happened made no sense to her, that some would judge it wrong. It felt like love. It *was* love. How could it be strange or wrong? Who should judge such things?

Marigold would not, at least not at the moment. She simply enjoyed it.

Later, much later, she asked, "Have you ever thought of going somewhere where nobody could use you?"

"Mari," he said, voice soft, lips in her hair, "people are affected by other people all the time. Usually, it's women being used. Nothing wrong happened here."

"Did we—?"

"No, but it seemed wrong for you to . . ."

A soft chiming filled the air. It was not overpowering or obtrusive. Marigold could feel it through his arms, and it made her feel something new. *Stronger?* "Wrong?" she asked, though she remained convinced that nothing was amiss.

"You had, uh, found us in Eydos, or what was happening there found you, and it was affecting you—"

It would have brought the dead gods to life. "And?"

He squeezed her harder through the blanket. "I thought you shouldn't be alone."

"Tell me about Brayden Fellows."

It was a question to spoil a nice ride. The capital was in sight, but they still existed in a space outside everyone else, a bubble of their own. Being asked about the actor should have been upsetting—it was a secret, after all—one of the greatest that Marigold had guarded for the Queen. And in a very real way, Marigold had carried that secret alone. She considered what she should tell him. How much pain it would cause him even while, perhaps, relieving some of hers.

Instead of answering him, she asked, "What's with the roses?" She remembered being stretched out on a bed of red roses, and Ezra there with her.

He did not answer right away. When he did, he spoke slowly, as if sorting out his ideas as he went along. "Every woman—no, that's not right—every *person* has, at their core, a central riddle."

Really.

"We are each of us a walking contradiction, made complex by the things that happen to us, the things we do and how we feel about them. How they change us or how we use them to change ourselves."

Marigold thought about the night she had left the castle when she should not have and how she had felt when she was allowed to return. She thought about how that event and Ezra's subsequent banishment led her to make a vow of loyalty to the Queen that not long after led to her carrying a body out of the castle in the night.

"It is a kind of story that we tell ourselves, Mari, *about* ourselves, about who we think we are. Of course, it's a dream of who we *want* to be, a dream of who we wish events had shaped us into."

"So are you saying this dream is horseshit?"

"No."

"So it's true, then?"

"No."

"Fuck you, Ezra."

He laughed and Marigold remembered his arms around her. She could still feel them now though hours had passed and she was wearing her armor now. *I don't need his arms.* But they had felt good. *Stolen time.*

"The story is aspirational, Mari. And it's a riddle, both true and false, though perhaps if held onto long enough . . . more true than false. But always there is a pain underneath it, and even as we reach for a better truth, the pain should be attended to also."

Dead gods. "You're supposed to be a knight, you know that, right?" Even out of his armor he looked like the perfect knight to Marigold. "Did you spend all the eleven years you were away isolated in your little hut, thinking?"

"I *was* banished," he said with a fleeting hint of a smile.

"*Fine,*" she said, drawing the word out long. "Everyone's a riddle, complex, full of lies, pain, and blah, blah, blahberty blah, reaching for some kind of better truth. Is that it?" She did not wait for a response. "So what on this godless world do roses have to do with it?"

"It's the heart of the riddle. Roses or thorns, what feels best." He sighed and added, "What we deserve."

"Well that explains *everything*," Marigold said and laughed.

Ezra gazed at her. His eyes seemed to penetrate deep into her. To the core of her being. "Yes. Well, that's a bit of a disagreement between her and me, played out each night as we meet a different aspect of each other."

Having been, for an all-too fleeting moment, on the bed of flowers, Marigold wondered how much talking was really going on.

"Tell me about Brayden Fellows."

Now his eyes were commanding.

This isn't a good story. Don't insist.

But he was still staring at her. She had to tell him. "After you left, the Queen, she became more . . . hungry. Addicted. She took a different man every night. And used them. Used them hard and sent them roughly out the back door when she was done with them."

He did not flinch, but Marigold could see a shadow cross his eyes. Pain. "One day she takes this actor, Brayden Fellows, into her bedchamber. I stand guard, and I hear them."

More pain in his eyes. But they stayed fixed on her.

"And then, a little while into it, all the ruckus just stops. She opens the door. Calls me in and . . . he's dead. Eyes wide. Blood on his neck."

"How much blood?"

"How much?" Marigold tried to remember. "I don't know." Her voice rose. "Enough to *notice*, enough to frighten me, Ezra."

I didn't know if I was going to be next.

She let him think on that for a moment while she tried to calm herself and take her voice down a step further away from hysterical. "I took him to the crypts under the castle. Put him in a tomb. Marked it and sealed it."

"You sealed it?" His face was tight, his eyes closed just a little.

"She *told* me to, Ezra. Mortared." *She's a vampire.* Marigold did not utter the thought. It was obvious enough, and he was in too much pain. *If I didn't know him so well, I might not know what agony he is in.*

Ezra's pain did not show in any way that Marigold could have explained. *That shadow over his eyes? A stiffness in the way he's sitting his horse? An almost imperceptible shrinking inward of the whole man?*

But she did not reach for him. What good would it do? Her armor was on, and his armor, and his pain, was for another woman. A monster.

As UGLY AS the memories had been, the conversation about Brayden Fellows had needed to happen. His name was being announced all over the squares. While she and Ezra had been absent from the capital, the Queen's Council, it seemed, had demanded that Brayden's body be exhumed.

"An answer to the accusations of Lady and Lord Paron to be delivered by spade!" was the bizarre announcement on the news posters.

That's what a dead noble and a room full of assassins will get you: a Commission of Inquiry. Especially when the noble is well liked and killed by "accident." The fate of Lady Jacqueline Paron at the siege of the palace was too suspicious to be ignored. And if it was on orders of the Queen, which Marigold suspected, it was strange indeed. For the most part, the Queen followed the rule of law.

Why would she have done something so clumsy?

Too busy. She's too damned busy, and now she's turned murderous again and at the exact wrong time.

Marigold had lived in the capital all her life and usually found its crowds and busyness exciting. Not so on this day. Perhaps it was the long, transporting orgasm that had rolled away with her that morning in the desert, perhaps the blessed simplicity of having her best friend all to herself in a way that could never happen in the city, but the crowds only seemed loud and rude as they clopped their way from square to square.

Can I capture a moment in a bottle and keep it forever?

The morning suddenly seemed far away, shrinking in the distance, lost from sight amid the tall buildings and heaped humanity.

A drunk collided with her horse and almost got tromped into mush by Ezra's. The derelict yelled an incomprehensible curse as he rebounded into a group of ladies.

No wonder Ezra retreats to this Eydos place.

They passed a late afternoon performance of "Saraith of the Nine Rings" that was only moderately attended and another of "The Vampire of Sangrea," which had attracted a much larger crowd, hungry, it seemed, to see the beautiful vampire staked.

Oh, oh.

"Calm down, Sir Ezra. They've been here a few weeks," said Marigold urgently as a low, dark rumbling rose from Ezra. His monster of a horse had stopped dead in the middle of the lane. "Come on, it's just a play," she said soothingly, then added jokingly, because the ominous sound continued to build, "let's not add a slaughter of mummers to the court proceedings this week."

His face was harder than Marigold's steel helm. The sound rose a little more, like a vast and slowly building wave, then reluctantly subsided. "You think this is a coincidence?" he asked through gritted teeth.

"Of course."

No dead-gods way. Do you think I'm stupid? I'll be checking into who their patron is as soon as I park you somewhere safe.

Marigold picked up the pace after that, reckless of further drunks, hoping to avoid any other troops of mummers or further philosophical introspection on the nature of time, happiness, or love. They made a quick stop at Gunning's Inn to see if Pontes was about, found a note saying he was with Lady Jayne Orton, and made for the palace.

"Took your time getting here, didn't you?" said Sir Jennifer Shryke when they arrived. She was in full plate, with two other knights behind her, and despite the saucy tone and casual language, no one looked casual. Eyes scanned the castle halls, and hands were close to swords.

"It's the prerogative of the new captain to decide where she goes," replied Marigold lightly. "And besides, I had orders."

"To play in the desert?" Shryke said archly. "How come I never get orders like those?" She shifted to Ezra and said, "Aren't you also required elsewhere?" Her eyes rolled up in the direction of the Queen's Tower.

"I'll be along soon enough," Ezra replied.

Marigold could hardly believe how easily he said it.

I thought he would have knocked down anyone remotely in his way when she called him.

The mystery of the two sets of orders swept over her once more, forgotten in the business with the farmers and the intimacy of the morning.

How did I forget this? What am I missing?

"When did she get back?" Marigold asked, watching Ezra stride away to find Pontes.

Shryke and the other two knights also watched Ezra go. "Not more than an hour ago. I'll get you her schedule when you're done with him."

"Damned right you will."

Can't do my job if I don't know where she says she'll be. Not that Corning ever seemed to get it straight.

And definitely can't do my job if I don't know who is sending the orders.

Part of her wanted to go to the captain's offices and look at the schedule. Another was fixed firmly on Ezra. He knew something, something about the orders, and it was telling that Marigold had not been able to drag it out of him on the ride back.

Enough of the navel fluff. Time to get some answers.

She found Ezra in one of the treasury conference rooms with Pontes, who was beaming and patting Ezra's shoulders. Lady Jayne Orton was with them, looking exhausted. Ledgers lay scattered all around the office, held open at certain pages by marking string. Several pages were held in place in the center of the table by ink bottles. Lines of writing were connected from page to page by bright strings and paste.

"There is something here, Sir Marigold," said Orton. "A pattern."

"Proof?" she asked.

Orton's face tightened. "Not actionable proof. Not yet, but somewhere for you or the constabulary to start."

"Boil it down for me," demanded Marigold, eager to hear what Ezra and Pontes were talking about.

That seemed to please Lady Jayne. With a flash of a smile, she said, "It's the *timing* of certain investments in the Paron family's estates and businesses. And then a very similar timing and set of investors in other estates and businesses. You see what happens—"

"Investors from Erle?" Marigold interrupted.

"Not directly," said Lady Jayne. "But we think the trail can be followed to Erle."

"Does it tell us who smuggled the swords into the Queen's audience chamber?"

"Not yet."

"Hmm." And with that, Marigold was already turning from her and crossing the room to join Ezra and Pontes. Glancing back to Lady Jayne, she said, "Good. Make a brief summary for my Knights of the Queen and for the constables, and a more detailed report for the Queen's Council." She stopped for a moment. "One other thing: send copies of the summary to be posted in all the squares of the capital."

I want everyone aware of this.

"This must be done as quickly as possible," she heard Ezra saying to Pontes.

"Yes, sir," Pontes responded, eyes sliding toward Marigold as she joined him and Ezra.

"And. As. Quickly. As. Possible." Ezra repeated with unusual emphasis. "And when you talk to them, you must take a written statement. Signed. With witnesses. Get a magistrate if you must."

"On whose authority?" asked Pontes.

"Lady Jayne Orton's," Ezra replied. "She can make you a writ."

"What are you two scheming about?" Marigold asked, feeling curiously unantagonistic toward Pontes for once.

Pontes must really have been in a good mood, perhaps because of Ezra's return, perhaps because of the evidence that he and Lady Jayne had uncovered, for he actually smiled at Marigold. "We are going to track down and sp—"

The loud, synchronous tromping of many boots on the polished floor made him abruptly pause. Marigold wheeled around. Through the open door of the conference room, Constable Bobby Archibald and a half-dozen subordinates could be seen quick-marching down the hallway, coming straight toward them.

"Knight of the Queen, Sir Marigold," Bobby said, long red hair streaming behind her.

"Knight Captain," Marigold corrected with a raised finger.

Bobby flashed a set of brilliant white teeth. "Knight Captain of the Queen, Sir Marigold—"

"So formal," interrupted Marigold. "Why do you always have to be so formal? Just spit it out."

"What is this?" demanded Pontes. "Are you arresting Sir Marigold?"

Marigold was surprised that Pontes appeared so indignant over the possibility. Less surprising, however, was Ezra, whose hand had gone to his sword hilt. A low, dangerous sound filled the air. Marigold was not sure if she scowled or smiled at him.

He's intent on needlessly slaughtering someone.

But the constables were a poor choice for slaughter, and Marigold liked Bobby.

"No—not arrested," said Bobby raising a hand diffidently. "But we do have to take Sir Marigold into custody. She is required to testify before the Queen's Council on the morrow."

Ezra's ringing deepened, rising above the possibly imaginary and entering the probably threatening. Bobby's eyes widened. "She will be kept in good stead, Sir Ezra, just in the Low Tower. For her own protection."

"From whom, exactly?" asked Pontes.

"We cannot say," Bobby said, trying not to wilt under the rising, ominous sound.

"This is quite inconvenient," said Marigold lightly, "but let's get on with it, then." She made a hushing motion to Ezra. *No need to ruin the memory of such a perfect day with misplaced violence.*

When his low tolling had subsided, Marigold said, "I appoint you Acting Knight Captain in my absence, Sir Ezra."

"Witnessed," said Lady Jayne.

With that, Marigold, marched quickly out of the room, parting the crowd of constables and forcing them to catch up with her.

Huh. He's actually going to see the Queen's schedule before I do.

CHAPTER 20
THE TALLEST TOWER

With Pontes off on his mission and Marigold in custody, Ezra had a rare moment to himself. Rare since leaving Lady Kristen's estates at least. Back there, he had usually been alone in his villa, quietly living out his banishment, dreaming of *her*, but too far away to think he might ever see her again.

Soon. I will see her soon. And ask her why.

But he knew why. Being loyal was a choice, not the inevitable outcome of stupidity and optimism. His quick mind and instinctive understanding of the Queen had led to an almost instantaneous and unspoken unravelling of her motivation. He knew why she had done it. However, knowing or not, loyal or not, some things demanded a hard conversation.

It's the riddle, the riddle of me, the riddle of you.

When thinking about the Queen, Ezra's mind sometimes fumbled its way to verse, not always of high quality. The riddle of the Queen, *that* he had thought about in a hundred ways while he had stood guard over her and a thousand ways during his banishment. But there was a riddle of himself to be examined also.

Any outsider would think I am insane giving so much for what seems so little in return. That I am a naïf. That I lack all pride and sense of self.

Marigold had said it herself. She had put it quite gently, for her, and now that their friendship—and more—was rekindled, she had to be thinking about it with greater intensity. And in more conflicted terms.

Love is difficult to explain or understand from the outside.

The central problem of loneliness is that no one else is truly on the inside. To understand another person, there must be both a storming of their castle and a supplication at its gates, an attack and a surrender, a long journey of imagination and a relentless, selfless effort.

This train of thought brought him to realize two things: first that he should visit the scholars again and learn more about Eydos. Travelling there seemed to make for an interesting solution to exploring feelings with another person. In a more elemental way.

And second, that Marigold did not have any comfortable clothes with her.

She can't sleep in her armor. And her padded undergarments had been worn in the desert for far too long.

The day was getting late—very late—and Ezra was exhausted, with a long list of things to do, but he prioritized his friend. Instead of ascending the Queen's Tower as he had intended, he jogged back down the polished corridors, returned to the stables, secured a relatively clean linen shirt and pants from Marigold's shelved saddle bags, and returned down the same corridors toward the Low Tower.

The Low Tower was the diplomatic wing of the palace complex. It was opulent and well-lit by windows and solar tubes set at angles in the thick stone. Rich carpeting ran from the gate to thicker carpeting inside. The apartments inside were spacious, high-ceilinged affairs with luxurious baths and hand-pumped plumbing. Marigold had been confined in accommodation second only to the Queen's.

But the enormous guard complement from the constabulary, arrayed inside and outside the gate, did not fit the decor. He counted twenty constables, and knew there were more that he could not see inside.

What are they so afraid of?

"You can't see her," Bobby Archibald told him after being summoned by the nervous constables. The portcullis was not down, and Ezra could simply have kept walking, except for the human wall in front of him. "Give me the clothes. I'll see that she gets them."

Ezra thought about that offer and then about the incongruous number of constables guarding Marigold.

"I don't think I will," he replied.

Bobby's long red hair might have been limp and a little damp from sweat, but her eyes had a determined glint. She said in a confident voice, "Don't make us stop you."

"You can't."

They could. Ezra knew that, but he also knew that he would learn something by standing firm.

After a tense few moments of staring silently at each other, Archibald shrugged. "It's not you we're worried about. Go on in, then" She stepped aside, inviting him to proceed with a theatrical, almost comical gesture.

Marigold's eyes were bright when he found her in a well-guarded but expansive bedchamber. Her helm was off, but she was still in her plate, and looking very out of place amid the rich, comfortable furnishings. "Thanks," she said, rolling her eyes at the crowd of constables forming at Ezra's back.

She turned full circle, showing him all the tight straps of her plate. "Are you going to help me out of this like you did in the desert?"

"A lot of things were easier in the desert."

"Yes," she said, her voice wistful. "Too bad we couldn't have stayed there."

"Well," Ezra winked at her and said in a voice meant to reach the audience behind him, "you want out of here, let me know. I'll knock these walls down."

"Ohhhh," she breathed, fluttering her eyelashes like one of the street mummers would have done, "you can come storm my walls anytime."

Bobby snorted behind him. Ezra glanced at her and saw genuine mirth on her face.

He laughed too, but wondered if the constables were keeping her prisoner, as he had at first assumed, or if they really thought she might be in danger. Or if it was simply the Council trying to show their power. It was becoming increasingly clear that Bobby and Marigold were friends, and that the red-haired constable genuinely seemed to think that Marigold was in danger. *But from whom?*

As he turned to go, Marigold called after him, "Get your armor back on, Ezra."

He nodded, though his armor was broken.

Leaving Marigold and those thoughts behind, he jogged back down the emptying corridors of a castle readying for night and ascended the much taller Queen's Tower. He was impatient to see her now, and the climb seemed endless.

When he leapt the last steps, he passed a page-captain leaving and nearly collided with Sir Jennyfer Shryke.

"Don't you sleep, Shryke?" he asked.

"Never on duty . . . my captain."

How did they find out so quickly? A problem for another day, but if Marigold was kept in protection for long, Ezra would have to learn how news could be travelling with such alacrity through the castle.

He left that question for the moment. It was time to see *her.* "Huh. Good." He thrust a chin toward the Queen's door. "Is she in?" He had not stopped to check the schedule at the Knight Captain's office.

"You just missed her."

"Story of my life."

"Story of *her* life."

An idea occurred to Ezra. "Do the Knights of the Queen have a legal counsel? I'd like to know if the constables have the right to hold Sir Marigold."

Shryke smiled, showing all her teeth. "Lady Kay could act in that capacity, though she's run off her feet. Should I try to find her?"

"Send her a note by one of these pages." Ezra gestured at the lineup of liveried servants waiting in the hallway. *Hmmm.* He gave Shryke a hard look and added, "But no one does anything without me being there."

"Where will you be?"

Ezra walked past her toward the princess's door. "Talking to her," he said and knocked on the door.

"You summoned me," Ezra said after the door closed behind him.

"It took you long enough," said Eryka. She was sitting on the floor, drawing in a large book. She wore a thick, cotton one-piece sleeping outfit in the shape of a tiger, complete with hood and ears.

"I was far away. In the desert."

She glanced up at him, one hand still working on her sketch. "I know. I felt you there."

Ezra crossed the room and crouched at her feet. She was drawing a castle whose walls seemed to stretch to infinity. "Where is your mother?"

"Working." She ground the nib of her pen into the paper, producing a bold vertical stroke. "Always working, always busy. Hardly *ever* here."

"It's a big job, being the Queen," Ezra said gently.

"It's as easy as growing a flower in the desert."

Goosebumps washed down Ezra's arms. Her intelligence staggered him. It also inspired a question. "Do you know why your mother is creating a water reservoir in the desert?"

Her bright eyes flashed toward him. "Same reason you grow a flower there."

Dead gods. Rocking back on his heels, Ezra thought about what he should say next and how he should say it. "You have been sending orders through your mother's page system," he said very quietly.

Those eyes flashed again. "You're smarter when all your blood is inside you." She continued drawing the endlessly tall walls and did not look at him when she added, "Don't let mother take too much."

The last remark made him shiver, but he ignored it and only said, "You have help. Sir Shryke does your bidding, I think."

Eryka declined to answer. He stared at her until she stopped drawing and looked up at him. "You ordered Shryke to execute Lady Jacqueline Paron," he stated.

"She asked a mob to stake my mother. Of the two requests, mine was just more effective."

Genuine fear settled on Ezra. *For Eryka.* "What am I going to do with you?" he asked.

She closed her book, hiding the tall castle from his eyes. "You can do my bidding, talk to me when I call you, play with me whenever I want, and guard me when I am frightened. When my mother cries, you can quietly hold *her.*"

"Most of that sounds . . . like it could be discussed." He cursed himself and added, "Though I don't know what your mother will say." *This child is way ahead of me.* "I'm not quite sure how I go from me being banished to taking on the role of your father." *I haven't even seen her yet.*

"Mother will just have to get used to it," Eryka said, her face determined.

Oh no. No, no, no. "Who ended my banishment? Was it you or *her?*"

Eryka smiled at him, bigger and wider than before. Her canines were long and pointed, just like her mother's. "She agreed to it after I sent the order out."

"She didn't want me to come back." Ezra felt the heat in his throat, in his eyes. His heart pounded.

Little arms went around his neck and her head rested against his. "Don't cry, father. She always wanted you to come back, she was just worried about Erle and me. But they finally realized I was not theirs."

"What?"

"Don't worry, they had already decided to kill us all. I am going to get them *first*."

Ezra found that his arms were around the little girl, who was still hugging him. What do you do when your child hugs you? You hug her back. But the question of what to do when you find out she is a murderous genius and that her mother does not love you eluded Ezra for the moment.

She doesn't love me. For eleven years, Ezra had survived by floating on the depth and density of his love for the Queen. It had been enough. But the dreams had intensified since his banishment had been lifted. They had met in Eydos. Every night. Ezra had become quite certain that she had loved him, even if she never said as much. But now . . .

"She does love you," said Eryka firmly, "but you'll never find her if you need to hear her say it."

"It doesn't matter either way," said Ezra, rallying. "I love her regardless." He gave Eryka a last squeeze and stood up, his mind busy. "It's very late, and I need to find some armor, get some new clothes, and look into a few things."

"No, you don't," said Eryka in a chirpy voice.

"What?"

"Mother has had the armorer working on something for you. It's almost ready. And I just ordered your clothes moved here."

"Does your mother know this?"

Eryka's head tilted. "By now? Probably."

If I move in here, the Queen is going to kill both of us.

"I'm not moving in anywhere without your mother's permission," Ezra said firmly. He then went down on one knee in front of his daughter. "You should not order people killed unilaterally."

Eryka looked like she was about to argue with him, and he quickly added, "You know why." *She knew. She had to know.* She was obviously smarter than him.

"I am the princess. You can't tell me what to do."

"I *am* telling you, Eryka."

"I'll have you sent away," she pouted.

Ezra knew he could not give her an inch. "Threaten me with something I haven't already lived through." He let that sink in before adding, "Killing is not something to take lightly."

She crossed her arms and spat, "I didn't!"

"You did," he said firmly. "Look at the legal mess we are in with the Queen's Council now. A very dangerous light is being shone upon the nature of your mother. It is a thing we may not be able to easily undo. We are in a crisis, Eryka! Promise me that you won't order anyone else killed unless your mother agrees." He hesitated, wondering what strange turn of events forced him to negotiate murders with a daughter he had not known he had, and said, "Or I do."

"No. You're just going to leave when she pushes you away."

Ezra once more marveled at her intelligence. "Eryka, I promise not to leave you, but you need to promise me this."

Her face darkened, but after a moment's angry silence, she said, "I promise. No killings without permission."

Dead gods! "Okay." *Help me.*

Ezra thought that he had gotten as much as he would, but a new thought flashed across his mind. "And definitely no killing Marigold."

"Father!" she said, exasperated now. "I would never hurt Mari."

Let it be so. He stood up and walked to the door, wondering if his daughter was a monster. Hand on the latch, he turned and asked her, "How can you feel me, and I cannot feel you?"

"You don't love me yet."

"COME HERE, SHRYKE," commanded Ezra after he closed Eryka's door.

A little smirk in the line of Shryke's mouth was visible through the opening of her helm. Ezra erased that when he grasped both sides of her breastplate, lifted her a foot off the polished floor, and smashed her back into the stone wall of the castle. A loud reverberation followed the sharp sound of steel on stone, as if Ezra had turned the plate-armored knight into a gong.

"You should know better," he said to her, still holding her off the ground. "No more, Jennifer. *Not one.* You ask *me* first."

He dropped her, and even though her return to the ground came with a crash, Shryke quickly regained her feet and her smirk. "I can see why she called you back, Captain," she said with obvious satisfaction.

"*She* didn't." Ezra's exhaustion deepened. "You know what happened." With that, he turned and walked away.

Shryke laughed. "Don't you think *she* had time to overturn that order? She wanted you back." Her voice rose to a roar as Ezra reached the landing of the private stairway down. "Keep climbing, Sir Ezra! She needs you!"

The Queen would be the first to disagree. And I would be the second. Ezra went down forty steps, his exhaustion growing heavier, thinking about the riddle of the Queen and what she needed—or did not need. Love.

He stopped.

And sat.

And thought.

Felt.

For.

Her.

The idea of her. The Eydos of her.

He fell asleep on the stairs, knowing that even if she had not called him back, he could never stop looking for her, or loving her.

CHAPTER 21

VAMPIRE

Much, much later, the man awakes in the midst of a mob. It is shuffling across rough cobble and gravel in the darkness, finding its way only by the light of torches held aloft and by the soft orange hue emanating from the castle. Outside of either halo, all is darkness.

It is peaceful in its way, this silent passage through night. It is also lonely, as the dark often is, the reduction of perception shining a brighter light on interior journeys. *Anything could be out there in the soft, silent dark, anything at all. And therefore,* nothing *is out there but what I put there.*

The man breathes it in, his separation from the world, and feels at once euphoric and elegiac. Loneliness is both relief and punishment.

"Dirty vampire!" someone in the crowd hollers crudely, smothering with uncouth words the soft crunch of feet on gravel and the moth-winged, flickering sound of the torches as they consume the air. The call reminds the man that he is with others, many others, not alone at all. More of those others are shouting now. "Vampire!" a child's voice near him bleats.

Vampire?

Where am I?

He looks ahead to the castle. It is not far away, and with every step the crowd eats the distance. It is a colossal stone edifice, surrounded by jagged rock and a deep, clear moat. Across the one drawbridge, a massive iron gate protects the entrance, and behind the gate rise nine circular towers, each with tiny windows leaking amber light, but the towers are high, and their light disappears up into the black, starlit sky. The man has seen many wondrous things: a mighty iceberg, towering high above the water and yet reaching a hundred times as deep below it, deeper than light could hope to reach, more awesome than imagination. A puma, a mighty huntress lurking in a garden, with bright eyes and sleek muscles, waiting to devour her prey. Other things, too, he has seen, great and wondrous, things to stagger the mind. This castle can now be added to that list. Despite the darkness that hides its full majesty, even just the shadowy suggestions of its battlements and merlons declare an unassailable impregnability. It is not a castle, it is *the* castle: the *idea* of what a castle should be.

With that realization, he knows where he is. *Eydos.*

A new, more powerful thought spears through uncounted dimensions into his mind.

I may not be alone here.

Hope kindles. His secret sharer might be there, somewhere in the dark.

Where is she?

There is only one real possibility in this night-bound world. The vast, shadowy fortress.

The drawbridge is just ahead, and the lead figures of a leaderless mob are already stepping onto its thick oak planks, their footfalls making a low drumming on it, a faint vibration of passing. They cross the clear waters of the moat and press up against the iron gates, ineffectual against them, going nowhere. No dirty, scratching fingers can hope to loosen even one of the mighty rivets in its enormous, blank face. Those gates, the man knows, are proof against any assault:

against the mob and their ignorant cries, against tears and recriminations and even—perhaps—against loneliness.

How to get inside? Not by this gate.

Entry can only be gained by a different kind of journey. Nearly across the moat, he spots a foot-wide rock outcropping along the wall just beyond the rounded edge of the gatehouse. He leaps across the water. One foot reaches the ledge, but the other misses and smashes against sharp stone, sending a lightning bolt of pain up his body, flashing across his eyelids. He stifles a gasp and takes the pain inside. He does not wish to be seen or heard. Not by the mob.

Sheltering in silence and shadow, the man perceives another way. Up, between the edge of the round gatehouse and the wall, where the shadow is deepest. He begins climbing, hands and feet pressed against the subtle imperfections of the rock, rising slowly above the throngs of angry villagers.

From the side and above, they look like paper-thin cut-outs, not real people at all. A few straining, silent movements later and the man can no longer see them.

THE HEIGHT of the wall defies measure. At first, the man counts his movements, thinks consciously about each one, wonders what will happen if he slips. Time drags on, *gravity* drags at him and looking up, he can see no top, no balustrade to surmount. No end.

This is not the way.

He closes his eyes and breathes deeply, sucking in the darkness, and gives himself to movement. He abandons time, place, necessity, every concern except the climb. He flows, stepping through and up, using a leg as a counterweight in a motion as smooth as a pendulum, hands crossing, feet pushing, finding the feel of the rock. He becomes one with its texture, with the night, with himself. As he flows up the stone wall of the castle, he *experiences* it, gets to know it, becomes one with it. It becomes—finally—impossible to fall.

But the wall is endless. At some nearly infinite height, its inclination turns past vertical, and Ezra fights to stay connected to the stone.

He realizes that, with every step he ascends, *she* is adding to the height and pitch of her walls. With every flowing movement, he knows her better, loves her more. With every new moment of beautiful revelation, her walls are melted and rebuilt, but the closer he gets, the more danger he is in from her. The more he is pushed away.

Reaching her is as easy as growing a flower in the desert. The man imagines watering the flower bed, imagines the iceberg and the woman at its heart.

The castle—the world—abruptly shifts, the incline moderates, and he sees an edge above. Only an arm's reach away. An instant later, his hands find the lip of a balustrade. It borders a dimly lit, open balcony. He understands the purpose of the wall.

Oooww!

It is the first stab of pain since he entered the flow. He looks down. A vine has wrapped itself around the top of the balustrade, and from its tendrils long, brown thorns sprout.

A fat drop of red blood balances on his finger pad.

"Why have you come?"

It is a rich voice, deep, smooth, and feminine. It does not part the air as much as flow over it, thrilling the man's ears, moving his blood. The fat drop of blood falls away from his finger and floats slowly downward into darkness, down the infinite wall.

Taking more care to avoid the thorns, the man surmounts the balustrade to face the woman.

She is naked, clothed only in dim amber light and her long, tawny hair. The play of shadow and light reveals sleek, long limbs and subtle curves. Her eyes shine bright blue, outdone only by her gleaming white teeth and full, red lips. She steps toward him with such subtlety that the man's eyes can scarcely comprehend the movement. One moment she was far away—barely discernible—and the next she has flowed across the distance between them and is within his arms' reach.

"For you," said the man. *I have come for you.*

A slow smile opens her lips like a sumptuous, incarnadine curtain across white teeth, revealing two dagger-like cuspids. They are as long and sharp as the thorn that bit his finger.

Her eyes move more slowly over the man than the blue ice of a glacier.

"Why?" she whispers. "Why climb so high in the dark? For *me*."

Because the wall was so high. "Because I love you."

She steps closer. Her eyes look into his. "What is that to me?"

"I would relieve your loneliness."

"I do not need you," she says, taking a half step back, eyes hard. "I am complete unto myself."

She had said this in every guise that he has found her in. She *is* complete. He knows that. But he also knows the feeling of being torn in half whenever one of these dreams ends. He knows there is more to loneliness—and more to *her*—than this.

"My soul vibrates for yours," he says. "I see you and am inspired. I see you and something happens to me. I create something."

She flows closer again. The breeze carries a few strands of her hair against his chest. "I am a vampire. Did they not tell you this?"

"I don't believe that."

She steps closer again, close enough that he can feel the tiny, invisible hairs of her bare skin against his body. "I am. I take what I want from men and toss them aside when they bore me. When I have taken all that they have."

"Take everything you want," the man says. He has a secret that gives him courage even in the face of her power. "I am yours for the taking. I have been yours since I first dived into the deep for you."

She presses into him. He can feel her hard nipples under her long hair as the strands flow over them like gossamer waterfalls over rocks.

The man finds that he is breathing rapidly. He cannot move. His courage is being tested again, but he remembers his secret.

Soft hairs brush his mouth and cheek as she presses her lips against his neck and kisses him. Electric pleasure flows from her lips, down his neck, igniting him. "I will destroy you," she says. She kisses him again. He moans, unable to move. "I am drawn to take you, man, to devour you . . . but I also find I do not wish to ruin you."

"You cannot," sighs the man, barely able to speak over the intense pleasure of her body against him as her lips pour icy pleasure down his neck. "You cannot devour me. I love you, and there will always be more."

"How?" she asks, kissing his neck again, but harder now, sucking.

The man's knees buckle. He would have fallen, but her powerful hands catch him and hold him up. "I will create even as you take," he whispers.

With one hand around his waist, holding him up, her other hand slides along his neck to the side of his head and holds it in place while she sucks still harder.

He gasps.

"Tell me how you would do this," she whispers in his ear.

"I simply will," breathed the man. "You create so much in me that I can never be drained. This place, that ocean, the gardens, in all of them, you are:

Words to light my mind on fire,
Thoughts to kindle heart's desire.
Ideas to consummate all reason,
Inspiration to lift me to Elysium.

Your unfathomable beauty
Your enigmatic perspectivity
Enable every breakthrough.

You are the oxygen,
Provoking, inspiring
My creative fire.

Is there any reciprocity
In your endless generosity?

In all the universe,
There is only one inferno
That burns as hot
But only creates.
And one emotion
that is devoured
But not destroyed.

I drink your fuel,
And fill your soul.

"Mmmm," she moans, moving against him. The man wants to put his arms around her, but he is powerless in her grip, in the pleasure she is pouring into him, in her strength. She nips his ear and says, "I believe that I will drink *your* fuel, man." She holds him fast, returns her lips to his neck, and sucks harder. Breathing louder, moaning once more, she bites him and begins to suck his blood.

THE MAN AWAKES ON A BED. She is astride him, legs to either side, smiling with a vast satisfaction. He can feel her heat on his abdomen. Her lips are redder than ever. A thin drop of blood falls through the long soft fan of her hair onto his chest.

"I can *feel* your love," she coos. "It is delicious."

He is just able to move his head enough to see that the bed is enormous. The soft blankets are woven into a pattern resembling a rose garden.

She moves slowly over him, rocking gently, her hair, like long daggers, falling down to the man's face. "It feels different from any other love I have tasted." She lowers herself onto him, still rocking back and forth.

Her nipples brushing his chest make satin feel rough.

She kisses his neck and bites it once more. His back arches and he screams in ecstasy. Releasing him just a little, she sits up, lips trailing little red drops over him, a dotted path from his neck to his navel. "Still, I am torn. I do not want to destroy you utterly. I do not want to take it all."

"You cannot," says the man.

"No? This again?" she says, smiling ferally. "I assure you that I can. I *own* you here, and your passion tastes delightful. No poem is going to protect you from my power."

"True love is a gift. You cannot take what is freely given."

"Ohhhhh," she whispers and kisses his lips, filling him with the taste of her mouth and his own blood, "That is sweet. I know you think you love me, but in the end, you will be terrified."

The man finds that his hands can move now, though the weight and potency of her pins the rest of him helplessly under her. He moves his hands up her sides, feeling her hair, his fingers moving over her nipples.

With easy strength, she takes his wrists and pins his hands to the bed. "I don't *want* you to fear me," she says, her lips inches from his, her eyes boring into his. "I think that would break my heart."

The man laughs. "I will not, vampire. I *know* you. I cannot fear the one I love utterly."

"You do not know what will come next," she answers in her deep voice.

"Neither do I fear it," he replies.

"You will be consumed." She kisses him deeply then, lips against his teeth, tongue deep, legs strong around him. "*Utterly*," she says, as if savouring the word.

She sits up, one hand on his chest, and pushes him deep into the bed, holding him inside herself. "This is your last chance. Go now."

Her words belie her intentions. The man can no more move her off him than he could lift an iceberg or overpower a puma. "You can't leave, can you?" she says with a sad smile. "I hold my hand on your chest while telling you that you are free. You have come too close, man. You have aroused my hunger too far."

Her legs wrap more tightly around his back, and she continues to rock slowly, but harder now. "You *are* mine, but I want to believe that you will somehow survive this night and not be destroyed."

"I wouldn't go even if I could," says the man. "I could not bear to leave you here in this castle, isolated and lonely. I am the other half of you, and you will not kill me, no matter what you take. I love you too deeply, vampire, to die by your lips."

"Oh. Alone! I don't want to hear about that," she growls. Then softening her voice, she says, "I want to hear more about this love and why you think you will survive." She lowers herself down until once more her nipples brush his chest and her eyes and lips are close to his. "Tell me."

The man knows this is a game for the vampire. She is like a cat with her toy. But it is, he knows, a complex game, part pleasure, part peril. She wants to dance on the edge of his death, to flirt with the idea that she is inimical. He realizes that she needs to come to this question, play this game again and again until she is ready to move past it.

He will answer as completely as he can and tell her as much as she is ready to hear. But he will hold back one secret. And hope that what he can offer will suffice until she is ready.

"Something has happened that never happened before," he says. "Not to me, and not anywhere that I have ever heard of. I loved a woman, as I had loved before, and listened to her stories as I have listened to so many before. But she showed me things about herself, in spare and parsimonious riddles, things, that were at once awe inspiring and harrowing. I wanted, at the same time, to lift her onto my shoulders in triumph and bathe her in tears, for she both lifted my mind up to heaven and shattered my heart on hard cobblestones. I felt she could do anything, achieve anything, *be* anything, while also feeling such terror and pity for her, such sadness on her behalf. She was an enigma of strength and calm fused with pain and abandonment.

"Yet she walked through it all with confidence and power, as if the pain was nothing more than preparation for her eventual triumph.

"That perception drove my soul deeper into a state of love for her. But I did not stop there, for the riddle of her possessed me. I knew I must dive deeper to work it out, to understand who she was *under* the story, *beneath* the riddles.

"I swam deeper and thought harder than I ever had about a human being. I thought about a woman who could cry alone, fill her own cups, fill them equally with ambition and with tears. I braved crushing depths, considered every aspect of her in all her incongruous guises— iceberg, puma, cyclone, tide, knight, vampire, woman. My consciousness passed through worlds of idea and metaphor to find her in every guise, and yes, I knew who she was. So of course I fell further in love, further than ever before.

"Then a new and more powerful force came to bear.

"My subconscious, that deep involuntary part of me, joined my conscious mind, and I began to dream of her every night. It was not to solve a problem, it was not from fear or angst. I was not dreaming in the fell grip of some inescapable trauma, I was dreaming in love and delight. I saw her lying in *this* bed, and she opened the covers for me— not to consume me, but to share passion and comfort, to be with the one man who *understood* her. I saw this beautiful, powerful woman invite me into her most secret spaces, places known only to her soul, her secret garden. To break both our loneliness's in a consummation beyond body or mind, but *of* both.

"All those dreams occurred because of love. I had too much love for her, I knew her *too* well. The conscious mind can be fooled about love, but the subconscious cannot. It *knows* love. It knows when the true other half appears.

"The deepest part of me therefore knew that I am hers and she is mine—my true love. My dreaming self could not bear to leave consideration of her behind. And so she came, every night like no vision before her. I dreamt of her again and again, and loved her more and more.

"In the end, there was not one part of me, not one cell in my body, that did not love her. Awake, asleep, until I am dead, I will love this woman.

"So drink my blood, vampire. Kill me now, if you can, feast on my love and see if you can devour me. I believe I will awake in the morning, and still we will both be less than full."

CHAPTER 22
BY ANY OTHER NAME

Ezra awoke in the early morning hours, naked, sore, and stiff from the hard stone that had been his bed. *How did I get here?* He only remembered stopping to think on the stairs above. He had apparently moved further down and found a landing, which was far more comfortable than the stone W of the steps would have been. And someone had slipped a luxurious red pillow under his head and a blanket over him. He realized, still groggily, that someone had found him in the night and covered him.

Very kind. But who?

Another thought came to him.

I would never have stripped naked here.

There were other sets of stairs, but he knew the pages occasionally used this private one. It was the secret passage that he and Marigold had climbed after the battle in the Queen's audience chamber.

He lay there reviewing the dream, his trip to the desert, and finally his current state.

I need a change of clothes. And the baths.

When he stood up to pull his rumpled clothes on, something small slipped off the blanket. He reached down to find it.

210

A thorn. Two inches long. Its tip was red.

He touched his neck. His fingers came away stained in blood. Fresh blood. Not much, just a few drops, but even a little blood always seemed like a lot. Goosebumps shot across his body.

Was she here? Just now?

Heart pounding, Ezra looked up the stairs. *How far away is her bedchamber? Far.* He had thought he had only descended a short distance down the tower stairs before sitting, but he realized he had come—or been carried—at least a third of the way down. A hundred and fifty stairs at least. Fighting an urge to run to her—a vastly inappropriate impulse—he looked down the stairs, vacillating, thinking of the absurdity of feeling he could not go to her after what had just happened in Eydos, and had probably happened on the landing too.

She is the Queen.

There was no appropriate way to storm her bedchamber. The only time he had ever forced the door was the night the Prince of Erle had died.

And yet, not walking up those stairs and seeing her—just seeing her awake and alive in the world outside Eydos—was killing him.

No. If she wanted me in her bedchamber, I would have been taken there.

Ezra inspected himself. He was a mess of blood, dirt, and the nine gods knew what else. He had not bathed in days. He could not look— or smell—very good at all. He finished dressing, belted on his sword, draped himself in the blanket, picked up the pillow, and began reluctantly to descend the stairs. Then he froze, remembering that Eryka had moved his belongings. Where?

He turned and walked up the stairs. Up and up the endless stairs.

"Where are my belongings?" he asked the knights and pages who waited in the hallway above.

The Knights of the Queen stood silent. Even with their helms on, he could tell they did not want to look at him either. Of the three female pages, only one met his eyes, but she stared at him boldly, with more than a hint of a smile.

I am not ashamed.

"Well?" he demanded.

"This way, Captain," said another of the knights at last. She introduced herself as Sir Valerie Simmons as she led him to the far end of the hall. It was two hours before dawn.

"A bath has been drawn for you inside," she told him, her voice sounding not embarrassed exactly, but awkward nonetheless. Uncomfortable. Ezra had no idea if she knew that the Queen had visited him in the night, or if she and the others had only felt him chiming while he dreamt. He wondered if they could have felt him from so far above.

It isn't important. "Have some breakfast brought up, Valerie, please" Ezra said, determined not to seem ashamed. He had been comfortable with Pontes and Marigold in the desert.

But they were trusted friends.

Why is anger so much easier? It had never occurred to him to feel ashamed after his destruction of the Paron Palace gates or the slaughter in the Queen's audience chamber. He had only been worried when he thought he might have killed the innocent. But love and passion were different. Projecting the sound and intensity of such personal emotions onto others felt wrong.

It shouldn't. Anger is so much worse.

"And see if there is any word of my secretary, Pontes," he added.

The chambers were expansive, at least as nice as the apartments the constables had confined Marigold in. There was a sitting room, an office, a dining table with rolls, fruit, cheese, and a bowl of boiled eggs arrayed on it, a bathroom with a claw-foot, copper tub—filled with steaming water—and a wide four-poster bed.

A cream-colored envelope sat on the center pillow of the bed. He opened it.

"For now, stay."

Feeling a little like a poorly used mistress, and laughing at the image, Ezra stripped and bathed. "For now," he said as he lowered himself into the warm water, wondering if he would ever see her in the waking world.

~

A FEW HOURS LATER, Ezra emerged clean and refreshed. He had fallen asleep in the bath. Luckily, drowning was out of the question after all his time swimming the ocean of Eydos. After checking with Sir Valerie and finding, of course, that he had already missed the Queen, Ezra jogged down the stairs to the Knight Captain's office.

He read the Queen's schedule—that paper he had been thinking about for so long—but restrained himself from feeling too much satisfaction. There was more going on than his desire to finally see her. He took a moment and thought about what was happening. He had been rushing from event to event with no other strategy. It was time to slow down and think.

The Queen's Council is holding an enquiry. Marigold has been called as a witness.

What is about to happen?

What can I do about it?

Pontes had already been sent on his mission, but there were other forces at work. The insiders who had smuggled weapons into the Queen's audience chamber. And the Erle forces who had used them. He found a feather pen and ink and began writing a series of orders. He had no sooner finished the last of these when there was knock on the door. It was Sir Shryke.

"Feeling rested?" she asked with a twinkle in her eyes.

He set aside his orders and held up the Queen's schedule. "I do now." Every moment of her day was accounted for. "I had this fantasy," he said to Shryke—she seemed to know everything, so why not confide in her?—"that once I knew where *she* was, I would have no problem just going and seeing her. But now that I have *this*," he shook the page, "I know I would feel bad even trying."

Shryke sat on the edge of the desk, her plate armor making a scratching sound against the protesting wood. "You just have to think about the timing of it and make your personal desires and your professional needs coincide."

He laughed. "Because there's no way for anything to go wrong with that."

It was strange laughing with a murderer, an aider and abettor, the hatchet woman of a child, but Ezra knew that loyalties were not simple things. He had killed dozens of people in his life, all of them without the slightest compunction, but he knew that the motivations and moralities of killing were as varied as the ways in which people loved. He knew he could be judged as easily as Shryke, and not just for his violence.

Was what I did to Marigold good or ill?

Holding her while she lay in ecstatic dreaming had *felt* right, but only time would tell if the love he had given would help or harm her.

No, it's not time *that will tell. Marigold is her own woman. She* will *tell.*

"How is Sir Marigold?" he asked and with one hand pushed Shryke off his desk.

Shryke saved herself from falling—barely—but the glint in her eyes shone brighter. "About to testify before the Queen's Council."

Before the Queen.

"And where is my secretary?"

"No idea."

This was frustrating. Ezra needed Pontes to succeed in his mission. And soon. "Make sure he finds me the instant he returns. He might have what we need to end this business."

"Yes, my captain."

Ezra stood up. "I'm going to the Pyracantha Institute. Keep an eye on things while I'm away." He gave her a hard look but refrained from reminding her not to execute anyone before he got back.

Before she could respond with some witticism to make him question her loyalties or morality again, the door opened. A page stepped inside.

She held a tray with a single, cream-colored envelope and blushed as she looked at him. "This message is for you, Sir Ezra. Passed from trusted hands to trusted hands and finally to mine."

"Not so far this time, though," Ezra said, recognizing her from the desert. He opened the heavy paper and read the letter. It said,

"See the armorer."

"Thank you," said Ezra, dismissing her. Marigold had said something days ago about his armor being repaired. In some ways, he had missed it. In others, he had not. More and more, it seemed that all his secrets were being laid bare.

It sure feels lighter without all that steel. But more dangerous.

The thought reminded Ezra of the orders he had written. He folded the Queen's letter, slid it into a trouser pocket, and took up the stack of papers. Holding them out to Shryke, he said, "These need immediate action."

She flipped through the pages, frowning. "This is going to strip every outlying town of their knights."

Ezra did not blink. "Everyone within a two-day ride, Jennifer. *Everyone.* And quietly. Use the Queen's pages to get the orders out as quickly as possible. I don't want to drain the personnel we have here on communications. They will be needed."

She smiled the wicked smile that Ezra was coming to realize was her natural expression. "She's going to kill you when she finds out you're absconding with her pages."

"Possibly, but at least she'll still be alive to do so."

He walked out the door to the sound of Shryke laughing.

It had been eleven years since Ezra had visited the castle armory. Going there brought back a host of memories from before the Night of Erle. Every step on the way took him deeper into a vast landscape of memory. Bittersweet, addictive memory. The armorer, Keaven Fawcett, was the same man from back then, except that the thick tangle of hair on his knotted forearms was white now instead of black, and he had a loud, persistent cough.

"Sir Ezra!" he bellowed. "It's about time you hauled your ass down here. I've been working on this for weeks." He crooked his neck and led the way to an armor stand. "It's fine work, but we still need to see if it fits."

The plate armor *was* fine work. It reflected the forge light brilliantly. Much of the plate had its own fine chain mail skirting mated to an accompanying piece, creating a fully protected, but still flexible, effect. The breastplate and backplate were one piece, connected by the chain mail, and the whole thing could be put on by simply lowering the assemblage over his head.

"I've got the felt," said Keaven, meaning the underlayers. "Why don't we see how it looks."

Halfway through the lengthy process of being strapped in, Ezra asked, "Weeks? You started this weeks ago?"

"More than a month."

What does that make this? A gift? If so, the decision to end my banishment was made well before Eryka decided to interfere.

Even after spending so many years thinking about the Queen, dreaming about her, communing with her in Eydos, he could not have predicted this.

She is a vast and powerful iceberg, floating on currents of her own making, deep beyond reckoning.

Beautiful beyond imagination.

"That's just about right," said Keaven, hands slapping down on Ezra's pauldrons.

Belting his sword over his hip, Ezra said, "I'm wearing this out of here."

The armor was made from a heavy-gauge steel alloy, but Ezra was so excited about wearing a gift from the Queen that he found himself jogging effortlessly down the palace halls. A page caught him just as he stepped out of the main gate of the castle.

"Sir Ezra!" she called. "Captain, sir. I have a message for you."

He waited patiently while she spoke the litany and received the envelope with a good grace despite wondering if he would ever manage to speak to the scholars. "Thank you," he said for the second time that morning and opened the envelope. In the now familiar, neat, bold print, it read,

"Marigold must answer."

"Where is Sir Marigold now?" Ezra asked the page.

~

"How DID you end up in the dungeon?" Ezra was more than a little exasperated. Angry too.

Marigold was back in her plate as well, but standing on the other side of a barred door. "And don't you ever take a day off?" he asked Bobby, who stood just a few steps away.

"Nice plate," purred Marigold, eyeing Ezra's armor enviously, refusing to take the situation seriously. "Is that an even more solid block on your left vambrace? It looks like it must weigh five pounds just by itself."

"It's not that heavy, but if you don't tell me what the problem is here, I might swat you with it."

"You're going to try sparring with me again?" Marigold asked with a wicked glint. "Because I have the gist of you now, and if we fight, you're the only one who is going to be holding wood."

That is so wrong.

He could barely hear himself object mentally to the innuendo over Bobby's uproarious laughter. "Why are you here, Mari?" he said, trying to ignore their mirth. "Does it seem like the Council is out to get the Queen?"

"I wouldn't say so, not necessarily," replied Marigold. "For most of them, this is a process they just seem to have decided they need to get through. Perhaps just to put behind them."

"And the others? Remember what Pontes and Lady Jayne were working on?"

Marigold looked at Bobby Archibald before replying. "Maybe," she said at last.

"How about the Queen?" Ezra found himself asking. He had not meant to.

Marigold's brows went up. "She looks like she is in charge. As usual. Commanding, graceful, beautiful."

The last two words might have been delivered with an undercurrent of jealousy, but Ezra did not know what to do with that. He forged on. "So why are you *here*?" He gave Bobby a harsh look. "In the dungeon of all places."

Thrusting her hands through the bars, Marigold pulled Ezra closer until his face was inches from hers. "They want to know where *the body* is," she whispered. "Lady Beatrice Whall is suggesting that if the Queen is a vampire, there will be no body there. Or if there is, it *will* not be . . . properly dead."

"Tell them," Ezra said.

"What?" Marigold looked genuinely frightened.

Does she think the Queen really is a vampire?

But his neck stung as he thought about the question. Trying not to touch the wound through his gorget, Ezra said, "The only way out is straight through."

"Ezra . . ." Marigold trailed off, eyes suddenly wet. "I can't betray her. Not again."

The night Erle died. It had been on Marigold's mind too—probably constantly since Ezra had returned.

"She ordered you to testify, didn't she?' he said. She nodded. He could see tears trickling along the lines of her helm beside her mouth.

"It's not a betrayal, Mari," Ezra said gently. "She knows there's no avoiding this." In truth, Marigold's refusal to testify had created some time that Ezra needed, but further delays could become a problem. "Just tell them."

"Okay."

It is difficult to wipe teary eyes in plate armor. First, one must remove the gauntlets and the helm—which reminded Ezra of something vitally important from a long time ago—and only then can the cleanup be attempted. By the time Marigold was halfway through the procedure, she had begun cursing and was once more her old self.

"Let her out," Ezra ordered Bobby, who had been watching in fascination. "Sir Marigold is ready to do her duty."

Ezra escorted Marigold, Bobby, and a contingent of twenty solemn constables to the narrow passageway leading into the Queen's High Court, set in an open square about five minutes' walk from the castle. He did not enter the square, even though he knew that *she* would be there, seated as befits a Queen in an imposing chair elevated high above the proceedings. He only looked around to confirm that certain of his orders were being followed.

Dozens of carriages lined the avenue outside the square, but they were the least of it. Hundreds of servants and house soldiers milled about, almost blocking non-court traffic. Many of the soldiers carried crossbows.

Dead gods.

Stifling the impulse to lay waste to these soldiers, Ezra looked for signs that his orders to Shryke were being followed.

We're still short.

A court page intercepted them at the passageway and whispered something in Bobby's ear. She nodded and dismissed the page, then turned to Ezra. "There is a new witness list. You're fifth on it." She shrugged. "I'm sorry, Captain. I did not expect this. You will have to stay here." Lamely, she added in a diffident voice, "Safe from harm."

You think my daughter is going to order me murdered to keep some secret about her mother?

Bobby of course had no idea it was a ten-year old girl who had ordered the opportunistic execution of Lady Jacqueline Paron.

Marigold caught Ezra's eyes. He smiled at her. "Take your time testifying Mari. I have a task to accomplish before I speak."

"Sir Ezra—" Bobby began, her hand going to the hilt of her sword.

Ezra laughed. "You're going to protect me with your sword? No. Tell them I'll be back . . . in due course. I am the Knight Captain thanks to this proceeding, and I intend to do my job." He knew that the constabulary's sequestration of Marigold had been done on shaky legal ground, and he could not allow them both to be detained at the same time.

Without waiting for Bobby to respond, Ezra winked at Marigold, turned, and marched quickly away, making a hole in the line of constables.

Moments later, having passed just as forcefully through the soldiers and servants crowding the street, Ezra put a hand on his sword hilt and started running. Children, birds, and idlers in the squares and byways he passed through scattered before the clanging of his plate and the nearly inaudible hum that rose off him.

"Anything from Pontes?" he asked Shryke, when he found her busy in the Knight Captain's offices coordinating his orders.

"Nothing," she said.

Dead gods damn it. "If he comes back, alert me immediately." He turned to leave, but added, "I have come directly from the court. I did not see there what I ordered done."

"Working on it."

"Did we get a legal opinion from Lady Kay?"

Shryke smiled her predatory smile and passed him an envelope. Ezra read the contents and passed it back to her.

Shaky ground indeed. But the timing was poor. They *might* win a legal challenge to release Marigold—at a separate forum—but likely not in time to make a difference. Ezra turned to matters he could deal with in the here and now.

"I'm going to the Pyracantha Institute now. When I am done there, I will be back at the court to testify." He looked at Shryke. *But not about you.*

She looked as unconcerned as usual.

"Have you seen *her* yet?" Shryke asked.

She was almost smirking at him. "Enjoy the paperwork," he said as he flung the door open and jogged back down the hallway. Once outside, he broke into a run again.

People in the palace square may have recognized him, but Ezra could not allow himself to be mobbed this time. Events were moving too quickly, and the space to maneuver was closing. The truth needed to come out, but the right truth at the right time.

If only I knew what that truth was.

He had an idea, and hoped he was right, but he could not be certain.

When he reached the square in front of the institute, he realized with dismay that he had no idea where exactly to find either Professor Olivia or Adjunct Parsons.

Whom do I ask? He didn't know anyone there.

Wait, that's not true.

Ezra ran into the main building, thinking about the Queen and chiming a soft, pleasant bell tone of love. He was not forcing the thought or feeling. It was no cheap trick or cynical manipulation. He simply allowed a small trickle of what he usually kept locked inside to leak out into the world. Doors up and down the long hallways opened and people emerged, curious and euphoric, as he went by. Ezra kept running, listening for the sound of his one other friend. The ground floor must have been devoted to classrooms, for its hallways slowly filled behind him as crowds of students emerged in his wake. The second floor seemed to have more offices. The doors here were closer together, and the people who emerged from them were older and either alone or in groups of only two or three.

He found her on the third floor. Almost as soon as he emerged from the stairs, he heard the birdsong. A familiar face poked out of a door a moment later. "Sir Ezra?" said a confused but clearly delighted Olivia, holding the covered birdcage.

The cage of his friend. For did the bird not always sing for him?

Feeling triumphant, Ezra said, "I need to know something."

Ezra slowed to a fast march about three hundred paces from the Queen's High Court. He knew it would be unseemly and might cause panic and even violence if he tried to charge straight through the security there—security that he himself had been quietly working to tighten. It would also be impossible, he realized. There were even more carriages, servants, and soldiers on the street than before. When he finally emerged from the press of armored or livered bodies and approached the narrow passageway into the court, a Knight of the Queen stepped between him and the entrance.

"Are they getting ready to send the constables after me?" Ezra asked.

The knight, a young man, hesitated for a moment, uncertain how to respond, or if he should respond at all. Finally, he confessed, "Yes, Captain, I believe they are."

He was not lying. Ezra could see Bobby and a dozen other constables at the far end of the passageway, clearly preparing for something. He waved to Bobby, then asked the knight, "What is your name?"

"Kenneth Kantor, Captain."

"Well, Sir Kenneth, have any of ours been able to take their swords in there?"

"No."

Not even Lady Kay could pull that one off, then. Ezra was tempted to test the constabulary's resolve but decided there was too little to be gained. He paused. *And the time isn't right.* "Okay, lay it out for me, Kenneth. What's happened and what's about to happen?"

"Uhm." Kenneth looked left and then right, buying time or perhaps just trying to think how to answer the question. Neither direction apparently coming to the rescue, he said, "Lady Kay has excluded questions of a personal nature or any suppositions about the Queen's . . . uh

. . . personal activities. They haven't gotten anywhere with the suspicious death of Lady Paron, so it is all coming down to the question of . . . whether or not the Queen is . . . a vampire. Sir."

This is dead-gods absurd. Ezra kept the thought to himself and only asked, "To be proven by?"

"Opening the tomb of the dead actor and ascertaining the state of the body. If, uhm, there is one."

"Solely?"

"To the best of my knowledge. Thus far."

"And this has been pushed by?

"Lady Beatrice Whall."

This fit with what Ezra had understood from Marigold and Bobby, and it also fit with what he had learned from the scholars. *Beatrice Whall pushing the undead vampire theory . . .*

I wonder if this was really her idea or if she brought that cousin of hers along. Gregory . . .

Ezra drew his sword and presented it to Sir Kenneth. "Hold this for me," he said to the awed young man.

When Ezra reached Bobby, he said, "I take it that you were about to come arrest me for truancy."

She snorted merrily but led him at once into the Queen's High Court. Stepping from the narrow corridor into that broad square was like entering another world.

It was a battleground, but not of a kind he had any experience of.

Row upon row of seats faced the witness boxes, the podiums, or stumps, of the speakers Rose and Thorn— of whom Kay was one—the high table for the nine members of the council, and the one seat elevated even above that. Ezra avoided looking at that seat for the moment, wanting first to take in the full space and geometry of the court.

Bobby's contingent of the constabulary guarded the entrance to the court and its witnesses until they had crossed the threshold, but they stood down at that point, and a specially constituted Court Constabulary took over. These special constables wore short swords, light mail, and red surcoats. They stood along the back walls, in front of the witness box and the stumps, and around the high table.

Ezra spotted a contingent of Knights of the Queen along the far wall, unarmed but not unarmored. Three of them had been allowed to stand to one side of the Queen's high seat. His eyes slid over her, refusing to settle.

Where are the rest of the knights? I ordered more than these to be deployed.

He scanned the rows of onlookers, the fascinated observers, the gossips, the ladies and lords of the Queendom. Hundreds of them. The enormous Sir Gregory Whall sat across two seats and towered over the expensively dressed, fashionable, hat-wearing lady beside him. Ezra noted the glint of a mailed sleeve shining out from the edge of a dark cloak. The scene reminded him ominously of the Queen's audience chamber, except that not a single chair was empty.

It is not every fortnight that your Queen is nearly assassinated, twenty soldiers are hacked down in her audience chamber, one Lady of the Queendom is decapitated, and the Queen is accused of being a murderer and a vampire. Loyalties were being tested. Some were being manipulated, Ezra was convinced, by the Kingdom of Erle. If Eryka was right and Erle now knew that she was no scion of theirs, then perhaps revenge of a broader scope was the goal.

Lady Jayne Orton and Pontes will find them out. Eventually.

But eventually is not good enough.

The court was in session *now*, and its enquiry had apparently been squeezed down into one strange and superstitious avenue.

There! Back behind the onlookers' rows stood another dozen Knights of the Queen, but search the room as he might, Ezra could not find any more of his knights. They had been excluded and would therefore be assembled at his secondary position, out of sight but not far away.

"Through here, Sir Ezra," said one of the special constables, a nervous, mustachioed older man. He pointed to the witness boxes. Ezra caught a fleeting glimpse of Marigold, seated in one of them.

"Who is to give evidence after me?" Ezra asked Bobby, the one member of the original contingent of constables who had been allowed to enter the court with him.

"You're the last," she said.

"Go find Lady Jayne Orton after I get to the box, will you?" Ezra said. "She may have something the constables need to look into." He had no idea if Jayne had finished her work or not, but the need for results was now urgent.

He did not see Bobby's nod as he marched past the Rose and Thorn stumps and took his place on the witness bench alongside Marigold.

Marigold pounded his shoulders with her gauntleted hands and whispered, "You took your time getting back."

He winked at her. "When are they bringing the tomb in?"

"Noon tomorrow. They want maximum sunshine in case there really is a vampire in there."

Ezra shook his head. "Can they have failed to notice that the Queen is here in daylight?"

Marigold snorted, "Did I ever say that any of this made sense?" She shrugged. "Though her high seat is actually in the shade."

"Sir Ezra," said Lady Kay in her role as the Rose stump, "would you please take your place on the witness platform?"

Ezra took up his position in the box and composed himself for interrogation by the Rose and the Thorn, Lady Kay and Lady Alanna Gill, posing alternating questions.

They began with the swearing in and routine matters, asking him, in rapid, staccato fashion, to confirm his name and date of birth, his years of service to the Queen—and correcting him on that, as even in banishment it seemed he had still officially remained a Knight of the Queen—his reason for returning to the capital, and his presence at the siege of Lady Jacqueline Paron's palace and in the battle of the Queen's audience chamber alongside Sir Marigold.

Without warning, the two interrogators moved abruptly to more contentious matters. Did he kill Lady Paron? No. Did he see who killed her? No. How did he know that assassins in the Queen's audience chamber were planning to kill her? Ezra explained. Did he know that nine of them were from Erle? He outlined his suspicions based on their appearance.

It was strange and off-putting to find himself in a formal court talking about death and mortal judgement in such a flat, matter-of-fact manner, while twenty paces away, the Queen whose life depended on his answers sat, upright and silent. He had travelled with her to the most secret places of the mind and body, to the inmost essence of things, a world far beyond and infinitely deeper than this mundane, yet fateful, material plane.

"Did you know that among of the Knights of Erle was one Sir Eamon Way, the so-called Unkillable Knight?" asked Lady Kay for reasons that Ezra did not at first understand.

"No," Ezra replied, bemused, "I have never heard of him. Until now. I killed him before I knew his epithet."

The lords and ladies erupted in laughter as the tension in the court broke like a window, like pieces of glass falling for an age. For all their high rank, the finely dressed onlookers laughed like jolly farmers. And they were in no hurry to stop.

Ezra watched the crowd, noting who was not laughing, who looked angry. Gregory Whall's arms were crossed and his face was stern. A few other men and women looked angry too.

Oh, I see.

Lady Kay's strange question suddenly made sense.

Lady Alanna protested that the question was irrelevant, but Kay, on her next turn to question, made another attempt at exposing allegiances. "You were not aware," she asked, with a scornful edge to her voice, "that you had already killed his older brother, Sir Jefferd Way, eleven years ago on the night when you also killed the Prince of Erle?"

"Was Sir Jefferd also unkillable?" shrieked a lady in the crowd.

Lady Alanna scowled at this indignity to the court and demanded that the question be struck down before Ezra could answer, perhaps fearing another jest. She quickly moved to a question she had apparently been saving.

"Have you ever seen the *Queen* kill anyone?"

Ezra scanned the onlookers, pausing to give the Knights of the Queen on the back wall a slow, keen regard, returned his gaze to Lady Kay for a moment, and after locking eyes with the enormous Sir Gregory Whall, finally found the Queen.

Rose.

Avoiding her eyes until that moment had taken a tremendous effort. She looked, as far as he could see, exactly the same as eleven years before. Long tawny hair like a lion's mane, proud face, eyes both hard and humane. Meeting her in Eydos as Iceberg, Puma, or Vampire was powerfully affecting, but seeing her live after all this time nearly dropped him. His knees failed for a moment, the colors of the world flared, his eyes widened, and his mouth opened.

An instant later, the pealing of Elysian Bells serenaded the court.

Ezra let them ring jubilant for exactly thrice eleven seconds—three peels for every year they had been apart—before slowly tamping down the soaring expression of his love.

As the ringing subsided, the court collectively exhaled, though several lords and ladies also fainted. Even Lady Alanna Gill swayed, staggered, and almost fell off her stump. Kay's pale face reddened, and the Councilors shifted in their seats, some obviously trying to conceal their more embarrassing physical reactions. The faces of Lady Beatrice Whall and Lady Emily Lang were wet with tears.

What the Queen felt was a mystery. Her face remained impassive and regal throughout these emanations of Ezra's pure love.

"Sir—" Alanna said, trying to collect herself, "Sir Ezra, I'll ask you again, have you ever seen the Queen kill anyone?"

"No."

CHAPTER 23

ELEVEN YEARS AGO

The narrow hallway was not to Ezra's advantage, burdened as he was by heavy plate armor and a long sword. He was also outnumbered four to one, but in this supernally intense state he did not care about such petty material considerations.

He did not think, "Fuck them!" as he cut through bodies with his sword or smashed faces with his reinforced left vambrace, or was struck in turn by his opponents' sharp, curved blades. He did not spell the words, "I'll kill you all" in bloody red letters across the topography of his mind. He did not speak of hate, betrayal, or dishonor. There were no words. He thought nothing. He was a creature of pure action, his being resonating solely to the frequency of fury and violence, to the need to save his Queen.

Cries of pain only fueled his soul and gave air to the fire of his savagery. *She* had cried out in fear and pain, and Ezra would answer with everything he had. The Queen's voice had called to him for years, and his honor had always checked the response that his heart and mind so urgently demanded. There had been no permissible response to the many times he had heard her in the throes of her raw passion, but as heartbreaking as those sounds had been for him, he could comfort himself in the knowledge that at least she was happy in her wild way.

He had also heard her weeping before this night. The sound of her crying had been the most painful thing that he had ever heard since Lilly had slipped away in death. The Queen's unanswerable tears were conflated in his mind with his helplessness in the face of his wife's suffering. They proved his inability to relieve the Queen's pain too.

But tonight's cries were different. Hearing her moan in pain and cry in mortal fear had ignited a side of Ezra that he had never let slip in his life before now. He had become, in an instant, an inferno of destruction.

Ezra had one of the Knights of Erle pinned to the stone wall of the castle and was pushing the nose from his face with a hard, sharp vambrace when another of the Prince of Erle's men tackled him from behind. One sword, no two, hammered into him, hitting hard plate, then finding the gaps between and separating the weaker chain, slicing through padding and lacerating skin. Against this hail of desperate blows, Ezra rocked hard and got to a knee.

His head rung from a blow to his helm that had snapped its laces, but he caught the next stroke with his vambrace, slid his forearm down along the sword, and caught the blade with his gauntleted fingers, chiming a tone of fury that shook the walls of the castle. Gripping the blade in bleeding fingers, Ezra projected his otherworldly wrath into the metal. The blade cracked in a brittle, widening spiderweb and fell away.

His attackers' gasps of shock and fear gave Ezra a moment of space. He exploded to his feet, sword whipping around faster than the eye could follow, adding a keening sound to his thunderous ringing.

A hail of teeth struck the wall behind one the Erlemen as Ezra's blade shattered his skull, sending bone fragments flying like kernels off a cobb of corn. The wet "glllaahhh!" sound of the falling man and the hoarse, gulping breaths of the last two soldiers of Erle were drowned by the pealing rumble rolling off Ezra.

But Ezra's opponents were not finished yet. He stumbled as the sharp edge of one of their swords somehow got up over his cuisse and under his mail skirt to bite deep into his left thigh. Fighting back the pain, Ezra chopped down, returning the blow in kind, separating rings of steel and hacking the man's shoulder halfway off. It was the same man whose nose Ezra had mauled from his face like a burst grape.

Blood spraying from his leg—scattering grim red art at wild angles as it shot through broken mail and bent plate—Ezra smashed the last man's sword from his hand and his hand from his arm, then shattered his skull as he fell away.

Clutching a hand to his thigh, vainly trying to hold the spurting blood inside his body, Ezra hobbled to the Queen's door and pounded on it. Inches of solid oak held it closed to him. Knowing it was barred from the inside, Ezra placed his free hand against the barrier and released the sound and pressure of his fury and desperation into it.

The door broke apart, brutally disaggregating, pieces of wood falling away like a dark waterfall. He pushed the bar up and out of the way and stumbled inside to see, at last, his Queen.

She stood in a red nightgown, facing the chain mail-clad Prince of Erle. Tall, dark-haired, and cruel, he waved his sword at her, barely turning his head in Ezra's direction, perhaps registering the gash in the intruder's thigh and deciding he must soon bleed out.

And Ezra was, indeed, bleeding out. He suddenly found himself down on one knee, cold and short of breath, growing desperately weak. His vision was blurring, the colours draining to gray, but seeing a trickle of blood from the Queen's hairline and mouth brought color and life back into him. With a scream of rage, he released his bleeding thigh and charged the Prince of Erle, colliding with him and sending him sharply into a desk. Both of them fell into a tangle on the hard floor.

Ezra barely registered what happened next. He had a sense of movement, of a red form, and a man's scream.

Seconds later, he was in her arms. Her hands were on him, and she was sobbing, **"Ezra! No, no, no."** It felt as if her dark smooth voice was carrying him to heaven.

His eyes closed, just for a moment, he thought, but when they reopened, the Queen was dressed in pants and tunic and pulling the prince's ill-fitting, too-long chain skirt over her head. Blood drenched her face and ran down her neck, glistening on the bright links of metal.

"Wha—?" Ezra mumbled, confused.

"You weren't hurt quite as badly as you imagined," the Queen said as if she could read his mind.

And it seemed to be true. Ezra found that he could move. He got back up on one knee. *Where is my sword?*

He turned, realizing that he must have left it in the hallway. Near the door his eyes caught what looked like a blood-soaked mop.

It was the head of the Prince of Erle.

Strong hands pulled Ezra to his feet. **"Come my love,"** she said in the voice of a dark angel. **"Let us kill them all."**

CHAPTER 24
UNTOMBED

"Where is Pontes?" Ezra asked Shryke the moment she arrived at the Knight Captain's offices.

She smirked the smile she always smirked, and answered with a question of her own. "You going to give that chair back to Marigold when they release her?"

It was a point of contention that the Queen's Council were still holding Marigold in what they called protective custody—though at least she was back in the opulence of the diplomatic wing rather than the dungeon. They apparently felt that she remained in danger until the tomb was opened. The council had uncovered no compelling evidence against the Queen—or anyone else—in the matter of Lady Jacqueline Paron's decapitation, and opening the tomb of Brayden Fellows would likely mark the conclusion of their investigation.

They did not know to question Shryke.

Ezra did not answer her. He was in no mood for her impertinence, having spent most of the night looking through ledgers with Lady Jayne Orton, chasing down details of his security arrangements, consulting with Marigold in her expansive chambers, dodging the unwanted gropings and pleas of strangers in the squares of the city, and asking after the whereabouts of his secretary. He had wanted to speak with the Queen and ask her to delay the opening of the tomb for a few days. Three should be the most that he and Jayne Orton would need to complete their investigation and, he hoped, stop the whole trial in its tracks. It was all the time that Pontes would need, Ezra hoped, to complete his secret mission.

He would also have asked the Queen to give him authority over the special constables in the court and see that his knights there were properly armed. But he had not seen her again after his testimony at court. At the conclusion of the day's proceedings, the Queen had vanished from her elevated throne and none of those questions had gotten asked.

Not in the waking world, anyway. If he had seen her that night in Eydos, he did not carry the memory forward. When his eyes had opened that morning, he had found himself lying sideways in bed as if some vast hand had reached down and spun him while he slept. His blankets had been twisted, and his neck was stained with blood.

I need to speak with her. In this *world now.*

But until then, he needed to find a way to do his job as Knight Captain and protect her.

"No sign of him," said Shryke, after finally seeing in his eyes that she had better answer his question. "You know . . ." she said, sliding unquietly up onto the desk again, "We could just go and take her out of the court. There are enough of us here now to just walk in and take the Queen away."

Ezra raised his eyebrows. "If she didn't want to be there, she wouldn't have left the castle."

"Why is she allowing this to go on?" Shryke asked, for once not smirking.

She has her reasons.

But Ezra did not want to speak his suspicions about the Queen's true plans aloud, and certainly not to Shryke. Instead, he pushed the knight off the desk—for the third time—and said, "Just make sure everyone is ready when I signal."

"Yes, my captain," she said landing neatly on her feet this time. With a laugh, she added, "And what would that signal be again?"

At that moment, the door opened. It was a page. Ezra waved away the page's speech about trusted hands and reached for the familiar cream-colored envelope on its gleaming tray. In neat bold printing, the message read:

"Come to me."

"I want you to go down there and stop the whole thing," said Eryka, stomping around her room. "Chop off heads if you have to, but put an end to it."

Did I not just have this conversation?

Eryka was about as mature as Shryke, Ezra realized.

Oh, wait!

Ezra realized, too, that Eryka must already have spoken to Sir Shryke.

"I can't do that," he told the pouting princess.

"Why not?" came the shrill reply.

Ezra sat down on a big, high-backed, padded chair. He patted the little space beside himself and waited for Eryka to sit there. "It's gone too far," he said. "It's a confidence issue now."

Eryka's neck craned to lift her head up in his direction. "But what about the postings you made in the squares?"

"Yes, those are helping I'm sure," Ezra allowed. "But it looks like the rumors have acquired a life of their own. Only a properly concluded trial can lay them to rest now. Your mother knows that too."

"But why is she risking a process that can still go either way?"

"I don't know for sure. She usually has reasons of her own," he said, then added, hesitating, "Perhaps . . . some part of her . . . *wants* to be punished."

"What for?"

"It's the riddle of her," Ezra said. "She knows that she does what she has to, she knows she is right, and beautiful, and loving. Calm. And worthy of love. But another part of her, a tiny, hidden part, sometimes works against all of that. It denies her beauty, pushes away love. Tells her she is a vampire." He smiled sadly at his daughter. "People are complex."

"Fuck your complexity," shot Eryka.

Ezra tried not to laugh. "How old are you anyway?"

"You know this," Eryka said, irritated. "I'm ten ye—" But Ezra had already folded her into his arms.

"THIS IS A GOOD THING," said Marigold as she stood with Ezra just outside of the court square. She had a cavalry horn tied to her sword belt. "Me being in protection means I am not part of the count of knights in there. One more, *highly skilled* body," she gave Ezra a pointed look, "could be enough to make the difference."

"Hmmm," Ezra said, not knowing how to reply to that. He looked up at the sun. *Not long now.* At any moment, the cart would roll up and nine sets of hands would carry the sealed tomb into the Queen's High Court. "You always make a difference, Mari."

Suddenly, Pontes appeared out of the crowd, looking sweaty, dirty, and disheveled. And very unlike himself. Beside him was Sir Valerie Simmons able, this time, to look Ezra in the eyes.

Rumpled as he was, Pontes looked triumphant. He was beaming from ear to ear, and as he crossed the remaining distance to the court entrance, he almost shouted. "I've got it," he exclaimed, waving a ledger.

"Whaddya know," said Marigold. "Your little plan might work after all, Ezra." She winked at him. "You may not be such a bad Knight Captain after all."

Ezra ignored that. "The affidavits?" he asked Pontes.

"*Five* of them," the secretary announced gleefully.

"That should be enough," Ezra replied. "None from in town, I take it."

Pontes pursed his lips. "No. But I found out that one member of the original troop is *here*, performing this very morning in a production of *Saraith and the Nine Rings*."

If we had only known that two days ago, this insanity could have been avoided altogether.

Ezra looked up at the sun. "Okay. Let's go get him."

"*Her*, sir."

"Give me that," Marigold said, reaching for the ledger. "You two go find this actress and I'll make sure Lady Kay gets the letters."

"Makes sense," said Ezra. "If I don't make it back in time and anything doesn't seem right, just blow the horn."

"Get going."

~

"Which way?" asked Pontes.

Ezra pointed, and they turned left. They had passed a showing of the *Saraith* play a couple of days ago, and Constable Bobby Archibald knew where each of the mummers' troops were playing in town, so its location was known. The *Saraith* venue, luckily, was not too far away, and yet Ezra's heart raced from more than just trying to run in heavy armor. He kept imagining the carriage and tomb arriving in his absence.

He tried not to think of the absurdity of it all. The trial. A tomb being exhumed. He and Pontes searching for an actress while the Queen was so unnecessarily exposed. *I can't change what's happened, only what will happen next. If we are fast enough.*

There! They emerged from a narrow, cobbled corridor into a wide square. At the far side, a crowd had gathered in front of a small stage—tiny, really—and on the stage, stood a woman with long, feathered, blue wings and even longer, black hair.

Ezra accelerated into a run, hurtled through the rows of onlookers, and leapt the three-foot height onto the stage to "Ooohhs," "Ahhs," and delighted clapping from the audience, who assumed his spectacular entrance was part of the play.

"And what god is this entering the nine rings?" boomed the dark-haired actress, staying in character despite the tremendous clatter that Ezra in full armor made as he landed on the cheap wooden platform.

"I am Sir Ezra, and I need to speak with you in the name of the Queen," Ezra said, not meaning to be part of any entertainment but unable to avoid giving that impression.

The actress whirled, fanning her raven hair and blue wings for the audience, and turned back to Ezra with dramatic intensity. "What earthly Queen demands the time of Saraith of the Nine Rings?"

What have I wandered into? He had travelled the oceans, gardens, and fields of Eydos and spoken to icebergs, pumas, vampires, and spinning storms, but right now this moment seemed even stranger.

A winded Pontes arrived, making urgent gesticulations at the stagehands, who were half obscured at the side of the platform. "Drop curtain! Drop curtain!" he shouted.

Not able to stop himself, Ezra answered the actress, "I need your help on matters of death and tragedy, for love, desire, and the health of kingdoms, and I need it *now*, Saraith!"

The actress spread her arms as if to take in the entire world—or at least the entire audience—and said in a loud, deep voice, "I am Saraith of the Nine Rings, and I am equal to any call."

"Drop the curtain," hissed Pontes, "Drop it!"

With a shrug, the stagehands complied. The curtain went down to thunderous applause from the audience.

"That was an incredible entrance," gushed Saraith as she led Ezra backstage. She turned around and said, "Help me out of these wings, will you. Whoever you really are."

As Ezra struggled to work the buckles that held the wide, feathery props to her back, he said, "It wasn't an entrance or audition or whatever it is that you seem to think. I really *am* Sir Ezra. And I really do need your help."

Saraith carefully set the wings aside, then laughed, and patted his breastplate. "No ordinary actor could have jumped the stage in real armor, *Sir* Ezra. Relax, you will definitely be an asset in our little troop." She placed the hand that had been on his breastplate onto her own chest and said, "Whooo, that was *wonderful.*"

"He really *is* Sir Ezra," said Pontes, finally jumping into the conversation.

"No," Saraith said, as her hand reached and traced along his pauldron, then the upper edge of his breastplate, feeling the thickness of the metal and realizing it was no prop. "How did you . . .? What is going . . ?"

"The Queen needs you," said Ezra.

"She does," said Pontes, nodding along earnestly.

"Why on earth?" asked Saraith, eyes huge, hand returning to her own breast. "A command performance?" she asked, looking hopeful.

"No, not for a show," said Ezra.

Saraith asked excitedly, "A solo recitation then?"

"We need to ask you a few questions to start with."

"And then the Queen?"

"Yes, if your answers tell us what we need to know," said Ezra, hoping that the insanity of the situation was on the retreat.

Saraith thrust her chin out bravely. "Okay. Ask."

Ezra looked to Pontes. The secretary asked, "Is your name Rosalyn Grey?"

Saraith's face went rigid. "Yes, it is," she said, a little huffily, "but do call me Saraith."

For dead gods' sake.

Pontes seemed unsurprised by this. He nodded affably and said, "Of course. And were you with Pepper Andrew's troop eleven years ago, Saraith?"

"Yes. How *is* dear old Pepper?"

"Unfortunately . . . he died," replied Pontes.

"Oh, dead gods, that's *such* a tragedy," Saraith said, nodding her head and breathing deeply. "He was such a dear." She glanced stealthily at her mirror and adjusted her hair. "Though getting on in years, of course," she added sadly.

"I'm so sorry to bring you the news," Pontes said. "It was a tooth infection, but everyone else seems to still be in good health, uh, according to them."

"So sad."

Ezra asked, "So you must have known Brayden Fellows?"

"Yes, certainly! He was the male lead in the *Vampire of Sangrea* when I was understudy to Doctor Messing."

"But he left the troop, right?" said Pontes.

Saraith smiled ruefully. "He left before Pepper could *fire* him. Saved a lot of trouble. Pepper hated firing actors." She suddenly grabbed both of Pontes's hands in hers and asked, "How is he doing?"

"He's dead too," said Ezra, then regretted his bluntness as Saraith's face crumpled like cheap paper and she began to cry. She had taken the death of the Pepper fellow so well, but he realized that he must have missed some element of subtext regarding Brayden. The Queen *did* like her men to be attractive . . .

"There, there," said Pontes, patting her back and giving Ezra an exasperated head shake. "We both deeply regret delivering this news, uh, Saraith, but could you tell us, please, why Pepper was going to fire Brayden?"

"He kept fainting on stage."

Ezra sprinted alone through the streets of the capital. Saraith could not run in her costume, so she and Pontes would follow along as quickly as they could. He ran faster and faster, his mood a strange mix of elation and anxiety. He was elated that they had found the actress. Her testimony would be the last mortar on the tomb, so to speak, but he feared that he might arrive too late.

He nearly tore a hole through a carriage that pulled up in front of him a square away from the Queen's High Court. He jumped over five liveried armsmen playing dice on the walkway just beyond that. Although no one could hear the low tone emanating from him, some could sense it, perhaps feeling it in their bones. They looked about in mild, confused alarm, not sure what might be wrong.

Sir Kenneth Kantor emerged from the narrow laneway outside the court in time to catch Ezra's tossed sword belt. "Where's Marigold?" Ezra asked, still running.

"Just under the high table!" called Kenneth to his back.

Slowing only to avoid testing his new plate on one of the drawn swords of the special constables, Ezra emerged into the court, pushing roughly past one of the red-tabarded constables who had raised a hand as if to stop him entering.

The stone coffin had been wheeled in on a stripped-down wagon and positioned between the Rose and Thorn stumps. Two special constables with iron mauls stood near its head.

They had been about to swing, but stopped as Ezra's anger leaked into the realm of perception. He slowed to a walk now and passed his rows of knights. As he proceeded past the lines of onlookers, every eye followed him. Marigold and the Queen stood tall as he approached them, Marigold standing near the high table, the Queen a level above her.

As Ezra reached the stumps, he placed one hand on the tomb and said, "Do you want me to save you the trouble and crack it open?"

He did not wait for an answer. Passing the two advocates, he rounded the base of the stands and reached the back area. A dozen special constables stood at attention there, guarding the wide set of stairs. Ezra passed them too and ascended to the level of the Lords of the Queen's Council. He caught Lady Beatrice Whall's eyes briefly as he continued up, step after step, until he stood, unchallenged, on the Queen's level.

This platform was five or six steps deep, about double that in width, and was dominated by the large, ornate wooden chair at its center. The Queen stood beside her throne, her head turned toward Ezra. A moment later, he found himself beside her, looking down on the court. There were about five hundred people in attendance, he estimated. Some were friends. Some were enemies. Many were simply there for the entertainment. Judging his Queen for their amusement.

A trickle more of his anger escaped. He was still in control of it, but it rumbled ominously like very distant thunder.

"Do you really want this?" he asked the Queen. They were the first words he had said to her in the world of the real for eleven long years.

"Yes," she said in her smooth, deep, untroubled voice.

Ezra nodded and shouted down to the lords and ladies below, "Is this truly what you want? To pry open a cold grave? To dig into old sorrow and misfortune?"

He stared at them coldly for a moment, then roared, "What you see here is a game constructed by the Kingdom of Erle and fueled by certain corrupt Ladies and Lords of the Queendom."

He gestured to the tomb. "That man, Brayden Fellows, was an actor with a known heart condition. That condition killed him, not some mythical creature. His death was tragic and untimely, but it was not murder. He had almost died on the stage several times. This has been witnessed and documented! In a few moments, one of those witnesses will enter this court to give testimony." He shook his head in disgust. "By all means, pry open his grave if you must, but it is *you* who will be judged."

The sound projecting from Ezra and the air around him was dreadful now, even though he was still restraining, using it only for effect. A murmur rose from the crowd. The onlookers were growing alarmed. Even the ever-cool Lady Allana, the Thorn, looked uncertain. "Perhaps," she ventured, "we could wait until—"

"Open it," said Lady Beatrice Whall.

"Yes, open it," came the dark voice of the Queen.

With fearful looks, the two constables swung their mauls. In three strokes, the seal of the tomb ruptured. Four additional constables rushed up, and together the six of them slid the lid off. It fell with a crash, breaking into five uneven pieces.

"It's just bones!" shouted Jonathan Sutton, one of the Lords of the Council.

Ezra was unsurprised. He had known. He also thought he knew what would happen next.

If I was part of a conspiracy involving many players, how would I arrange the signal to act? Something that could not be missed. That could not be misunderstood.

Whatever it is, this is surely when it will happen.

He was proven correct.

As if on cue, "Death to the vampire!" roared dozens of voices in unison from the crowd of onlookers. "Stake her! Stake the vampire!"

In a mob, slogans are contagious. The chant was taken up by more and more onlookers. "Stake the vampire! Stake the vampire!"

Under cover of the confusion created by these shouts, carefully distributed members of the audience, some of them assassins from Erle, the rest rebels against their own Queen, now threw off their cloaks, revealing chain armor and the short swords that someone had conspired to smuggle into the proceedings. A knot of these murderers, positioned strategically in the center of the court, appeared to be hurriedly assembling something.

In its outlines at least—the moment, for Ezra—was predictable. And for the conspirators of course. For everyone else, it was shocking and incredible. They had thought they were in a court of law. They thought the Queen was being judged. Perhaps some of them had even expected a vampire to tumble out of the tomb or a perfectly preserved body. Or for the tomb to be empty. But all that was left of the actor Brayden Fellows was desiccated skin and bones. It was his final dramatic entrance. And now armed assassins were about to turn the trial into a violent, real-life tragedy

Ezra had planned for this moment, but it was still shocking. And viscerally upsetting.

"Stake the vampire!" enraged him. And so many of them were in on it, scattered all about the court in small, tight groups. More than he had planned for. Ezra let his rage loose. In a matter of moments, it was ten times more powerful, shaking the square so hard that both Lady Alanna and Lady Kay had to quit their stumps for fear of falling. He turned to the three other knights on the narrow platform. "Block the stairs. Now!"

"With what?" asked one of the knights in a shaky voice, his hand reaching toward a sword hilt that was not there.

"Step back, my lady," Ezra said to the Queen. "Away from the ledge." She did not move. Ezra put a hand on her shoulder. She was stiff and cold. "Let us do our jobs, Rose!" he growled, his face close to hers.

She relented and stepped back from the edge of the platform, but her expression was hard. Cold.

Kneeling beside her heavy, throne-like chair, Ezra took hold of the two front legs. They were made of thick, tan-colored hardwood, each leg carved into the shape of a puma claw. With a tremendous heave, he broke the legs off. Flipping the chair over, he snapped the other two legs from it.

"Here," he said to the knights, passing a leg to each of them and keeping one for himself. "If any of them reach the stairs, you will only need to hold them for a few minutes."

He *hoped* it would only be a few minutes. There were a *lot* more assassins than he had planned for. The operation to smuggle arms and Erlemen into the court had been more successful than Ezra could have imagined, and the local opposition to the Queen's projects had clearly been higher than anyone had suspected. Keeping the Queen well behind him, Ezra stepped forward to see how the battle was going.

It was pandemonium below. A group of the special constables was fighting a traitorous group of their colleagues, some of whom were armed with crossbows. Bolts flew at close range but to uncertain effect. Bobby's constables were filtering in, charging the armored men of Erle and their allies, but at least two had been cut down at once by treacherous special constables. Innocent lords and ladies were being hacked indiscriminately in the melee.

A bolt from a light crossbow rang off the top of Ezra's breastplate.

He heard the knights on the stairs fighting, but he stayed where he was in front of the Queen.

"You *wanted* this," he said to her.

"Yes," she calmly replied. He felt her hands on his pauldrons as she pressed herself into his back. Only a few inches of air and a thin layer of steel separated her lips from his neck. **"This is how it must be,"** she said.

He wondered at the complex layers of guilt, self-punishment, and cold calculation that had gone into her decision to pull out the root of betrayal in this way. When had she decided to do it this way? Or had she simply adapted to the situation, converting what happened in the audience chamber and even her daughter's mistake in ordering Lady Paron's death into a new opportunity. He realized he could never know. Not unless she told him, and perhaps even then she herself might not fully know. It was that complexity that Eryka had cursed. Ezra did not like it either, but he knew he had to accept it. The situation would unfold in the way it had to regardless of his feelings.

Let's hope to the nine gods that the plan works, then.

There were an astonishing, a frightening, number of enemies in the melee below, but Ezra knew that reinforcements were on their way.

Screams ripped the air.

How did this get so bad? Why did I let it?

His Knights of the Queen, secreted from both groups of constables in a building one street away, would have heard his ringing and must be halfway to them now. The assassins should not be able to win unless they could so in the next few moments. He had outmaneuvered them in advance, but there were more of them than he had expected. More than they had deduced from the ledgers. Far more than he had feared.

A ragged, desperate scream spoke to Ezra's most immediate concern. Careful not to move away from the Queen, he wheeled and saw one of his knights go down, clutching her knee and rolling left and then right. The other two knights were hard pressed by special constables in their red tabards. Ezra realized with horror that the entire troop guarding the back steps were assassins.

The knight with the injured knee rolled into her fellow, knocking him off balance. A sword across his gorget produced a desperate, new, gurgling scream and a thick spray of blood. He hit the side of the platform and fell awkwardly away out of sight. Other blades sought for gaps in the plate of the first downed knight, stabbing, stabbing, and stabbing until she stopped moving. The last of Ezra's knights hacked off a chain-mailed arm with one brilliant stroke, but took a thin blade through his visor in return and fell forward, plank-stiff, into the crowd of constables below him.

Ezra charged, unleashing all of his fury into the heavens, into the air, and into the constables. It emanated from him with a new power. The Queen was here at last, with him, and although it was likely that she had never really needed him in all those eleven years, she surely did *now*. Ezra held nothing back. A tall woman raised her short sword overhead to meet him and was swept off the platform in a blast of deep, rumbling fury. Her desperate, keening shriek went unnoticed in the maelstrom of Ezra's rage.

The intensity of his rage was so overwhelming that instead of being impaled on a thicket of constables' swords as he plunged into their line, Ezra delivered a crushing overhead blow to the first one he swung at. The man was too busy covering his eyes from the thunder emanating from Ezra to see the heavy wooden leg before it crushed his head. Leaving the cracked wood buried in the constable's skull right down to his now-bulging eyes, Ezra plucked the sword out of the man's spasming hands and chopped short and hard into the teeth of the skinny, red-haired, older man beside him. Another scream was swallowed up in the raging inferno of sound.

Ezra swung into whoever he could reach, choosing his targets unconsciously, moving with preternatural speed now, pouring out his rage and hatred upon them all. They died without knowing that they were being destroyed by the inferno of a decade and more of frustration and denial.

To his right, he saw the Queen grappling with a woman who had somehow gotten past him. To no avail. His lady shook the red-tabarded constable from side to side and hurled her like an empty shirt into the unquiet air and the long drop below.

Some instinct warned Ezra, and he raised his left vambrace in time to catch a crossbow bolt and deflect it, broken in pieces, away from his visor.

"Step back!" he roared to the Queen and launched into Carried by the Cyclone, rotating into a living maelstrom of carnage. Turning and tolling, striking, shouting, Ezra lost track of time and consciousness, carried entirely on rage, passion, and his compulsion to protect *her* at any cost.

No helm, no arm, no shirt of mail, shirt of cloth, thin layer of skin, or mad courage protected them from him. He hit one man so hard that an eye burst from his skull, snapping off the optic nerve and splattering wetly like an unprotected egg in the thunder of Ezra's percussive hate.

Teeth, hair, fingers, blood, and pieces of broken chain flew in all directions. Swords and hacked-off arms spun into the air, severed from hands, separated from bodies, out of sight and mind. At a strange and unknowable still point, a long string of blood and a handful of teeth circled Ezra, moving hypnotically back and forth on some unpredictable, atmospheric tide before shattering abruptly from a sharp detonation of sound and blowing off into infinity.

His rage did not make Ezra invulnerable. He was hit again and again, blows coming like hail on steel, denting and breaking metal. But he did not fall, too deep in the cyclone to be stopped even as his own blood sprayed the air. It was the mindless chaos of rage, utterly loosed and let slip from sanity or restraint, the horrific opposite of unconditional love.

"Stop, Ezra," some immeasurable time later, came the dark voice of the Queen,

He awoke to himself on the stairs, three steps down, surrounded by grievously hacked bodies, random limbs, a few stray heads, and what seemed like a waterfall of blood. A flash of urgent movement revealed three constables at the base of the stairs, fleeing.

Someone's red-streaked head lay at the Queen's feet. Blood streaked her own mouth and her neck. Ezra was too deep in the moment to wonder if anyone had seen his Queen tear or bite that head off, as she must have done with the Prince of Erle's all those years ago. He was still rage personified, beyond thinking and speculating.

The tower was shuddering violently, coming apart under his fury, brutally breaking apart.

"Take it in, my knight, take it in before you destroy us both."

Ezra remembered her saying that once before to him. And holding him tight. It had been the first time he had felt an answering love from her.

Yes.

Love brought him back to himself, soothed his unquantifiable, appalling fury, tempered the thunder still rolling in continuous standing waves off him. Pacified his rage. Quelled his power. He mounted the platform again and stood close to the Queen.

"It should be clear to our backs now," Ezra grunted, able to hear himself now that he had pulled in much of his rage. He had no sword sheath, so he kept the hilt in his grip as he crossed to the front of the platform. The Queen's eyes were bright with a frightening excitement, shining from her blood-spattered face, but she fell quietly in behind him.

Below, as if from nowhere, three assassins charged the high table, but Marigold stepped out. She was unarmed and took one blow off a vambrace, stepping sideways with the stroke to avoid a broken arm, only to be hit on the backplate by another man.

Lord Gregory Whall charged into the melee and tackled one of Marigold's assailants, knocking the man's sword free and pounding his head into the cobblestones as Bobby and another constable entered the fray.

Out of the corner of his eye, Ezra spotted Pontes and the wide-eyed actress, Saraith, enter the court with a crowd of new constables. Pontes held Saraith's hand, not, Ezra assumed, as a romantic gesture. He could only imagine how frightened they both must be to push through into the maelstrom of carnage that was unfolding around them.

You should have stayed back, Pontes!

But he understood that Pontes would have done anything to help, even enter a domain of violence and disorder that was the opposite of his orderly world of numbers and lists.

And it *was* violent and disordered. It was furious and chaotic, but it also seemed as if the assassins' moment had passed its zenith. A flash of bright armor reflected from the side, signaling that the first of the knightly reinforcements had arrived at last.

What am I missing?

Even as the assassins fell away from the center of the gallery like petals from a spent flower, the thing he had seen them assembling rose into view. It was a scorpion—an oversized spear launcher—with but one long spear that must have been screwed together. The treachery of the special constables had gone deeper than Ezra imagined possible. To smuggle those parts into the court would have required coordination by many hands. Even so, their time was running out. The assassins were quickly overwhelmed by the arriving knights, but not before the last of them to die reached the trigger and got the shot off. Meant for the Queen, the enormous spear flew through the air at tremendous speed and smashed into Ezra's breastplate, penetrating his chest from front to back.

"You have come for a reason, Sir Ezra," Professor Olivia had said as she followed him into her office away from the eager gaze of the crowd of students who had begun filtering out of the stairway and cautiously moving toward the knight. His bell sound had aroused both their emotions and their scholarly curiosity.

Olivia carefully placed the ecstatically warbling bird on the top of a bookshelf near the window. "Should we wait for my colleague?" she asked. "He's teaching a class in our other wing at the moment."

"We have no time to lose," replied Ezra. Parsons was a nut in any case.

Olivia gestured to a heavily padded, high-backed leather chair and walked around her book-heavy desk to take a seat in an identical chair. "How can I help you, then?"

"You said that I am a rare human."

"Yes. Though exactly how rare we do not know."

Ezra smiled. Olivia was easier to speak with when Parsons was not around. And she seemed to be sensitive to his state of mind. "So that I'm not the only one," he continued. "And I can meet with others like me in Eydos."

"Indeed," she stated. "Or at least that is what some accounts state."

"*What* are we?"

Olivia tittered at this. "Wouldn't we like to know."

Seeing Ezra's impatient expression, she stopped laughing. "No, we really *would* like to know." She pointed vaguely at the books on her table. "There are stories and legends in plenty about the . . . heaven-sent, as my colleague calls you, but no solid research has ever been done." Her face was regretful as she added, "Some of you have been imprisoned and uh . . . used. Or use has been attempted of you, uh, them, but no one as yet has made an empirical study of a rare human."

"So you don't know what we are," said Ezra, frustrated. "Whether we are good? Or evil?"

Olivia looked at him sadly. "I truly don't know, but I can speculate. I think your morality is no more intrinsically defined than anyone else's. You simply have a unique set of capabilities and perception. Not everyone agrees with that opinion, however." The sadness slipped away as she leaned forward, excited. "Sir Ezra, I apologize. Perhaps I have understated what I do not understand. You *are* connected somehow to the world beyond matter, to feelings and fundamental natures. And that in itself is a beautiful, powerful thing."

"But what about the other 'heaven-sent'? What about . . . the vampires?"

"Oh," Olivia said knowingly. "The Queen. She really is quite remarkable. Unique, I would imagine. And yes, frightening." She looked pointedly at the bird cage. "But the bird sings for her too, so I suspect your 'vampire' is no more intrinsically evil than you are."

"But everyone fears vampires. They say that they kill innocents and make others cursed like themselves."

"I think," Olivia said, with a trace of superiority in her voice, "that some part of this may be the voice of jealousy speaking. Men who could never control a vampire. Women who could not become one." She raised her left index finger pedantically. "Each of these rare humans—save only one as far as we know—appears to have a dual nature. *You* are love and fury. *She* is life and death, loving the taste of life, *capable* of giving much greater life back, yet also of consuming the life of another utterly."

EZRA DROPPED TO HIS KNEES, skewered, but he did not collapse entirely. She had caught him.

I am in your arms at last.

"You aren't a vampire," he said to the Queen. *Stop punishing yourself!* "I love y—"

"Still your mind," she said. Letting him lean against her, she grasped the spear at the front and back and snapped the thick heavy wood as if it were a dry twig. Then, without pausing, she yanked the remnant of the broken spear from his body and tossed the pieces away.

Blood gushed from Ezra in gouts. His vision turned cloudy and dim.

But he felt something. *Her.* Her healing hands.

Breathing deep despite the exquisite pain, Ezra felt, finally, content. He was once more *hers.* His eyes closed. He was at peace.

CHAPTER 25
FORCE OF NATURE

Stretching to break the warm surface with one last stroke, the man drifts exhausted onto the sandy shoreline. He has been in the ocean for as long as he can remember and does not have the strength to drag himself up the beach.

His memory is fractured, and a deep pain and weariness press upon him. But there is also contentedness, as if he has fulfilled some vital role.

Am I hurt? Or just tired? He does not know. There is so little of him left, washed up there, helpless on the sand. And yet. And yet, that feeling of satisfaction persists. *Has this been my last journey on the ocean?*

The tide is far more powerful. It is above such concerns and questions. It carries out its will on the man, regardless of his ruin or his triumph, pulling him back and forth, lifting his legs, moving his body. The man is too tired, too beaten, to resist its workings. Time passes imperceptibly but the tide continues working him, lifting and lowering him, back and forth, sometimes gently, sometimes not. The strength of many worlds and minds are behind it, and no man can resist its power. This man does not try, only giving himself to its smooth, changing motions. He is dying.

251

A tall, sharp shadow falls across him. It has an opaque tip like a thorn. The water rises in a surge, and the tide pulls him back into the depths. He slides, limp, unresisting, and passive, back out into the vast endlessness of idea toward a colossal, umbral figure. It is *her*. *She* has found him again.

"I cannot let you go," she says. **"Not yet. Not *nearly* yet."**

THE MAN STANDS in an endless field of wheat, a single golden stalk protruding from his chest. The field's pastel yellow tapestry waves gently in a soft wind that sweeps from horizon to horizon, creating a wave of thought and feeling. He coughs painfully, and kernels blow in a cloud from out of his mouth.

Something hurts, sharply, intensely, agonizingly, deep in his chest, in his heart, but he keeps his feet, watching the grain grow and dance slowly to the wind in its season.

My season is up.

He feels it in his chest, when he breathes, when he coughs. The pain rides every heartbeat. But he keeps his feet, equal now to whatever may come.

On the horizon, a purple-black anvil coalesces into being. A thundercloud of infinite height, reaching from the tips of the wheat up through the sky, boiling out over the edges of the atmosphere. With horrifying speed, the colossal storm front slides across the field toward the man.

The underside of the thunder cell is white, like frilly lace except that it flows and undulates. *It's like the froth from the sea,* the man thinks, awed at the immeasurable power bearing down on him.

There is something arresting and fascinating about this force of nature. The man should run, but he does not. He cannot. He cannot tear his eyes from its majesty and grandeur even as he hears the violent winds whipping around its periphery and the warning thunder hidden within its depths.

"So beautiful," he breathes as it grows ever closer.

A moment later, it is too late. When the storm reaches him, the bulk of it seems almost to rear up, and something like a spinning hand reaches down, stretching toward him, closer and closer. He does not know if the storm has come to crush him, consume him, or possess him, but he knows there is no escape. Nor does he seek one.

"Come to me," the dark voice of a goddess calls, and the man's feet gently leave the ground. He rises in the soft grip of an irresistible power, turning, rotating slowly in the air, and is carried off in the cyclone.

CHAPTER 26

ELEVEN YEARS AGO

The page opened the thick oak door. Her bedchamber. And left. No guard now. No Knights of Erle. Tomorrow, no Ezra.

The knight stepped inside.

"Shut the door, Knight."

Ezra obeyed his Queen. He looked for her but could not see her. In the bath? No, that was too far. He would have heard the distance in a voice he was so closely attuned with. His senses always strained to make out her location, however far away she might be. His instinct was always to close that distance, whatever it was.

The curtains were drawn around her enormous bed. Was there a silhouette behind them? The curtains were too thick. He could not be sure. Was she hidden there, about to deliver some final message before he was sent into exile?

His heart leapt at the thought of her saying anything. His body thrilled to her voice. Any words, however cold or perfunctory or commanding, would be gold, for they would be the last words from her that he would likely ever receive. Her simple, 'Shut the door, Knight' had nearly burned him alive in his plate armor.

I will gather what treasure I can from her words, no matter their content.

Even if she had only called to remind him never to speak of what had happened in her bedchamber on the night that the Prince of Erle had died.

I will never tell.

I will speak any lie for you.

"Take off your armor, Ezra."

Confusion.

Hesitation, as never on the battlefield.

But his hands were already at work, on their own, unfastening his vambraces. His body always knew what should be done.

His strong heart pounded, hard and loud. Did the walls reverberate with those beats? His strong hands trembled with terrible potential, with the gathering of power, a reckless mix of feelings. Disbelief, lust, nervousness. Above all, love. Soaring love.

"Here, let me help you."

The curtains parted, and she emerged from the great bed, long and lean, her hair hanging down like the mane of a lion. She wore a diaphanous blue gown. He could see another layer of blue underneath, covering her loins. Her breasts were only thinly draped by the transparent gown, her nipples erect.

His armor started to chime like a bell, but only from his shaking. Quickly, another deeper ringing arose, the precursor and warning of a vast potential energy about to become kinetic, of an internally constrained passion about to become unbound.

"You should have started with your helm," the Queen said, business-like, though her breath came fast. She removed his helmet and threw it forcefully across the room where it crashed in a riotous cacophony.

"Don't cry," she said next.

Ezra felt the hot tears now. He had not realized he was crying.

What a mess I've become!

He was hot everywhere now, bell notes chiming both from his body and the metal encasing it.

"After that, you should have taken off your gauntlets," she said, unlacing these. Her voice was serious, her face intense, half-hidden by her long, intoxicating hair. Hair that he could now smell. He felt on the verge of collapsing in his fifty pounds of metal just from being able to smell her hair.

But he did not. He stood tall and chimed like the bells of spring.

He heard the swish as her gown and nipples brushed across his breastplate. There was no smile on her face as she unlaced the gauntlet of his right hand, only a dreadful concentration, a life-or-death sincerity.

The gauntlet flew somewhere and crashed loudly, though not as loudly as Ezra was ringing now.

He brought his right hand around her gently. As soon as he felt her skin, the hand vibrated at a new, softer frequency, though the rest of him continued its more savage pulsations. He leaned down to sift through her hair, an adventure into what felt like endless, stretched-out time and space. It seemed impossible that he could actually be touching her—like a heavenly dream. He found her lips and kissed them. They were still puffy from the night the Prince of Erle had died.

Small strong hands directed his mouth to her long neck and then went back to removing his armor.

Ezra nuzzled her hair again, hair he had long dreamt of touching, hair he would have died for the sake of touching, hair he was now *alive* within. He kissed her neck and felt her body move to its own frequency from the pleasure of his kisses and the reverberations he imparted to her smooth skin. The tiniest of shivers. Could she also be as excited and aroused . . . as afraid as him as he of her? His left hand was free of metal now, and he brought it around her, touching her back, tracing her ribs through the thin gown, moving up to the back of her neck, into her hair, sifting strands of dream, hardly believing that he was truly touching her whom he had loved so distantly and so achingly for so long.

"Kneel," she said, still serious, still commanding, and he knelt. As she worked the straps on his back, Ezra grasped her ass with both hands and pulled her forward, kissing her through the gown and the thin layer that covered her stomach.

This time her trembling was unmistakable.

He could feel his hands on her hips, then her backside, making dents in her skin, parting flesh. He felt her yield and relax her hips toward him.

The breastplate fell with a clang.

Ezra stood and kissed her lips again, pulling her to him.

Once more, small hands wrapped around his face and pushed him where she wanted him, to her neck. He kissed and sucked and nuzzled, chiming louder, kissing harder. The more she quivered from pleasure, the tighter he held her and the deeper he searched her mouth with his tongue.

And with every kiss, more armor came off and was flung across the room.

And with every turning and repositioning that she guided him tersely toward, he saw her face, so intense and purposeful.

So frightening.

A new sound arose from within the cold stone of the castle. It was darker, harder, hungrier. It was not a chime like his, but something else, a deeper tone. Ezra had heard a bar of it once before, a year in the past, when he had revealed himself to her, and again on the night that the Prince of Erle had died. But her dark gift had been silent except for those two times. Never with her other lovers, amid their screams and hers, had he heard it. This dark song was under a more powerful control, more disciplined than his, and seemingly tuned to a different purpose. He did not feel her emotions. Only her frightening hunger.

Ezra sang back, joining in counterpoint with her ominous tones.

When she had him kneel again to remove some final forgotten piece of metal, he slipped his hands up from the base of her breasts over her nipples. He moved gently and kissed her thighs through impossibly thin cloth. He could feel her wetness and heat, and he moved into her, sucking gently, then in a slower tempo, tonguing her hot opening through satin, pushing on something infinitely softer and more precious than the most luxuriant silk.

She pushed back at him then, moaning, hands on his chest, but he held her tight with both hands around her ass, slid her gown up, got under it, and freed one hand to slide the panty down, down, halfway down. He licked and sucked harder, tasting honey with lips and tongue that moved to the melody and the ringing of his internal rapture. She was breathing in rapid gasps and moans now, and for several long seconds, grabbed his ears and worked him, guiding him as he kissed her. At the apex of an intake of breath, she pushed his head back, pulled her undergarment up, and pulled his chain mail off in one smooth, powerful motion. She tossed it recklessly away, and it obliterated a painting on the wall, mashing it as both painting and metal fell to the ground with an ugly crash.

Ezra felt her grasp his ears a second time and pull him to her left breast while she worked on his padded underlayers. He could still hear the sound of his bells and her dark, thunderous notes as he alternated between being manipulated and undressed by her and sucking her breasts or her neck.

When his armor and his underclothing were finally gone, the Queen held him still for a moment and gazed at him, intensely, ferociously, as if at the threshold of a vast precipice. A dark density pulsed with her song.

"*I will take everything from you.*"

"Take."

"*I am a vampire, Ezra, not an Elysian Bell. I will suck you dry*."

"Try," he said.

"*I will hurt you.*"

"Destroy me."

"*Then tell me you love me, Ezra. Tell me with no words,*" she said. Then her lips were on him, on his lips, then his neck, sucking hard, almost painfully, just below his ear. He spasmed in pleasure, moaned louder than from any injury, cried louder than from birthing as he was reborn in pleasure, in the full realization of her love.

There was a brittle, shattering sound as the mirror in her bathroom exploded from his ringing.

He spun her around and laid hands on her from behind, pushing his erection against her backside and her warm, wet panties. His hands slid up once more over her breasts. He caressed her to the rhythm of his ringing, and the Queen pulsated against him in turn. She put one hand around his neck and pulled his face to her neck, then pulled them both to her bed.

She released his neck, turned and put her hands on the bed, then bent forward, presenting her ass and pushing herself against his erection, rhythmically, fiercely.

She turned her head to look at him. Wild eyes through long blonde hair gazed into his soul, staring a hole into him as she ground back and forth and around, sensual and terrifying, immensely powerful.

"Aaahhhhhhhh," moaned Ezra. He lowered one of his hands from her breasts and began stroking her through her thin underlayer. He kissed her neck and worked his way to her ears as she ground him into heaven.

He tongued her left ear. She screamed and bucked as if trying to squirm free, but he had her right breast in one hand and her hot wet opening, softly, in the other. His penis was hard against her. She was going nowhere. He slid his hand under the thin layer of silk, and as he tongued her ear again, he entered her with a single finger, gently, and cupped her breast hard. He tongued her ear again, and entered a little deeper, cupping her breast a little harder.

She turned her face toward him again, and through the mystery of long strands of hair, gave him a look of such intensity and ferocity that he froze. In that instant, she regained her balance, stepped out of her undergarment, grasped his throbbing cock, and pushed backward, guiding him into her.

They both gasped.

He returned to tonguing her as she moved back and forth, from her waist, the corresponding motions from his waist fusing them together. Ezra switched hands. Now his left was on her breast, his right sliding into the top of her honeypot just above his penis, stroking her gently in the little place that throbbed, letting his kinetic, musical vibration work on her. He tongued her again and ground harder with his hips, stroked faster with his finger, cupped her breast with his other hand. Her eyes kept finding his as she pushed into him harder, and every time they did, he knew that it was *her* driving his movements, not *him*. Her feral eyes held his as they moaned and gasped for breath in raw, wild magic and ecstasy.

At last, she screamed and he exploded, gripping her hips hard with both hands. They slowed, still together as if dissolving into one another, their movements growing smaller and smaller, less and less urgent but still rhythmically perfect, a slowly diminishing standing wave of transcendent love and raw sex. She whimpered and uttered other little sounds that made him hold her harder. He continued moving just a little, just a tiny bit, not quite stopping.

She looked back at him fiercely and in a voice deeper and more inexorable than the tide, said only, "***Give me more***."

Ezra slipped out of her and began kissing her back. The Queen crawled further up onto the bed and lay down face first in her pillows. Ezra followed her, still kissing her back, then licking her from the center of her derriere to the back of her neck. He paused and kissed each lovely ass cheek while working his fingers around the inside of her thighs, kissing her ass until goosebumps stood out upon it, and slid his hands under her once more to find her breasts. She raised herself up as he reached under and gained her elbows and knees as he kissed her backside again, then her back and neck, cupping her breasts as he did so. She raised her ass higher, and as a hand somehow came around his neck, Ezra found himself releasing her breasts and tonguing her from behind.

"**You are *mine*, Ezra**," she moaned, looking back at him. Her eyes were a hard, intense contrast to the rich croon of her voice. Her long, soft, golden hair half veiled those cold blue orbs, a fervid, enigmatic presence.

Ezra felt his cock harden again, saw her eyes move eerily toward it.

Her tiny hand found his and she pulled him effortlessly on top of her, pulling him into her again as she began moving through her waist once more, gasping and moaning.

Ouch.

Ezra's left hand felt a sharp pinch cut through the pleasure she was giving him elsewhere. He looked and saw that pinkie finger impaled on something. He raised himself up, even as she pushed back to take him deeper into her, and examined it. A two-inch-long thorn was embedded in the finger. A fat drop of blood welled from its tip.

The Queen turned to see what had happened. Her coldly feverish eyes widened, her pupils expanding until her eyes looked black. Her dark song swelled then, and suddenly Ezra found himself on his back, hardly aware of how he got there. She straddled him and slid him into her in a succession of gasps, and as she began slowly rocking and undulating, she lifted his hand to her breast, rested it there, and pulled the thorn out. Almost reverently, she took Ezra's finger into her mouth and began to suck on it.

She moaned around his finger, eyes boring into his, frightening him, and kept sucking, harder and harder, rocking against him. Then her mouth was on his, bloody and tasting of copper, and her tongue thrust deep into him as she rocked harder yet. Even when fighting four men and bleeding by quarts, Ezra had never felt so weak or helpless. He sank into a helpless kind of surrender, but it was a surrender of pleasure, a sacrifice of himself to her whom he had loved for so long. He felt her kissing his neck, hard, then harder still, squealing and moaning as she rode him into ecstasy.

Her eyes blazed blue as she came again, screaming wildly.

When Ezra awoke, she was lying on his chest crying and repeating, "I'm sorry, Ezra, I'm so sorry."

CHAPTER 27

LOVE OF ANOTHER KIND

Ezra awoke in the dark, still shaking from the memory of being with the Queen that fateful night that had sealed his future.

Why such an ungentle dichotomy between the Queen in Eydos and the Queen in her bedchamber that night?

He had only been with her that one solitary time. As raw and rough —and pure—as their lovemaking had been—and terrifying too—it had also been utterly transporting. Life-changing in every possible sense. Ezra had always been a man of pure passions—he rang with them in the tones of heaven—but the Queen had brought him to a new, unfiltered, *naked* reality.

He had dreamt of her often before that first night, but had never stopped dreaming of her afterward. And he had never entered Eydos without meeting her in it somewhere, in some guise. *Without Rose, I never would have known the world inside the world. A reality both deeper and higher.*

It was wonderful and strange, arousing and unsettling, both frightening and comforting, and a hundred other paradoxes. How could he reconcile having felt the vast pleasure of her touch in two realms, one colored softly like a children's book, the other in the sharp tones and strokes of the real and of a life that could end at any moment.

It is the riddle of her.

Real love and deep fulfillment had eluded her. Or she thought that it had. Love was no simpler a thing than it was important. It manifested in diverse ways, could be denied in more ways than the sun rose, could be put away in the dark or brought out into the air. *Perhaps when it is held at arm's length for so long, it is realized with a reciprocal power and ferocity when it is finally released.*

Ezra felt once more her powerful sexual intensity . . . and remembered the calm, loving strength and vertiginous depths of the Iceberg. She was a riddle that he would ponder for all of his days.

"Sir?"

It was Pontes. Ezra felt a flood of relief at hearing his voice. He opened his eyes.

"No, Sir Ezra, don't get up," Pontes said, his skinny, long-fingered hands on Ezra's shoulders, pushing him back gently into the soft bed of the castle infirmary.

"The actress—Saraith—is she okay?" Ezra asked.

Pontes sat down, his back rigid. "She is fine, sir. And she testified. After the, er, dust had settled. It may not surprise you to hear that she did not break character once in doing so."

Ezra laughed at that, though it hurt.

"Sir . . ."

"Yes, Pontes?"

"Will you be staying with the Queen now?"

Trying not to laugh, because for once in his life, Ezra was trying to learn a lesson, he said, "I suppose that I will try." The laugh would have been rueful anyway. *She will try to push me away.*

"She doesn't deserve you, sir," Pontes said in that harder voice he rarely used. "What happened at the court. It should not have. *Need* not have." His hands went to his hair as if he wanted to pull the thin strands out. "It was reckless. It was . . . irresponsible, sir."

Ahhh. The riddle of the Queen.

Ezra knew he could not begin to explain it to his precise, prosaic, invaluable secretary. Not if he had a year. How can you explain that what had happened was part accident, part trap, and part something so much more complex? Instead of trying the impossible—he was far too weak for that in any case—Ezra said, "Sometimes it's not about what we deserve, my friend."

The tension seemed to crest in the thin man. His hands did, for a moment, clutch at his thinning hair. But in the next moment, he relaxed. "Yes sir," he said resignedly.

Ezra gave him a moment before saying, "Pontes, I have been wondering why you hated the scholars so much." Before the thin man could answer, Ezra added, "I know you weren't secretly working on behalf of Lady Kristen or any other agency."

"Ah, well . . ." Pontes did not say more for a long moment. The secretary massaged his right wrist with his left, and Ezra remembered that his friend sometimes had trouble with his hands. "They seemed . . . wrong somehow. Their behavior seemed wrong. No. It seemed *obscene*," Pontes said with curious emphasis, "to reduce to paper what you do."

He leaned forward onto his elbows, his face close to Ezra's chest. "I do not know if it is a sound of heaven or if you are a piece of god, or what other worldly or unworldly thing it is about you, sir, but whatever it *is* should not be analyzed or used like a one-trick pony. Or a packhorse," he added, at a loss for the right metaphor. "You should not be made small by such a gift."

He leaned back. "It is a wonderful thing."

"Not like numbers in a ledger, hey, my friend?"

"No, sir."

"Well . . . that's nice." Ezra was fading. Even with the Queen's healing touch, he was far from on his feet again. His eyes felt heavy, and he thought he might have lost a moment. Or more than one.

"I suppose that it is time I took the ledgers back to Lady Kristen," said Pontes softly. "She will be wondering what has happened to them."

"Thank you for staying with me through this," said Ezra, feeling it. He deeply appreciated this man who had stayed by his side for his own, secret reasons. There were more riddles in the world than just the riddle of the Queen, and exhausted though he was, Ezra needed to tickle Pontes's riddle. "It must have been difficult wading into all these battles, chasing across the countryside by yourself to find witnesses, sleeping in the cold desert just for friendship. And so far from home."

Pontes smiled, stood up, leaned forward, and gently kissed Ezra on the forehead.

"Well," Pontes said, seeming to stand taller than he ever had. "I hear the chimes of heaven." He paused. "Goodbye." And walked away.

CHAPTER 28

THE DREAD QUEEN

Naked of plate, and still far from full strength and health, Ezra stood before the Queen's door and the armored knights who guarded it. One, Sir Jennifer Shryke, he knew as a smiling provocateur and a murderer, or the tool of one. *My daughter's tool.* The other, Sir Marigold, he knew to be a friend, and a tool of the Queen.

"You should not enter," said Marigold, her voice ringing hollow out of her closed helm.

"Both messages said the same thing this time," replied Ezra, though he knew that Marigold was not referring to the letters that had summoned him. Letters from both the Queen and her daughter this time.

"Come to me," the notes had said.

He had decided to answer the Queen's summons first. He was yet to have a proper conversation with her in the waking world.

Marigold's armor told no tale. But that in itself was a story. She knew that a decision had been reached and was closing herself up to pain.

Oh, Marigold.

With gentle reassurance, Ezra said, "Everything is okay, now Mari. We won." The bulk of Erle's poisonous influence had been cleared away. Saraith had testified about Brayden's fainting—which other actors had confirmed, in affidavits, was a result of a weak heart—and the guardsmen, special constables, Lords and Ladies suborned by Erle had been exposed thanks to the work of Pontes and Lady Jayne Orton. Those not captured at the Queen's High Court had been arrested in the days following. It had all worked out very neatly, if the butcher's bill— the massacre in the Queen's High Court—could be ignored.

Did she know that it would happen in this way? Was this her plan?

If so, he realized, she must have had tremendous confidence in him.

Or was it more complicated than that?

He thought about Marigold.

Like many things are. His relationship with her was complicated in a way that his tryst with Danielle Stonehouse had not been. He *did* love Marigold, as a friend and—though in a complicated way—more than a friend.

Right now at least, whatever Marigold felt remained a mystery hidden behind steel plate. Her voice gave nothing away either. "If you go in," she warned, "you may never come out."

Ezra stepped up to her and put his arms around her. The hard edges of her plate armor bit into his skin and hid her from him, but the gesture felt necessary.

"No one comes away from her the same," he said, his head against her helm.

He closed his eyes, still holding Marigold, then reaching inside himself, slowly allowed his feelings for her to rise up from his soul. Love found soft expression in the air, rousing it from the cool stillness induced by thick, stone walls into something alive and warm. The soft vibrations penetrated her plate, caressing her skin, resonating infinitely with her inner self.

It was the sound and feeling of deep, ideal friendship and uncondi- tional support. It was the tone of strength that built bones and made hearts stronger but that also caressed the soul to sleep, knowing it would always be loved. The chiming sound danced softly down the hallways of the fortress, demanding nothing, giving everything.

"This will always be here for you, Marigold." Ezra said, releasing her.

She swayed for three heartbeats, then raised her helm and showed him her glistening eyes.

"So. You have obeyed my last command to you."

The soft, deep voice of the Queen thrilled Ezra. As he had known it would. His heart pounded at the sound, his eyes widened at the sight of her at her desk, dressed in a thick nightrobe. Her long, tawny hair spilled down her back.

He looked around her bedchamber, noting the absence of conventional mirrors and the highly polished metal that hung in their stead upon the walls. But his eyes quickly returned to the woman he had never stopped thinking and dreaming about for eleven years. The gentle chiming that had begun with his embrace of Marigold had never quite ceased, but now it rose to a deeper, richer harmony.

"I will always do as you ask," he said, breathing deeply, calming his heart, moderating the Bell-ringing of his soul.

She closed the ledger she had been working on and rotated on her chair to give him her full attention. **"You should take Sir Marigold's hand and leave. Go away from here and be happy. Or return to Lady Kristen and be all the things she dreams you could be to her."** After a pause, she added bitingly, **"Or that seamstress of yours. Stonehouse."**

"You'll get no apology from me for loving," said Ezra, annoyed but unsurprised that even now she would try to push him away. As alluring and powerful as she was, a thousand men would have walked away from her at this, not understanding, perhaps bearing a poisonous grudge for such an ego-crushing dismissal.

But Ezra *knew* her. "It has been eleven years."

"So leave, then. I've been with enough people to know that . . . they come and go."

And knowing her, Ezra could see the bitterness on her face that spoke of secret wounds. "You made a bed of them. Your bed of thorns," he said.

"Yes."

Images of the vast sea, the lush garden, and the tall castle flashed across Ezra's mind. "So it's true," he breathed. "You really were with me in Eydos." He had known it was true, had always known it, but he needed to hear her confirm it.

"Of course."

"I don't want to go," said Ezra. "I *will not* go. You will not sacrifice me a second time."

For a painfully long moment, she did not answer. A single clear tear ran down her cheek, which she ignored. When it finally dropped down onto her robe, she said, **"You can never be my husband. I have had three and that is enough."**

Her words felt like a punch to the stomach. But the greater question had been answered. "You were going to bring me back quickly. But then you found that you were pregnant."

"Do you hate me for it?"

"No." He understood the necessary fiction that had kept the peace with the Kingdom of Erle for so long. They believed that the murderer of their prince had been punished. And they did not want to act while they thought they had a daughter of Erle they could someday exploit. But that he had been sacrificed still hurt. Such is the pain that tests love.

Her face was still, as if made of ice. **"If you stay, you will be kept like a mistress in Erle, given no special rank."**

"I am content simply to be a Knight of the Queen and Vice-Captain to Marigold."

"But no more than that."

"You will keep me informed of your schedule, and notify me if it changes."

"I am too busy to make that promise."

"You have pages aplenty. You *will* do this."

"So be it." Her eyes blazed, wide and bright. **"You will be in *my* orbit, you will have rooms in the castle and may come to me in dreams or—when my schedule allows—when *I* send for you."**

At that last phrase, he looked at her almost reproachfully and held the gaze until her expression faltered. But he knew he did not need to fight every statement of hers like Pontes and Lady Jayne had fought to understand every point on the ledgers. Instead, he said, "You will love no one other than me."

"I *have* loved no other than you." She frowned, her expression all icy angles. **"But you mean the verb. Yes. You will suffice. If you stay."**

If Ezra had expected his ego to be stroked, he had come to the wrong woman. But he knew her too well. He balanced the coldness of her tone against the implication of the statement.

I need one more thing.

"I want to help Eryka."

"Yes. She needs you. But let us be clear. You can never be publicly acknowledged as her father."

Every word of that hurt, but behind the words he felt a dam breaking. He laughed. "I will be her father in private. I'll let *you* explain the rest to her."

Did her expression soften at this? Perhaps for an instant. But then it hardened more even than before.

"How can your pride accept this position? Why do you not leave and go away forever to some place where you will be loved as you should be? Why endure what will surely be a special kind of torture?"

Ezra smiled, and his chiming deepened further. There was one secret he had never fully explained. He had told her of love in long soliloquys and poems, in metaphor and verse. But he had never told her all. "You have seen me grow flowers for your bed?"

"Yes."

"Then you know how I feel about you, and you know I believe you deserve a more comfortable resting place at night."

She said nothing, gazing steadily at him. Ezra walked to her and knelt at her feet, his head level with her breasts. His chiming soared, louder and more beautiful, but the Queen did not flinch. Her arms lightly encircled his neck. Ezra said, "*I* am the flower in your bed. Allow me to speak love to you again as I might if we were in Eydos:

Love is the poetry of the soul.
Constructed by will
And a magic of mind.

You told me of yourself.
Your concerns and cares you spoke.
I listened, separating the truths
That you willingly tell
From those you won't.

Making a voyage on an ark
From those words, said and unsaid,
Using imagination in kind
To build a vision in my mind
Of who it is you truly are.

A trip upon a sea,
Diving into the deep
Embracing everything
That you have been:
Full cups,
Lost loves,
Far more deceit,

Than can be believed,
Broken trust,
Addiction's rust,
Immeasurable passions,
A torrential rain,
Of overcoming pain.

And with wisdom these make
An ascending strength.

In the Eydos of you, I see:
A colossal, vertiginous iceberg
A devouring puma
An overwhelming storm
A rising tide
An all-consuming vampire
A commanding Queen.

I have thought so hard and true
On all the wondrous things you've been
Until my inner and my outer mind agree
The only thing that I can dream
Is the transcendent beauty of you."

It was all of a piece with the other things he had said to her in Eydos. It had to be so, for he was speaking of the same being and the same love. And though she had heard it before, her eyes streamed with tears.

"I love others," Ezra said, "but I love you *utterly*, Rose. I am not going anywhere."

Her legs parted and she pulled him in until he was pressed tight against her and his face was buried in the soft cloth that hugged her breasts. **"I love you, Ezra. But you know that I need to do this on my own."** She did not push him away.

"Why always on your own?" he asked.

"It is my task. I would die to create a better world."

"Let me help you."

Her hands tightened on his back. **"You will be destroyed, Ezra. Everyone I come close to dies. I am a vampire. I destroy them all."**

Were you not sure what would be in that tomb?

He had known. He had never believed she was a murderer and certainly not a monster. Professor Olivia had helped him understand, a little, but then she also did not fully understand what either the Queen or he really was. Pontes was right. She *could* not.

In Eydos, Rose had been so many things, puma, cyclone, tide, iceberg. Vampire. Things of mind and feeling, of passion and idea. Ezra was certain that he had seen only a tiny portion of all that she was. *I don't think I'll learn the rest from some scholars at an institute.*

Ezra sighed, thinking carefully about how to respond to her strange and complex self-punishment. "You aren't really. We both know that." He laughed softly into her breasts. "The scholars at the institute think you are like me, but instead of love and fury, you are life and death."

"So you see, then," she said as if that answered him completely.

"I do not," Ezra replied. "You cannot destroy *me*. Let me ease your loneliness, Rose."

She pulled his head away from her breasts. **"A leader *must* be lonely,"** she said. Then, putting the lie to her words, she kissed his mouth.

Ezra kissed her back, feeling lightning rush through his veins at her touch. Pulling away for just a moment, he said. "Being lonely won't make you a better leader, it is just something you have learned to endure. And doing too much alone has not helped. Look at this latest crisis of multiple misunderstandings."

He ran his hands through her long hair and kissed her neck. She moaned and shuddered. Pulling slowly back, he breathed, "Having love won't make you weak." He sucked hard on her neck, as she had done to his and slid his hands around her ass. "It will not hold you back from your goals."

He kissed her mouth again, harder this time, and pulled her hips into his, grinding against her, entering deep into her mouth. He untied her robe and pushed it back over her shoulders and off her hips. "Take off *your* armor. Hold my hand. Embrace our connection."

The castle shook with soaring music, the sound of wedding bells, of joy, of pure love.

THE MAN ENTERS THE GARDEN, walking easily despite the trembling ground. He sees the puma on her bed of roses, lounging there, waiting for him as tremors rock the world and rose petals dance. He sinks into the red flowers. Long lean limbs, velvet paws and dagger-sharp claws enfold him. Two-inch-long, sharp, curved teeth touch his neck.

HE STANDS in the violently quaking wheat field. The grain, the field, and the very ground begin to shake apart even as an anvil storm rears overhead, adding thunder to the urgent, exigent sound. An indigo hand reaches down, twirling columns of air for fingers. The cyclone engulfs the man. Carries him up into the air. Slowly turning him, spinning him, once, twice, gently and slowly at first, then faster and faster, carrying him higher into heaven.

THE VAMPIRE HOLDS him in her embrace, sliding kisses along his neck, one hand on his cheek, the other around his ass. Fangs puncture skin. Her castle tilts to one side and shudders. The stones crack and dust fills the air as level after level collapses, as she tastes his love and gives him hers.

THE MAN REACHES her once more, in the depths, the water turbulent and frothy now, and sees her asleep on her bed of thorns. He presses against the clear, cold barrier. He breaks through, pushing aside the shattered ice, and steps inside.

She opens her eyes.

He kisses her softly, carefully lowers himself onto the thorns beside her. The loud ringing of bells softens as its ice-shattering power sublimates into something beautiful, complete, creative. She slides over top of him, resting on his body, taking him into her.

The iceberg, the castle, the wheat field, and the garden shake gently to the rhythm of their passion.

LATER, much later, straddling him on her bed, Rose asked, **"Is this truly all you want?"**

That she even asked again, *now*, after the matter had so clearly been settled, showed how much her icy walls had melted. It was all he had dreamt of, growing this flower, but he had not known he had a daughter then. "I want to help Eryka," he said. The thought of Lady Paron's execution surfaced. *We must be very careful with her.*

"She may need some guidance," the Queen allowed.

"She is something new," Ezra said. *Something we don't understand. My daughter.*

"Yes." She watched him through those strands of perfect hair coiling on his chest. **"Why do you love me?"**

"In a sentence?" Ezra asked.

"Indeed."

It was Ezra's last secret. "When I understood you, I loved you. And when you understood me, you loved me too. We may each be the only other that *could* understand. But it's more than just comprehension.

We both saw a complicated, depthless other that thrilled our hearts and made us complete."

"That is nice."

"And do you know why you can never suck me dry, vampire?" It was finally time to tell her the secret, the one thing he had never divulged. "It isn't just because I always have more."

"No?" She smiled curiously. **"Why then?"**

"Because you love me too. Because I am the only one you have ever loved."

She did not feel compelled to answer the obvious. She did, however, move her hand gently on his chest. **"What else do you want?"** she asked.

Oh, that was a question. There were a thousand ways that Ezra could have answered her. Despite the accord they seemed to have reached, there was still pain. Despite his loyalty to her, he was not a slave. There was another side to him that he might have spoken of then and gained some sour satisfaction from speaking of it. He could have spoken of all his needs, how the Queen had spent so little concern over them, of his hot, sick jealousy of her other lovers, of the immense pain at having been sent away, the deep feelings of anger and hurt over being kept from his daughter.

But his greatest strength had never been fighting the Queen's enemies. It had always been how he *felt* about her. His soul vibrated to hers. He loved her too much and too deeply for any of those poisons to take root.

And even though he loved her with an intensity to shatter steel and pulverize stone, Ezra knew there was still more to be discovered. There was *infinitely* more to Eydos. Above all, there must be a reason for it, a purpose to it. And as much as there was more to the universe of perception that was Eydos, Ezra felt that there was something vastly more important: there was more to *her*. He had glimpsed depths beyond imagining in the freezing waters of the ocean, and he felt compelled to swim for them. *For her.*

There was really only one answer to give, an answer that spoke across all worlds, across all time, a response to loneliness, duty, abandonment and betrayal: an answer to the woman at the heart of all his dreams.

Looking up at her long hair cascading down toward his chest, Ezra let chime and said, "Perhaps it's time you had someone who is here solely for you, for the Iceberg, the woman at its heart, for the Puma and the Vampire, someone who loves every aspect of your innermost self, your soul."

Acknowledgments

Thank you to my test readers. I cannot express how much your suggestions have meant to me, except by using some of them. You made this book better, and you did it by donating two precious things: your time and your creativity.

ABOUT THE AUTHOR

Born with only one working lung, and having had the last rites read to him as he lay dying of an influenza-related viral pneumonia, 25-year-old geophysicist Lee Hunt experienced several near-death dreams. The power of communication and the need to both understand and be understood was at the heart of each. He had already found that nothing was more important than being able to cross the distance between people.

Lee's interests are eclectic. He is an Ironman Triathlete, hiker, traveler, and an enthusiastic sport rock climber. Lee also continues to work as a geophysicist on Carbon Capture and Sequestration projects, and is a writer for BIG-Media.ca.

The dream of understanding and being understood has never left his mind, and Lee continues that quest in his works of fiction through metaphor. His works include *The Dynamicist Trilogy*, *Last Worst Hopes* and *Bed of Rose and Thorns*.

9 781777 973438